THE GIVER
Lois Lowry
WITH RELATED READINGS

THE EMC MASTERPIECE SERIES

Access Edition

EMC/Paradigm Publishing
St. Paul, Minnesota

Staff Credits:

Laurie Skiba
Managing Editor

Lori Coleman
Editorial Consultant

Brenda Owens
High School Editor

Nichola Torbett
Associate Editor

Becky Palmer
Associate Editor

Jennifer Anderson
Assistant Editor

Jennifer Wreisner
Senior Designer

Paul Spencer
Art and Photo Researcher

Valerie Murphy
Editorial Assistant

Sharon O'Donnell
Copy Editor

Gia Marie Garbinsky
Educational Writer

Parkwood Composition
Compositor

Photo credits: cover, © George D. Lepp / CORBIS
page xvi, Lois Lowry

© 1993 by Lois Lowry.

Reprinted by arrangement with Houghton Mifflin Company

Library of Congress Cataloging-in-Publication Data

Lowry, Lois.
 The giver / Lois Lowry.
 p. cm. – (The EMC masterpiece series access editions)
 Includes related readings, creative writing activities, critical writing
 activities, and projects.
 Summary: Given his lifetime assignment at the Ceremony of Twelve,
 Jonas becomes the receiver of memories shared by only one other in his
 community and discovers the terrible truth about the society in which
 he lives.
 ISBN 0-8219-2406-0
 [1. Science fiction.] I. Title. II. Series.

PZ7.L9673 Gi 2002
[Fic]—dc21

                                                          2001055672

ISBN: 0-8219-2406-0

Copyright © 2003 by EMC Corporation

Published by EMC/Paradigm Publishing
875 Montreal Way
St. Paul, Minnesota 55102
800-328-1452
www.emcp.com
E-mail: educate@emcp.com

Printed in the United States of America.
 12 xx 15 14 13

Table of Contents

THE LIFE AND WORKS OF
Lois Lowry

Lois Lowry

Lois Lowry is an award-winning author and an accomplished photographer. Lowry was born Lois Hammersberg in Honolulu, Hawaii, on March 20, 1937, the second of three children—an older sister Helen, Lois, and a younger brother Jon. On being the middle child in her family, Lowry has said, "That left me in-between, and exactly where I wanted to be: on my own. I was a solitary child who lived in the world of books and my own imagination."

Because Lowry's father was a military officer—an army dentist—her family traveled often. During World War II while her father was away, Lois lived with her mother's family in Amish country in central Pennsylvania. (She later used the house and town that she lived in as the setting for her autobiographical novel *Autumn Street*.) After the war, at the age of eleven, Lois and her family joined her father in Tokyo, Japan. She attended high school in New York City, then Brown University in Rhode Island, leaving in 1956 to marry.

Lowry married a naval officer, and their travels took them to California, Connecticut, Florida, South Carolina, Massachusetts, and Maine. By the time they reached Maine, Lowry and her husband had four children—Alix, Grey, Kristin, and Ben. She returned to college in 1972 at the University of Southern Maine, earning her bachelor's degree. She went on to pursue some graduate courses and began to write professionally.

Lowry published her first novel, *A Summer to Die*, in 1977 and then continued to publish one and sometimes two books per year. In 1979, she published *Anastasia Krupnik*, the first of many books about a girl named Anastasia and her family. Lowry has said that the first book actually grew from what was supposed to be a short story, but that she liked the characters of Anastasia and her family so much that she "didn't want to see them disappear into a magazine story."

In 1990, Lowry was awarded the Newbery Medal for *Number the Stars*, a story set during the German occupation of Denmark during WWII and seen through the eyes of a ten-year-old girl whose family aids Jews trying to flee to safety. Lowry published *The Giver* in 1993. It received the Newbery Medal in 1994.

Today, Lowry lives in Cambridge, Massachusetts, with her dog Bandit, a Tibetan terrier. On the weekends, she relaxes in her 1840s farmhouse in rural New Hampshire. Besides writing, Lowry enjoys gardening, cooking, and reading.

Lowry has found the inspiration for many of her stories in her personal experiences. *A Summer to Die,* which tells the story of the death of a young girl as witnessed by her younger sister, draws on Lowry's experience of losing her own sister, Helen, at a young age to cancer. The idea for *The Giver* came to her while she was visiting her father, who had lost his long-term memory. Lowry recognized that without memory there is no pain, and she began to contemplate the idea of a society that erases its past to avoid pain. Of her work, Lowry has said, "My books have varied in content and style. Yet is seems to me that all of them deal, essentially, with the same general theme: the importance of human connections."

Books by Lois Lowry

A Summer to Die
All About Sam
Anastasia, Absolutely
Anastasia Again!
Anastasia, Ask Your Analyst
Anastasia at this Address
Anastasia at Your Service
Anastasia Has the Answers
Anastasia Krupnik
Anastasia on Her Own
Anastasia's Chosen Career
Attaboy, Sam!
Autumn Street
Find a Stranger, Say Goodbye
Looking Back: A Book of Memories
Number the Stars
Rabble Starkey
See You Around, Sam!
Stay!: Keeper's Story
Switcharound
Taking Care of Terrific
The Giver
The One Hundredth Thing About Caroline
Us and Uncle Fraud
Your Move J. P.!
Zooman Sam

Time Line of Lois Lowry's Life

1937	Lois Lowry is born Lois Hammersberg on March 20, 1937, in Honolulu, Hawaii.
1948	Lois and her mother, sister, and brother move to Tokyo to join her father.
1954	Lois attends Brown University in Rhode Island.
1956	Lois leaves Brown University to marry Donald Lowry, a naval officer.
1956–1972	Lowry and her husband move around, living in several different states before settling in Maine in 1972. They have four children: Alix, Grey, Kristin, and Benjamin.
1972	Lowry enrolls at the University of Southern Maine and earns her B.A.
1977	Lowry publishes *A Summer to Die,* her first novel. She and her husband are divorced.
1978	*A Summer to Die* is awarded the International Reading Association Children's Book Award. *Find a Stranger, Say Goodbye* is published.
1979	*Anastasia Krupnik* and *Autumn Street* are published.
1980	*Autumn Street* receives an ALA Notable Book citation.
1981	*Anastasia Again!* is published.
1982	*Anastasia at Your Service* is published.
1983	*Taking Care of Terrific* is published. *Anastasia Again!* is nominated for an American Book Award.
1984	*Anastasia, Ask Your Analyst* and *Us and Uncle Fraud* are published.

The One Hundredth Thing About Caroline and *Anastasia on Her Own* are published.

1985

Anastasia Has the Answers is published.

1986

Rabble Starkey and *Anastasia's Chosen Career* are published. *Rabble Starkey* receives numerous awards, including the Boston Globe/Horn Book Award.

1987

All About Sam is published.

1988

Number the Stars is published.

1989

Number the Stars receives numerous awards, including the Newbery Medal.

1990

Anastasia at this Address is published.

1991

Attaboy, Sam! is published.

1992

The Giver is published.

1993

The Giver is awarded the Newbery Medal.

1994

Anastasia, Absolutely is published.

1995

See You Around Sam! is published.

1996

Stay!: Keeper's Story! and *Looking Back: A Book of Memories* are published.

1998

Zooman Sam is published.

2001

Context for *The Giver*

The **setting** of *The Giver*—that is, the specific time and place in which it occurs—is not clearly defined. The novel is not set in the past, present, or future. Instead, it occupies an imagined world. *The Giver* is considered **science fiction**, highly imaginative writing that contains fantastic elements based on scientific principles, discoveries, or laws. Science fiction allows writers to suspend or alter certain elements of reality in order to create fascinating and sometimes instructive alternatives.

Imagine a world free of suffering and inequality, a world in which war is unknown and everyone lives in harmony. Can such a place exist in real life? Great thinkers over the centuries have believed it is possible and have attempted to design their own ideal societies, or **utopias**. The term *utopia*—derived from Greek words meaning "good place" and "no place"—was coined in the 1500s by Sir Thomas More in his novel *Utopia*. The concept, however, was around long before More's time.

One of the first people to create a vision of a utopian society was the Greek philosopher Plato, writing in the third century B.C. In his book *The Republic,* he outlines an ideal society divided neatly into three classes: the philosophers, the warriors, and the commoners. The philosophers and the warriors would be the guardians of the state, leading a life without luxury so that the commoners would not envy their power. The commoners would each be assigned occupations best suited to him or her, so that everyone would live in peace. No one would want for anything, because everyone's needs would be met.

Plato's perfect world did have a dark side, however. The rulers, he believed, had a responsibility to keep some secrets from the people in the interest of creating the best possible society. For example, no one would know that the children of the higher classes were being selectively bred, like animals, to encourage the most advantageous traits. Parenting would be permitted only through a lottery system, so that some people considered undesirable would be prevented from having children. Those so-called undesirables would be made to believe it was their own bad luck, and not the will of the state, that denied them that right. Children who were considered inferior, or who were deformed in some way, would simply be taken away to some "mysterious, unknown place" so that they would not taint the pure society. Information would be controlled in many other ways as well. For example, texts for schools would be strictly censored so that children could not be exposed to ideas that were not "good for them." So while Plato's "perfect society" looked perfect on the outside, ugly things were happening in secret.

Through the ages, people have attempted to set up real utopian communities around the world. Amos Bronson Alcott wanted to create a spiritual community untouched by society and its evils. In 1842, he began Fruitlands, a farm near Harvard, Massachusetts. The rules at Fruitlands were strict, allowing no animals for labor and no animal products. The community was designed to be self-sufficient, so members could only eat what they grew. Eventually, the community disintegrated, as it was impossible to grow enough food for everyone without the help of animals. Louisa May Alcott, daughter of the community's founder, wrote about the doomed experiment in her short story "Transcendental Wild Oats."

One might say that the trouble with utopian societies is that in order to maintain harmony and perfection, certain freedoms and certain individuals must be eliminated. A number of well-known science fiction novels— including *1984* by George Orwell, *A Brave New World* by Aldous Huxley, and *Fahrenheit 451* by Ray Bradbury— have explored the faults and falsehoods of utopia.

The Giver also presents a utopia that isn't as perfect as it might seem at first glance. To everyone in Jonas's community, life is good. There is no crime, suffering, or serious conflict. Anyone who disrupts the peaceful, predictable way of life is "released," free to go "Elsewhere." Differences of race, religion, or ideology do not exist. Jonas begins to see the dark side of this utopian society as he learns from the old man he knows as The Giver.

Characters in *The Giver*

Major Characters

Jonas. Jonas is eleven years old and about to turn twelve at the opening of the book. At the Ceremony of Twelve, he is selected to become Receiver of Memory, the most honored position in his community. His experience as Receiver profoundly changes his life and his relationship with others in the community. Jonas is the main character of the book, and although he is not the narrator, the events of the story are seen through his eyes.

The Giver. The Giver is an old man. He has served the community as Receiver of Memory since he was twelve years old, and it is his job to train Jonas by passing on his knowledge of the past and the world outside the community.

Gabriel. Gabriel is a newchild at the Nurturing Center where Jonas's father works. Because Gabriel is maturing more slowly than the other newchildren, Jonas's father receives permission to bring him home in the evening to give him special care and attention. Jonas develops a special relationship with Gabriel.

Minor Characters

Jonas's father. Jonas's father is a Nurturer in the community. It is his job to take care of the newchildren in the community before they are assigned parents. Jonas's father requests and receives special permission to bring Gabriel, one of the newchildren, home in the evenings for additional care. Jonas's father is also the father of Lily, Jonas's younger sister.

Jonas's mother. Jonas's mother works at the Justice Department. She is also Lily's mother.

Asher. Like Jonas, Asher is eleven years old and about to turn twelve at the opening of the book. Asher is known throughout the community for his good sense of humor and his imprecise use of language. He is a friend of Jonas.

Lily. Lily is Jonas's sister. She is seven years old and about to turn eight at the opening of the book. Lily talks a great deal, sometimes saying things that Jonas considers rude.

Fiona. Like Jonas and Asher, Fiona is about to turn twelve at the opening of the book. Fiona spends many volunteer hours with the elderly at the House of the Old. Fiona is a friend of Jonas and Asher.

The Chief Elder. The Chief Elder is the leader of the Committee of Elders. The Committee of Elders makes all major decisions in the community. The Chief Elder presents Assignments to all twelve-year-old citizens of the community. The Assignments dictate what each person's life occupation will be.

Rosemary. Rosemary was selected ten years before Jonas's selection to become Receiver of Memory.

Echoes

Quotes on themes from The Giver

Color possesses me. I don't have to pursue it. It will possess me always, I know it. That is the meaning of this happy hour: Color and I are one. I am a painter.

—Paul Klee

Memory and forgetfulness are as life and death to one another. To live is to remember and to remember is to live. To die is to forget and to forget is to die.

—Samuel Butler

O memory! thou midway world
'Twixt earth and paradise,
Where things decayed and loved ones lost
In dreamy shadows rise.

—Abraham Lincoln

Who controls the past controls the future: who controls the present controls the past.

—George Orwell

The moments of the past do not remain still; they retain in our memory the motion which drew them towards the future, towards a future which has itself become the past, and draw us on in their train.

—Marcel Proust

There can be no knowledge without emotion. We may be aware of a truth, yet until we have felt its force, it is not ours. To the cognition of the brain must be added the experience of the soul.

—Arnold Bennett

I think there is choice possible at any moment to us, as long as we live. But there is no sacrifice. There is a choice, and the rest falls away. Second choice does not exist. Beware of those who talk about sacrifice.

—Muriel Rukeyser

Life is pain and the enjoyment of love is an anesthetic.

—Cesare Pavese

I don't avoid pain by not remembering something; I try to remember. . . . Memory is empowering, and it's what gives you your sense of continuity in the world.

—Melinda Worth Popham

Love is life. All, everything that I understand, I understand only because I love. Everything is, everything exists, only because I love. Everything is united by it alone. Love is God, and to die means that I, a particle of love, shall return to the general and eternal source.

—Leo Tolstoy

Love is a great thing. It is not by chance that in all times and practically among all cultured peoples love in the general sense and the love of a man for his wife are both called love. If love is often cruel or destructive, the reasons lie not in love itself, but in the inequality between people.

—Anton Pavlovich Chekhov

Truth always rests with the minority, and the minority is always stronger than the majority, because the minority is generally formed by those who really have an opinion, while the strength of a majority is illusory, formed by the gangs who have no opinion—and who, therefore, in the next instant (when it is evident that the minority is the stronger) assume its opinion . . . while Truth again reverts to a new minority.

—Soren Kierkegaard

The truth must dazzle gradually
Or every man be blind.

—Emily Dickinson

Truth never damages a cause that is just.

—Mohandas K. Gandhi

The original cover of *The Giver* features photographs taken by Lois Lowry.

THE GIVER

For all the children
To whom we entrust the future

Chapter 1

IT WAS ALMOST December, and Jonas was beginning to be frightened. No. Wrong word, Jonas thought. Frightened meant that deep, sickening feeling of something terrible about to happen. Frightened was the way he had felt a year ago when an unidentified aircraft had overflown the community twice. He had seen it both times. Squinting toward the sky, he had seen the sleek jet, almost a blur at its high speed, go past, and a second later heard the blast of sound that followed. Then one more time, a moment later, from the opposite direction, the same plane.

At first, he had been only fascinated. He had never seen aircraft so close, for it was against the rules for Pilots to fly over the community. Occasionally, when supplies were delivered by <u>cargo</u> planes to the landing field across the river, the children rode their bicycles to the riverbank and watched, <u>intrigued</u>, the unloading and then the takeoff directed to the west, always away from the community.

◀ Why was Jonas fascinated at first by the aircraft?

But the aircraft a year ago had been different. It was not a squat, fat-bellied cargo plane but a needle-nosed single-pilot jet. Jonas, looking around <u>anxiously</u>, had seen others—adults as well as children—stop what they were doing and wait, confused, for an explanation of the frightening event.

Then all of the citizens had been ordered to go into the nearest building and stay there. IMMEDIATELY, the rasping voice through the speakers had said. LEAVE YOUR BICYCLES WHERE THEY ARE.

Instantly, obediently, Jonas had dropped his bike on its side on the path behind his family's dwelling. He had run indoors and stayed there, alone. His parents were both at work, and his little sister, Lily, was

---

words for everyday use

car • go (kär´ gō) n., goods carried by ship, plane, or vehicle. *Food supplies, drinking water, and materials to build temporary shelters were among the items of <u>cargo</u> that the plane carried to the devastated country.*

in • trigue (in trēg´) v., excite interest or curiosity. *The tour guide was able to <u>intrigue</u> visitors to the old house by relating its eerie history.* **intrigued,** *adj.*

an • xious (ank´ shəs) *adj.,* worried or eager. *Nina became extremely <u>anxious</u>, suffering sweaty palms and a dry mouth, before her first vocal solo.* **anxiously,** *adv.*

at the Childcare Center where she spent her after-school hours.

Looking through the front window, he had seen no people: none of the busy afternoon crew of Street Cleaners, Landscape Workers, and Food Delivery people who usually <u>populated</u> the community at that time of day. He saw only the abandoned bikes here and there on their sides; an upturned wheel on one was still revolving slowly.

He had been frightened then. The sense of his own community silent, waiting, had made his stomach churn. He had trembled.

But it had been nothing. Within minutes the speakers had crackled again, and the voice, reassuring now and less urgent, had explained that a Pilot-in-Training had misread his <u>navigational</u> instructions and made a wrong turn. Desperately the Pilot had been trying to make his way back before his error was noticed.

▶ What will happen to the pilot? Why is this a grim future?

NEEDLESS TO SAY, HE WILL BE RELEASED, the voice had said, followed by silence. There was an <u>ironic</u> tone to that final message, as if the Speaker found it amusing; and Jonas had smiled a little, though he knew what a grim statement it had been. For a contributing citizen to be released from the community was a final decision, a terrible punishment, an overwhelming statement of failure.

Even the children were scolded if they used the term lightly at play, jeering at a teammate who missed a catch or stumbled in a race. Jonas had done it once, had shouted at his best friend, "That's it, Asher! You're released!" when Asher's clumsy error had lost a match for his team. He had been taken aside for a brief and serious talk by the coach, had hung his head with guilt and embarrassment, and apologized to Asher after the game.

---

words for everyday use

pop • u • late (päˊ pyə lāt) v., occupy, inhabit. *Human beings <u>populate</u> even the most rugged landscapes on Earth.*

nav • i • ga • tion (na və gāˊ shən) n., science of getting ships, aircraft, or spacecraft from place to place. *A compass is one of the most important tools for the <u>navigation</u> of ships, planes, and people.* **navigational,** adj.

i • ron • ic (ī ränˊ ik) adj., meaning the opposite of what is actually said or expressed. *Lynn's mother's comment, "I love what you've done with your room!", was an <u>ironic</u> comment, as the room was a disaster from a huge slumber party.*

Now, thinking about the feeling of fear as he pedaled home along the river path, he remembered that
moment of <u>palpable</u>, stomach-sinking terror when the
aircraft had streaked above. It was not what he was
feeling now with December approaching. He searched
for the right word to describe his own feeling.

Jonas was careful about language. Not like his
friend, Asher, who talked too fast and mixed things
up, scrambling words and phrases until they were
barely recognizable and often very funny.

◄ How does Jonas
approach language?
How does Asher
approach language?

Jonas grinned, remembering the morning that Asher
had dashed into the classroom, late as usual, arriving
breathlessly in the middle of the chanting of the morning <u>anthem</u>. When the class took their seats at the
conclusion of the <u>patriotic</u> hymn, Asher remained
standing to make his public apology as was required.

"I apologize for inconveniencing my learning
community." Asher ran through the standard apology phrase rapidly, still catching his breath. The
Instructor and class waited patiently for his explanation. The students had all been grinning, because
they had listened to Asher's explanations so many
times before.

"I left home at the correct time but when I was
riding along near the hatchery,[1] the crew was sepa-
rating some salmon. I guess I just got <u>distraught</u>,
watching them.

"I apologize to my classmates," Asher concluded.
He smoothed his rumpled tunic[2] and sat down.

---

1. **hatchery.** A place for hatching eggs (as of poultry or fish)
2. **tunic.** A slip-on garment once worn by men and women of ancient
Greece; a long jacket worn as part of a uniform

**words
for
everyday
use**

pal • pa • ble (pal´ pə bəl) adj., noticeable; capable of being felt. *When I walked
in the kitchen, I knew my parents must have
been having an argument because the tension between them was palpable.*

an • them (an´ thəm) n., song of praise or
gladness. *In the United States, the national
anthem is sung before all sports events.*

pa • tri • ot • ic (pā trē ä´ tik) adj., inspired
by love for one's country. *People around*
the world often demonstrate their *patriotic*
feelings by displaying their country's flag.

dis • traught (di strôt´) adj., extremely
troubled. *Emma became increasingly distraught as each cleaning product she tried
failed to get the dark stain out of the white
carpet.*

▶ How do the students respond to Asher's apology?

"We accept your apology, Asher." The class recited the standard response in <u>unison</u>. Many of the students were biting their lips to keep from laughing.

"I accept your apology, Asher," the Instructor said. He was smiling. "And I thank you, because once again you have provided an opportunity for a lesson in language. 'Distraught' is too strong an adjective to describe salmon-viewing." He turned and wrote "distraught" on the instructional board. Beside it he wrote "distracted."

Jonas, nearing his home now, smiled at the <u>recollection</u>. Thinking, still, as he wheeled his bike into its narrow port beside the door, he realized that frightened was the wrong word to describe his feelings, now that December was almost here. It was too strong an adjective.

He had waited a long time for this special December. Now that it was almost upon him, he wasn't frightened, but he was . . . eager, he decided. He was eager for it to come. And he was excited, certainly. All of the Elevens were excited about the event that would be coming so soon.

But there was a little shudder of nervousness when he thought about it, about what might happen.

Apprehensive, Jonas decided. That's what I am.

"Who wants to be the first tonight, for feelings?" Jonas's father asked, at the conclusion of their evening meal.

It was one of the <u>rituals</u>, the evening telling of feelings. Sometimes Jonas and his sister, Lily, argued over turns, over who would get to go first. Their parents, of course, were part of the ritual; they, too, told their

---

words for everyday use

u • ni • son (yü´ nə sən) *n.*, at the same time, in perfect agreement so as to harmonize exactly. *The cheerleaders called out in perfect <u>unison</u> even as they jumped and twirled and performed backbends.*

rec • ol • lec • tion (re kə lək´ shən) *n.*, memory. *The strong, sweet smell of red roses often stirs in me <u>recollections</u> of summers spent at my grandmother's house, which was surrounded by rose gardens.*

ap • pre • hen • sive (a pri hent´ siv) *adj.*, viewing the future with nervousness or alarm. *After doing poorly on her English test, Janie was very <u>apprehensive</u> about the upcoming math test.*

rit • u • al (ri´ chə wəl) *n.*, a customarily repeated act or ceremony. *Rising at 7 a.m., eating two poached eggs, and walking two miles has been my father's Sunday morning <u>ritual</u> for ten years.*

---

feelings each evening. But like all parents—all adults—they didn't fight and <u>wheedle</u> for their turn.

Nor did Jonas, tonight. His feelings were too complicated this evening. He wanted to share them, but he wasn't eager to begin the process of sifting through his own complicated emotions, even with the help that he knew his parents could give.

◀ Why doesn't Jonas argue with Lily about being first to share his feelings?

"You go, Lily," he said, seeing his sister, who was much younger—only a Seven—wiggling with impatience in her chair.

"I felt very angry this afternoon," Lily announced. "My Childcare group was at the play area, and we had a visiting group of Sevens, and they didn't obey the rules at *all*. One of them—a male; I don't know his name—kept going right to the front of the line for the slide, even though the rest of us were all waiting. I felt so angry at him. I made my hand into a fist, like this." She held up a clenched fist and the rest of the family smiled at her small defiant gesture.

"Why do you think the visitors didn't obey the rules?" Mother asked.

Lily considered, and shook her head. "I don't know. They acted like . . . like . . ."

"Animals?" Jonas suggested. He laughed.

"That's right," Lily said, laughing too. "Like animals." Neither child knew what the word meant, exactly, but it was often used to describe someone uneducated or clumsy, someone who didn't fit in.

◀ What word don't Jonas or Lily exactly know the meaning of? How is the word often used?

"Where were the visitors from?" Father asked.

Lily frowned, trying to remember. "Our leader told us, when he made the welcome speech, but I can't remember. I guess I wasn't paying attention. It was from another community. They had to leave very early, and they had their midday meal on the bus."

Mother nodded. "Do you think it's possible that their rules may be different? And so they simply didn't know what your play area rules were?"

Lily shrugged, and nodded. "I suppose."

---

words for everyday use whee • dle (hwē´ dəl) v., coax, flatter. *The owner used a soft, calming voice to <u>wheedle</u> his dog into her cage.*

"You've visited other communities, haven't you?" Jonas asked. "My group has, often."

Lily nodded again. "When we were Sixes, we went and shared a whole school day with a group of Sixes in their community."

"How did you feel when you were there?"

Lily frowned. "I felt strange. Because their methods were different. They were learning <u>usages</u> that my group hadn't learned yet, so we felt stupid."

Father was listening with interest. "I'm thinking, Lily," he said, "about the boy who didn't obey the rules today. Do you think it's possible that he felt strange and stupid, being in a new place with rules that he didn't know about?"

Lily pondered that. "Yes," she said, finally.

"I feel a little sorry for him," Jonas said, "even though I don't even know him. I feel sorry for anyone who is in a place where he feels strange and stupid."

"How do you feel now, Lily?" Father asked. "Still angry?"

"I guess not," Lily decided. "I guess I feel a little sorry for him. And sorry I made a fist." She grinned.

Jonas smiled back at his sister. Lily's feelings were always <u>straightforward</u>, fairly simple, usually easy to resolve. He guessed that his own had been, too, when he was a Seven.

He listened politely, though not very attentively, while his father took his turn, describing a feeling of worry that he'd had that day at work: a concern about one of the newchildren who wasn't doing well. Jonas's father's title was Nurturer. He and the other Nurturers were responsible for all the physical and emotional needs of every newchild during its earliest life. It was a very important job, Jonas knew, but it wasn't one that interested him much.

"What gender is it?" Lily asked.

▶ Once Lily is finished talking to her parents and Jonas, how does she feel about the boy who made her angry?

▶ About what is Jonas's father concerned? What job does Jonas's father do? How does Jonas feel about his father's job?

---

words for everyday use

us • age (yü´ sij) *n.*, firmly established practice or procedure. *The rules for correct <u>usage</u> of "who" and "whom" can be confusing.*

straight • for • ward (strāt fōr´ wərd) *adj.*, clear-cut, easy to understand, direct. *"I'd like to know why I wasn't invited to your party," Myra asked in her usual <u>straightforward</u> way.*

"Male," Father said. "He's a sweet little male with a lovely <u>disposition</u>. But he isn't growing as fast as he should, and he doesn't sleep soundly. We have him in the extra care section for <u>supplementary nurturing</u>, but the committee's beginning to talk about releasing him."

"Oh, *no,*" Mother murmured sympathetically. "I know how sad that must make you feel."

Jonas and Lily both nodded sympathetically as well. Release of newchildren was always sad, because they hadn't had a chance to enjoy life within the community yet. And they hadn't done anything wrong.

There were only two occasions of release which were not punishment. Release of the elderly, which was a time of celebration for a life well and fully lived; and release of a newchild, which always brought a sense of what-could-we-have-done. This was especially troubling for the Nurturers, like Father, who felt they had failed somehow. But it happened very rarely.

◀ On which two occasions is release not a punishment?

"Well," Father said, "I'm going to keep trying. I may ask the committee for permission to bring him here at night, if you don't mind. You know what the night-crew Nurturers are like. I think this little guy needs something extra."

◀ For what does Jonas's father plan to ask the committee permission? Why?

"Of course," Mother said, and Jonas and Lily nodded. They had heard Father complain about the night crew before. It was a lesser job, night-crew nurturing, assigned to those who lacked the interest or skills or insight for the more <u>vital</u> jobs of the daytime hours. Most of the people on the night crew had not

---

words for everyday use

dis • po • si • tion (dis pə zi´ shən) *n.*, mood or temperament one most often displays. *Usually, Dad has a very pleasant disposition, but when he's sick, he is cranky and whiny.*

sup • ple • men • ta • ry (sə plə men´ tə rē) *adj.*, additional. *The teacher asked the students to complete their homework and two supplementary activities to prepare for the upcoming test.*

nur • ture (nər´ chər) *v.*, educate, foster, further the development of; supply nourishment to. *Students at the wildlife center learn how to nurture ill, injured, and orphaned birds and animals.* **nurturing,** *n.*

vi • tal (vi´ təl) *adj.*, necessary, essential; important. *Nutrition is a vital part of good health.*

even been given <u>spouses</u> because they lacked, somehow, the essential <u>capacity</u> to connect to others, which was required for the creation of a family unit.

"Maybe we could even keep him," Lily suggested sweetly, trying to look innocent. The look was fake, Jonas knew; they all knew.

"Lily," Mother reminded her, smiling, "you know the rules."

Two children—one male, one female—to each family unit. It was written very clearly in the rules.

Lily giggled. "Well," she said, "I thought maybe just this once."

Next, Mother, who held a <u>prominent</u> position at the Department of Justice, talked about her feelings. Today a repeat offender had been brought before her, someone who had broken the rules before. Someone who she hoped had been adequately and fairly punished, and who had been restored to his place: to his job, his home, his family unit. To see him brought before her a second time caused her overwhelming feelings of frustration and anger. And even guilt, that she hadn't made a difference in his life.

▶ How does Jonas's mother feel about the repeat offender who is brought before her? Why?

"I feel frightened, too, for him," she confessed. "You know that there's no third chance. The rules say that if there's a third <u>transgression</u>, he simply has to be released." Jonas shivered. He knew it happened. There was even a boy in his group of Elevens whose father had been released years before. No one ever mentioned it; the disgrace was unspeakable. It was hard to imagine.

Lily stood up and went to her mother. She stroked her mother's arm.

words for everyday use

spouse (spous´) n., married person: husband or wife. _Employees are encouraged to bring their <u>spouses</u> to the holiday party._

ca • pac • i • ty (kə pa´ sə tē) n., individual's mental or physical ability. _Iman has a remarkable <u>capacity</u> for remembering numbers and dates._

prom • i • nent (prä´ mə nənt) adj., leading, widely and popularly known. _Carole is a <u>prominent</u> figure in the community, best known for her years of volunteer service._

trans • gres • sion (trans gre´ shən) n., violation of a law, command, or duty. _Mr. Hui enforces strict classroom rules, and three <u>transgressions</u> within a month, gets you a week of detention._

From his place at the table, Father reached over and took her hand. Jonas reached for the other.

One by one, they comforted her. Soon she smiled, thanked them, and murmured that she felt soothed.

The ritual continued. "Jonas?" Father asked. "You're last, tonight."

Jonas sighed. This evening he almost would have preferred to keep his feelings hidden. But it was, of course, against the rules.

◀ What would Jonas prefer to keep hidden? Why doesn't he?

"I'm feeling apprehensive," he confessed, glad that the appropriate descriptive word had finally come to him.

"Why is that, son?" His father looked concerned.

"I know there's really nothing to worry about," Jonas explained, "and that every adult has been through it. I know you have, Father, and you too, Mother. But it's the Ceremony that I'm apprehensive about. It's almost December."

Lily looked up, her eyes wide. "The Ceremony of Twelve," she whispered in an awed voice. Even the smallest children—Lily's age and younger—knew that it lay in the future for each of them.

"I'm glad you told us of your feelings," Father said.

"Lily," Mother said, beckoning to the little girl, "go on now and get into your nightclothes. Father and I are going to stay here and talk to Jonas for a while."

Lily sighed, but obediently she got down from her chair. "Privately?" she asked.

Mother nodded. "Yes," she said, "this talk will be a private one with Jonas."

---

words for everyday use
beck • on (be´ kən) v., summon or signal typically with a wave or nod. *Keesha flailed her arms wildly, in an effort to beckon her friends, who were across the stadium.*

Chapter 2

JONAS WATCHED AS his father poured a fresh cup of coffee. He waited.

"You know," his father finally said, "every December was exciting to me when I was young. And it has been for you and Lily, too, I'm sure. Each December brings such changes."

Jonas nodded. He could remember the Decembers back to when he had become, well, probably a Four. The earlier ones were lost to him. But he observed them each year, and he remembered Lily's earliest Decembers. He remembered when his family received Lily, the day she was named, the day that she had become a One.

▶ What happens each December to the newchildren born the previous year?

The Ceremony for the Ones was always noisy and fun. Each December, all the newchildren born in the previous year turned One. One at a time—there were always fifty in each year's group, if none had been released—they had been brought to the stage by the Nurturers who had cared for them since birth. Some were already walking, wobbly on their unsteady legs; others were no more than a few days old, wrapped in blankets, held by their Nurturers.

"I enjoy the Naming," Jonas said.

His mother agreed, smiling. "The year we got Lily, we knew, of course, that we'd receive our female, because we'd made our application and been approved. But I'd been wondering and wondering what her name would be."

"I could have sneaked a look at the list prior to the ceremony," Father confided. "The committee always makes the list in advance, and it's right there in the office at the Nurturing Center.

"As a matter of fact," he went on. "I feel a little guilty about this. But I *did* go in this afternoon and looked to see if this year's Naming list had been made yet. It was right there in the office, and I looked up number Thirty-six—that's the little guy I've been concerned about—because it occurred to me that it might enhance his nurturing if I could call him by a name. Just privately, of course, when no one else is around."

"Did you find it?" Jonas asked. He was fascinated. It didn't seem a terribly important rule, but the fact that his father had broken a rule at all awed him. He glanced at his mother, the one responsible for adherence to the rules, and was relieved that she was smiling.

◄ By what is Jonas awed?

His father nodded. "His name—if he makes it to the Naming without being released, of course—is to be Gabriel. So I whisper that to him when I feed him every four hours, and during exercise and playtime. If no one can hear me.

"I call him Gabe, actually," he said, and grinned.

"Gabe." Jonas tried it out. A good name, he decided.

Though Jonas had only become a Five the year that they acquired Lily and learned her name, he remembered the excitement, the conversations at home, wondering about her: how she would look, who she would be, how she would fit into their established family unit. He remembered climbing the steps to the stage with his parents, his father by his side that year instead of with the Nurturers, since it was the year that he would be given a newchild of his own.

He remembered his mother taking the newchild, his sister, into her arms, while the document was read to the assembled family units. "Newchild Twenty-three," the Namer had read. "Lily."

He remembered his father's look of delight, and that his father had whispered, "She's one of my favorites. I was hoping for her to be the one." The crowd had clapped, and Jonas had grinned. He liked his sister's name. Lily, barely awake, had waved her

---

words for everyday use

en • hance (in hants´) v., increase or improve in value or quality. *The previous owners had taken great care of the house, which served to enhance its overall appearance.*

ad • her • ence (ad hir´ ənts) v., steady of faithful attachment; loyalty. *At the banquet, Solomon was recognized for being a top-notch lawyer and also for his longtime adherence to the ethics of his profession.*

ac • quire (a kwīr´) v., get as one's own; come into possession or control of. *My brother put an advertisement in the local paper in an effort to acquire a used lawnmower at a good price.*

as • sem • ble (ə sem´ bəl) v., bring together. *After reading the directions, Lila's parents easily assembled the dollhouse.* **assembled,** adj.

small fist. Then they had stepped down to make room for the next family unit.

"When I was an Eleven," his father said now, "as you are, Jonas, I was very impatient, waiting for the Ceremony of Twelve. It's a long two days. I remember that I enjoyed the Ones, as I always do, but that I didn't pay much attention to the other ceremonies, except for my sister's. She became a Nine that year, and got her bicycle. I'd been teaching her to ride mine, even though <u>technically</u> I wasn't supposed to."

Jonas laughed. It was one of the few rules that was not taken very seriously and was almost *always* broken. The children all received their bicycles at Nine; they were not allowed to ride bicycles before then. But almost always, the older brothers and sisters had secretly taught the younger ones. Jonas had been thinking already about teaching Lily.

There was talk about changing the rule and giving the bicycles at an earlier age. A committee was studying the idea. When something went to a committee for study, the people always joked about it. They said that the committee members would become Elders by the time the rule change was made.

Rules were very hard to change. Sometimes, if it was a very important rule—unlike the one governing the age for bicycles—it would have to go, eventually, to The Receiver for a decision. The Receiver was the most important Elder. Jonas had never even seen him, that he knew of; someone in a position of such importance lived and worked alone. But the committee would never bother The Receiver with a question about bicycles; they would simply fret and argue about it themselves for years, until the citizens forgot that it had ever gone to them for study.

His father continued. "So I watched and cheered when my sister, Katya, became a Nine and removed her hair ribbons and got her bicycle," Father went

▶ What rule is almost always broken?

▶ Who sometimes decides whether to change very important rules?

▶ What happens to most rules studied by the committee?

words for everyday use

tech • ni • cal (tek´ ni kəl) *adj.,* based on strict interpretation. *I understand in very general terms how my computer works, but my sister can tell you about all the <u>technical</u> details that I don't really understand.* **technically,** *adv.*

on. "Then I didn't pay much attention to the Tens and Elevens. And *finally,* at the end of the second day, which seemed to go on forever, it was my turn. It was the Ceremony of Twelve."

Jonas shivered. He pictured his father, who must have been a shy and quiet boy, for he was a shy and quiet man, seated with his group, waiting to be called to the stage. The Ceremony of Twelve was the last of the Ceremonies. The most important.

◀ What does Jonas assume his father must have been like as a boy? Why?

"I remember how proud my parents looked—and my sister, too; even though she wanted to be out riding the bicycle publicly, she stopped <u>fidgeting</u> and was very still and attentive when my turn came.

"But to be honest, Jonas," his father said, "for me there was not the element of suspense that there is with your Ceremony. Because I was already fairly certain of what my Assignment was to be."

Jonas was surprised. There was no way, really, to know in advance. It was a secret selection, made by the leaders of the community, the Committee of Elders, who took the responsibility so seriously that there were never even any jokes made about Assignments.

◀ Who decides what one's Assignment in life will be?

His mother seemed surprised, too. "How could you have known?" she asked.

His father smiled his gentle smile. "Well, it was clear to me—and my parents later confessed that it had been obvious to them, too—what my <u>aptitude</u> was. I had always loved the newchildren more than anything. When my friends in my age group were holding bicycle races, or building toy vehicles or bridges with their construction sets, or—"

◀ Why was Jonas's father fairly certain of what his Assignment would be?

"All the things I do with my friends," Jonas pointed out, and his mother nodded in agreement.

"I always participated, of course, because as children we must experience all of those things. And I studied hard in school, as you do, Jonas. But again

---

words for everyday use

fidg • et (fiˊ jət) *v.,* move or act restlessly or nervously. *Our little sister sat quietly during the first hour of the concert, but after that, she began to fidget.*

ap • ti • tude (apˊ tə tüd) *n.,* natural ability, talent. *Calvin has a strong aptitude for math, but history gives him trouble.*

and again, during free time, I found myself drawn to the newchildren. I spent almost all of my volunteer hours helping in the Nurturing Center. Of course the Elders knew that, from their observation."

▶ Of what has Jonas been aware during the past year?

Jonas nodded. During the past year he had been aware of the increasing level of observation. In school, at recreation time, and during volunteer hours, he had noticed the Elders watching him and the other Elevens. He had seen them taking notes. He knew, too, that the Elders were meeting for long hours with all of the instructors that he and the other Elevens had had during their years of school.

"So I expected it, and I was pleased, but not at all surprised, when my Assignment was announced as Nurturer," Father explained.

"Did everyone applaud, even though they weren't surprised?" Jonas asked.

"Oh, of course. They were happy for me, that my Assignment was what I wanted most. I felt very fortunate." His father smiled.

▶ Which Assignments would disappoint Jonas?

"Were any of the Elevens disappointed, your year?" Jonas asked. Unlike his father, he had no idea what his Assignment would be. But he knew that some would disappoint him. Though he respected his father's work, Nurturer would not be his wish. And he didn't envy Laborers at all.

His father thought. "No I don't think so. Of course the Elders are so careful in their observations and selections."

"I think it's probably the most important job in our community," his mother commented.

"My friend Yoshiko was surprised by her selection as Doctor," Father said, "but she was thrilled. And let's see, there was Andrei—I remember that when we were boys he never wanted to do physical things. He spent all the recreation time he could with his construction set, and his volunteer hours were always on building sites. The Elders knew that, of course. Andrei was given the Assignment of Engineer and he was delighted."

"Andrei later designed the bridge that crosses the river to the west of town," Jonas's mother said. "It wasn't there when we were children."

"There are very rarely disappointments, Jonas. I don't think you need to worry about that," his father <u>reassured</u> him. "And if there are, you know there's an appeal process." But they all laughed at that—an appeal went to a committee for study.

"I worry a little about Asher's Assignment," Jonas confessed. "Asher's such *fun*. But he doesn't really have any serious interests. He makes a game out of everything."

◀ What worries Jonas?

His father chuckled. "You know," he said, "I remember when Asher was a newchild at the Nurturing Center, before he was named. He never cried. He giggled and laughed at everything. All of us on the staff enjoyed nurturing Asher."

"The Elders know Asher," his mother said. "They'll find exactly the right Assignment for him. I don't think you need to worry about him. But, Jonas, let me warn you about something that may not have occurred to you. I know I didn't think about it until after my Ceremony of Twelve."

"What's that?"

"Well, it's the last of the Ceremonies, as you know. After Twelve, age isn't important. Most of us even lose track of how old we are as time passes, though the information is in the Hall of Open Records, and we could go and look it up if we wanted to. What's important is the preparation for adult life, and the training you'll receive in your Assignment."

◀ What ceases to be important after one become Twelve?

◀ What becomes one's focus once one is Twelve?

"I know that," Jonas said. "Everyone knows that."

"But it means," his mother went on, "that you'll move into a new group. And each of your friends will. You'll no longer be spending your time with your group of Elevens. After the Ceremony of Twelve, you'll be with your Assignment group, with those in training. No more volunteer hours. No more <u>recreation</u> hours. So your friends will no longer be as close."

◀ What changes take place after the Ceremony of Twelve?

---

words for everyday use

re • as • sure (rē ə shùr´) v., comfort; give confidence to; free from doubt. *I did my best to <u>reassure</u> Jeannie that she would find a new job, but I could tell she didn't really believe me.*

rec • re • a • tion (re krē ā´ shən) n., means of refreshment of strength and spirit that is separate from one's work. *Some pursue swimming as a sport, others as a means of <u>recreation</u>.*

Jonas shook his head. "Asher and I will always be friends," he said firmly. "And there will still be school."

"That's true," his father agreed. "but what your mother said is true as well. There will be changes."

"*Good* changes, though," his mother pointed out. "After my Ceremony of Twelve, I missed my childhood recreation. But when I entered my training for Law and Justice, I found myself with people who shared my interests. I made friends on a new level, friends of all ages."

▶ What became less important to Jonas's mother once she became Twelve?

"Did you still play at all, after Twelve?" Jonas asked.

"Occasionally," his mother replied. "But it didn't seem as important to me."

"I did," his father said, laughing. "I still do. Every day, at the Nurturing Center, I play bounce-on-the-knee, and peek-a-boo, and hug-the-teddy." He reached over and stroked Jonas's neatly trimmed hair. "Fun doesn't end when you become Twelve."

Lily appeared, wearing her nightclothes, in the doorway. She gave an impatient sigh. "This is certainly a very *long* private conversation," she said. "And there are certain people waiting for their comfort object."

▶ What is taken away when one becomes an Eight?

"Lily," her mother said fondly, "you're very close to being an Eight, and when you're an Eight, your comfort object will be taken away. It will be recycled to the younger children. You should be starting to go off to sleep without it."

But her father had already gone to the shelf and taken down the stuffed elephant which was kept there. Many of the comfort objects, like Lily's, were soft, stuffed, imaginary creatures. Jonas's had been called a bear.

"Here you are, Lily-billy," he said. I'll come help you remove your hair ribbons."

Jonas and his mother rolled their eyes, yet they watched <u>affectionately</u> as Lily and her father headed

---

words for everyday use   af • fec • tion • ate (ə fek´ shə nət) *adj.*, caring, kind, warm-hearted, tender. *Our mother is very <u>affectionate</u>, hugging us and saying she loves us often.* **affectionately,** *adv.*

to her sleeping-room with the stuffed elephant that had been given to her as her comfort object when she was born. His mother moved to her big desk and opened her briefcase; her work never seemed to end, even when she was at home in the evening. Jonas went to his own desk and began to sort through his school papers for the evening's assignment. But his mind was still on December and the coming Ceremony.

Though he had been reassured by the talk with his parents, he hadn't the slightest idea what Assignment the Elders would be selecting for his future, or how he might feel about it when the day came.

◄ About what is Jonas still uncertain?

Chapter 3

▶ What does Lily point out about the newchild's eyes?

"OH, LOOK!" Lily squealed in delight. "Isn't he cute? Look how tiny he is! And he has funny eyes like yours, Jonas!" Jonas glared at her. He didn't like it that she had mentioned his eyes. He waited for his father to <u>chastise</u> Lily. But Father was busy unstrapping the carrying basket from the back of his bicycle. Jonas walked over to look.

It was the first thing Jonas noticed as he looked at the newchild peering up curiously from the basket. The pale eyes.

Almost every citizen in the community had dark eyes. His parents did, and Lily did, and so did all of his group members and friends. But there were a few exceptions: Jonas himself, and a female Five who he had noticed had the different, lighter eyes. No one

▶ What is considered rude? Why does Jonas decide that Lily will soon need to learn this?

mentioned such things; it was not a rule, but was considered rude to call attention to things that were <u>unsettling</u> or different about individuals. Lily, he decided, would have to learn that soon, or she would be called in for chastisement because of her insensitive chatter.

Father put his bike into its port. Then he picked up the basket and carried it into the house. Lily followed behind, but she glanced back over her shoulder at Jonas and teased, "Maybe he had the same Birthmother as you."

Jonas shrugged. He followed them inside. But he had been startled by the newchild's eyes. Mirrors were rare in the community; they weren't forbidden, but there was no real need of them, and Jonas had simply never bothered to look at himself very often even when he found himself in a location where a

▶ Of what is Jonas reminded about light eyes?

mirror existed. Now, seeing the newchild and its expression, he was reminded that the light eyes were not only a rarity but gave the one who had them a certain look—what was it? *Depth,* he decided; as if one were looking into the clear water of the river,

---

words for everyday use

chas • tise (chas´ tīz) *v.,* criticize severely; punish. *I didn't like to <u>chastise</u> my younger brother, but sometimes his rude behavior demanded it.*

un • set • tling (ən set´ liŋ) *adj.,* having the effect of upsetting or disturbing. *I find loud thunder and lightning storms particularly <u>unsettling</u>.*

down to the bottom, where things might <u>lurk</u> which hadn't been discovered yet. He felt <u>self-conscious</u>, realizing that he, too, had that look.

He went to his desk, pretending not to be interested in the newchild. On the other side of the room, Mother and Lily were bending over to watch as Father unwrapped its blanket.

"What's his comfort object called?" Lily asked, picking up the stuffed creature which had been placed beside the newchild in his basket.

Father glanced at it. "Hippo," he said.

Lily giggled at the strange word. "Hippo," she repeated, and put the comfort object down again. She peered at the unwrapped newchild, who waved his arms.

"I think newchildren are so cute," Lily sighed. "I hope I get assigned to be a Birthmother."

◀ What does Lily's mother tell her not to say? Why?

"Lily!" Mother spoke very sharply. "Don't say that. There's very little honor in that Assignment."

"But I was talking to Natasha. You know the Ten who lives around the corner? She does some of her volunteer hours at the Birthing Center. And she told me that the Birthmothers get wonderful food, and they have very gentle exercise periods, and most of the time they just play games and amuse themselves while they're waiting. I think I'd like that," Lily said <u>petulantly</u>.

◀ What is life like for Birthmothers?

"Three years," Mother told her firmly. "Three births, and that's all. After that they are Laborers for the rest of their adult lives, until the day that they enter the House of the Old. Is that what you want, Lily? Three lazy years, and then hard physical labor until you are old?"

"Well, no, I guess not," Lily acknowledged <u>reluctantly</u>.

words for everyday use

lurk (lərk´) v., lie hidden. *Our cat likes to* <u>lurk</u> *under beds and other furniture in the house.*

self- • con • scious (self kän´ shəs) adj., intensely aware of oneself as an object of the observation of others. *Much attention was focused on me after I won the award, and I couldn't help feeling <u>self-conscious</u>.*

pet • u • lant (pe´ chə lənt) adj., rude in speech or behavior. *Ron's <u>petulant</u> remarks were obviously made out of jealousy.* **petulantly,** adv.

re • luc • tant (ri lək´ tənt) adj., feeling or showing hesitation or unwillingness. *The dog was <u>reluctant</u> to give up its bone.* **reluctantly,** adv.

Father turned the newchild onto his tummy in the basket. He sat beside it and rubbed its small back with a <u>rhythmic</u> motion. "Anyway, Lily-billy," he said affectionately, "the Birthmothers never even get to see newchildren. If you enjoy the little ones so much, you should hope for an Assignment as Nurturer."

"When you're an Eight and start your volunteer hours, you can try some at the Nurturing Center," Mother suggested.

"Yes, I think I will," Lily said. She knelt beside the basket. "What did you say his name is? Gabriel? Hello, Gabriel," she said in a <u>singsong</u> voice. Then she giggled. "Ooops," she whispered. "I think he's asleep. I guess I'd better be quiet."

Jonas turned to the school assignments on his desk. Some chance of *that,* he thought. Lily was *never* quiet. Probably she should hope for an Assignment as Speaker, so that she could sit in the office with the microphone all day, making announcements. He laughed silently to himself, picturing his sister <u>droning</u> on in the self-important voice that all the Speakers seemed to develop, saying things like ATTENTION. THIS IS A REMINDER TO FEMALES UNDER NINE THAT HAIR RIBBONS ARE TO BE NEATLY TIED AT ALL TIMES.

He turned toward Lily and noticed to his satisfaction that her ribbons were, as usual, undone and dangling. There would be an announcement like that quite soon, he felt certain, and it would be directed mainly at Lily, though her name, of course, would not be mentioned. Everyone would know.

Everyone had known, he remembered with humiliation, that the announcement ATTENTION. THIS IS A REMINDER TO MALE ELEVENS THAT OBJECTS

▶ *What did everyone know about the announcement? Why did no one mention it?*

rhyth • mic (rith´ mik) *adj.,* marked by or moving in pronounced rhythm. *The drummers led the marching band with a loud and <u>rhythmic</u> cadence.*

sing • song (siŋ´ sän) *adj.,* having a uniform rhythm. *Two children in the playground clapped hands together as they repeated nursery rhymes in <u>singsong</u> voices.*

drone (drōn´) *v.,* talk in a persistently dull tone. *I gasped as I watched my mother's eyes close for several seconds as she continued to listen to Aunt Rose <u>drone</u> on about her various health problems.*

ARE NOT TO BE REMOVED FROM THE RECRE-
ATION AREA AND THAT SNACKS ARE TO BE EATEN,
NOT <u>HOARDED</u> had been specifically directed at
him, the day last month that he had taken an apple
home. No one had mentioned it, not even his parents, because the public announcement had been
sufficient to produce the appropriate remorse. He
had, of course, disposed of the apple and made his
apology to the Recreation Director the next morning,
before school.

Jonas thought again about that incident. He was
still <u>bewildered</u> by it. Not by the announcement or
the necessary apology; those were standard procedures, and he had deserved them—but by the incident itself. He probably should have brought up his
feeling of bewilderment that very evening when the
family unit had shared their feelings of the day. But
he had not been able to sort out and put words to the
source of his confusion, so he had let it pass.

It had happened during the recreation period,
when he had been playing with Asher. Jonas had
casually picked up an apple from the basket where
the snacks were kept, and had thrown it to his friend.
Asher had thrown it back, and they had begun a
simple game of catch.

There had been nothing special about it; it was an
activity that he had performed countless times:
throw, catch, throw, catch. It was effortless for Jonas,
and even boring, though Asher enjoyed it, and playing catch was a required activity for Asher because it
would improve his hand-eye coordination, which
was not up to standards.

But suddenly Jonas had noticed, following the
path of the apple through the air with his eyes, that
the piece of fruit had—well, this was the part that he
couldn't adequately understand—the apple had

◀ *What did Jonas
suddenly notice
about the apple?*

**words
for
everyday
use**

hoard (hōrd´) v., store up and hide away
a supply for oneself. *My brother likes to
hoard any chocolate that comes into our
house, but I found his secret hiding place
and help myself to whatever I want when
he's not around.*

be • wil • der (bi wil´ dər) v., perplex or
confuse. *My mother stared at the directions
for assembling the computer station, and I
could tell all the drawings and charts did
nothing but bewilder her.*

changed. Just for an instant. It had changed in mid-air, he remembered. Then it was in his hand, and he looked at it carefully, but it was the same apple. Unchanged. The same size and shape: a perfect <u>sphere</u>. The same <u>nondescript</u> shade, about the same shade as his own tunic.

There was absolutely nothing remarkable about that apple. He had tossed it back and forth between his hands a few times, then thrown it again to Asher. And again—in the air, for an instant only—it had changed.

It had happened four times. Jonas had blinked, looked around, and then tested his eyesight, squinting at the small print on the identification badge attached to his tunic. He read his name quite clearly. He could also clearly see Asher at the other end of the throwing area. And he had had no problem catching the apple.

Jonas had been completely mystified.

"Ash?" he had called. "Does anything seem strange to you? About the apple?"

"Yes," Asher called back, laughing. "It jumps out of my hand onto the ground!" Asher had just dropped it once again.

▶ Why did Jonas take the apple home?

So Jonas laughed too, and with his laughter tried to ignore his uneasy conviction that *something* had happened. But he had taken the apple home, against the recreation area rules. That evening, before his parents and Lily arrived at the dwelling, he had held it in his hands and looked at it carefully. It was slightly bruised now, because Asher had dropped it several times. But there was nothing at all unusual about the apple.

He had held a magnifying glass to it. He had tossed it several times across the room, watching, and then rolled it around and around on his desktop, waiting for the thing to happen again.

words for everyday use

sphere (sfir´) *n.*, globular body such as a ball. *A globe presents the most accurate representation of the world because it is a sphere, like Earth.*

non • de • script (nän di skript´) *adj.*, lacking distinctive or interesting qualities: dull, drab. *Selena's bright and unique way of dressing is anything but nondescript.*

But it hadn't. The only thing that happened was the announcement later that evening over the speaker, the announcement that had singled him out without using his name, that had caused both of his parents to glance meaningfully at his desk where the apple still lay.

Now, sitting at his desk, starting at his schoolwork as his family <u>hovered</u> over the newchild in its basket, he shook his head, trying to forget the odd incident. He forced himself to arrange his papers and try to study a little before the evening meal. The newchild, Gabriel, stirred and whimpered, and Father spoke softly to Lily, explaining the feeding procedure as he opened the container that held the formula[1] and equipment.

The evening proceeded as all evenings did in the family unit, in the dwelling,[2] in the community: quiet, reflective, a time for <u>renewal</u> and preparation for the day to come. It was different only in the addition to it of the newchild with his pale, <u>solemn</u>, knowing eyes.

◀ How do all evenings in the family unit proceed? What is different about this evening?

---

1. **formula.** Milk substitute for feeding an infant
2. **dwelling.** Shelter; home

words for everyday use

hov • er (hə´ vər) v., move to and fro near a place; to remain suspended over a place or object. *The bee <u>hovered</u> above the flower before slipping inside it.*

dwell • ing (dwe´ liŋ) n., shelter (as a house) in which people live. *The types of <u>dwellings</u> in which people around the world live often depend on the landscape and climate of the area.*

re • new • al (ri nü´ əl) n., act or process of restoring to freshness, vigor, or perfection. *The relaxing vacation left me with a refreshing sense of <u>renewal</u>.*

sol • emn (sä´ ləm) adj., somber; serious; thoughtful; intense. *I expected people to be <u>solemn</u> at the funeral, but instead, they told stories and laughed.*

Chapter 4

▶ Why doesn't Jonas normally do volunteer hours with Asher?

JONAS RODE AT a <u>leisurely</u> pace, glancing at the bike-ports beside the buildings to see if he could spot Asher's. He didn't often do his volunteer hours with his friend because Asher frequently fooled around and made serious work a little difficult. But now, with Twelve coming so soon and the volunteer hours ending, it didn't seem to matter.

The freedom to choose where to spend those hours had always seemed a wonderful <u>luxury</u> to Jonas; other hours of the day were so carefully regulated.

He remembered when he had become an Eight, as Lily would do shortly, and had been faced with that freedom of choice. The Eights always set out on their first volunteer hour a little nervously, giggling and staying in groups of friends. They almost invariably did their hours on Recreation Duty first, helping with the younger ones in a place where they still felt comfortable. But with guidance, as they developed self-confidence and maturity, they moved on to other jobs, gravitating toward those that would suit their own interests and skills.

▶ Which duty do most Eights choose for their volunteer hours at first? Why? Toward what do the Eights ultimately gravitate?

A male Eleven named Benjamin had done his entire nearly-Four years in the Rehabilitation Center, working with citizens who had been injured. It was rumored that he was as skilled now as the Rehabilitation Directors themselves, and that he had even developed some machines and methods to hasten <u>rehabilitation</u>. There was no doubt that Benjamin would receive his Assignment to that field and would probably be permitted to <u>bypass</u> most of the training.

Jonas was impressed by the things Benjamin had achieved. He knew him, of course, since they had

words for everyday use

lei • sure (lē´zhər) *n.*, time free from work or duties. *My father recently retired and so has more <u>leisure</u> time now to pursue activities other than work.* **leisurely,** *adj., adv.*

lux • u • ry (lək´shə rē) *n.*, indulgence in something that provides pleasure, satisfaction, or ease. *My friend's mom indulges in the <u>luxury</u> of a massage once a month.*

re • ha • bil • i • ta • tion (rē ə bi´lə tā´shən) *n.*, restoration to a condition of health. *Taji was in a very serious automobile accident a few days ago, and doctors say her path to <u>rehabilitation</u> will be long and difficult, but they expect a full recovery.*

by • pass (bī´pas) *v.*, avoid; to manage to get around. *Tanya takes a different route home from school now to <u>bypass</u> her old boyfriend's house.*

always been groupmates, but they had never talked about the boy's accomplishments because such a conversation would have been awkward for Benjamin. There was never any comfortable way to mention or discuss one's successes without breaking the rule against bragging, even if one didn't mean to. It was a minor rule, rather like rudeness, punishable only by gentle chastisement. But still. Better to steer clear of an occasion governed by a rule which would be so easy to break.

◀ Why has Jonas never talked with Benjamin about his accomplishments?

The area of dwellings behind him, Jonas rode past the community structures, hoping to spot Asher's bicycle parked beside one of the small factories or office buildings. He passed the Childcare Center where Lily stayed after school, and the play areas surrounding it. He rode through the Central Plaza and the large Auditorium where public meetings were held.

Jonas slowed and looked at the nametags on the bicycles lined up outside the Nurturing Center. Then he checked those outside Food Distribution; it was always fun to help with the deliveries, and he hoped he would find his friend there so that they could go together on the daily rounds, carrying the cartons of supplies into the dwellings of the community. But he finally found Asher's bicycle—leaning, as usual, instead of upright in its port, as it should have been—at the House of the Old.

There was only one other child's bicycle there, that of a female Eleven named Fiona. Jonas liked Fiona. She was a good student, quiet and polite, but she had a sense of fun as well, and it didn't surprise him that she was working with Asher today. He parked his bicycle neatly in the port beside theirs and entered the building.

"Hello, Jonas," the attendant at the front desk said. She handed him the sign-up sheet and stamped her own official seal beside his signature. All of his volunteer hours would be carefully <u>tabulated</u> at the

---

words for everyday use

tab • u • late (ta´ byə lāt) v., count, record, or list systematically. *We watched our teacher carefully <u>tabulate</u> each team's points twice before declaring the winner.*

▶ *What once happened long ago to an Eleven?*

Hall of Open Records. Once, long ago, it was whispered among the children, an Eleven had arrived at the Ceremony of Twelve only to hear a public announcement that he had not completed the required number of volunteer hours and would not, therefore, be given his Assignment. He had been permitted an additional month in which to complete the hours, and then given his Assignment privately, with no applause, no celebration: a disgrace that had clouded his entire future.

"It's good to have some volunteers here today," the attendant told him. "We celebrated a release this morning, and that always throws the schedule off a little, so things get backed up." She looked at a printed sheet. "Let's see. Asher and Fiona are helping in the bathing room. Why don't you join them there? You know where it is, don't you?"

Jonas nodded, thanked her, and walked down the long hallway. He glanced into the rooms on either side. The Old were sitting quietly, some visiting and talking with one another, others doing handwork and simple crafts. A few were asleep. Each room was comfortably furnished, the floors covered with thick carpeting. It was a <u>serene</u> and slow-paced place, unlike the busy centers of <u>manufacture</u> and <u>distribution</u> where the daily work of the community occurred.

▶ *Why doesn't Jonas have any idea of what his assigned career will be?*

Jonas was glad that he had, over the years, chosen to do his hours in a variety of places so that he could experience the differences. He realized, though, that no focusing on the one area meant he was left with not the slightest idea—not even a *guess*—of what his Assignment would be.

He laughed softly. Thinking about the Ceremony again, Jonas? he teased himself. But he suspected

---

words for everyday use

se • rene (sə rēn´) *adj.*, calm; restful. *Once the tourists have left, summer evenings on the beach are quiet and <u>serene</u>, with only sounds of the ocean to break the silence.*

man • u • fac • ture (man yə fak´ chər) *n.*, act or process of making products by hand or machinery. *The automobile company announced that next year they will begin to <u>manufacture</u> a car that runs on electricity.*

dis • tri • bu • tion (dis trə byü´ shən) *n.*, act or process of dispensing or doling out. *While one group of students is responsible for planning the winter festival, another group of students is responsible for creation and <u>distribution</u> of the posters announcing the festival.*

that with the date so near, probably all of his friends were, too.

He passed a Caretaker walking slowly with one of the Old in the hall. "Hello, Jonas," the young uniformed man said, smiling pleasantly. The woman beside him, whose arm he held, was hunched over as she shuffled along in her soft slippers. She looked toward Jonas and smiled, but her dark eyes were clouded and blank. He realized she was blind.

He entered the bathing room with its warm moist air and scent of cleansing lotions. He removed his tunic, hung it carefully on a wall hook, and put on the volunteer's smock that was folded on a shelf.

"Hi, Jonas!" Asher called from the corner where he was kneeling beside a tub. Jonas saw Fiona nearby, at a different tub. She looked up and smiled at him, but she was busy, gently washing a man who lay in the warm water.

Jonas greeted them and the caretaking attendants at work nearby. Then he went to the row of padded lounging chairs where others of the Old were waiting. He had worked here before; he knew what to do.

"Your turn, Larissa," he said, reading the nametag on the woman's robe. "I'll just start the water and then help you up." He pressed the button on a nearby empty tub and watched as the warm water flowed in through the many small openings on the sides. The tub would be filled in a minute and the water flow would stop automatically.

He helped the woman from the chair, led her to the tub, removed her robe, and <u>steadied</u> her with his hand on her arm as she stepped in and lowered herself. She leaned back and sighed with pleasure, her head on a soft cushioned headrest.

"Comfortable?" he asked, and she nodded, her eyes closed. Jonas squeezed cleansing lotion onto the clean sponge at the edge of the tub and began to wash her frail body.

---

words for everyday use
stead • y (steˊ dē) v., make or keep stable, firm in position, or sure in movement. *The young girl's father ran behind her on the bike, keeping a hand lightly on the back of her seat to <u>steady</u> her if needed.*

▶ Of what does bathing Larissa remind Jonas?

Last night he had watched as his father bathed the newchild. This was much the same: the fragile skin, the soothing water, the gentle motion of his hand, slippery with soap. The relaxed, peaceful smile on the woman's face reminded him of Gabriel being bathed.

▶ To whom do the rules of nakedness not apply?

And the nakedness, too. It was against the rules for children or adults to look at another's nakedness; but the rule did not apply to newchildren or the Old. Jonas was glad. It was a <u>nuisance</u> to keep oneself covered while changing for games, and the required apology if one had by mistake glimpsed another's body was always awkward. He couldn't see why it was necessary. He liked the feeling of safety here in this warm and quiet room; he liked the expression of trust on the woman's face as she lay in the water unprotected, exposed, and free.

From the corner of his eye he could see his friend Fiona help the old man from the tub and tenderly pat his thin naked body dry with an absorbant cloth. She helped him into his robe.

Jonas thought Larissa had drifted into sleep, as the Old often did, and he was careful to keep his motions steady and gentle so he wouldn't wake her. He was surprised when she spoke, her eyes still closed.

"This morning we celebrated the release of Roberto," she told him. "It was wonderful."

"I knew Roberto!" Jonas said. "I helped with his feeding the last time I was here, just a few weeks ago. He was a very interesting man."

Larissa opened her eyes happily. "They told his whole life before they released him," she said. "They always do. But to be honest," she whispered with a <u>mischievous</u> look, "some of the tellings are a little boring. I've even seen some of the Old fall asleep during tellings—when they released Edna recently. Did you know Edna?"

▶ What does Larissa say about Edna and her release celebration?

| **words for everyday use** | **nui • sance** (nü´ səns) *n.*, something that is annoying or unpleasant. *Sometimes weeding the garden is a* <u>*nuisance*</u>*, but at other times I find it calming and satisfying.* | **mis • chie • vous** (mis´ chə vəs) *adj.*, irresponsibly playful. *The puppy was quite* <u>*mischievous*</u>*, getting into the garbage or climbing up on the furniture whenever no one was looking.* |

Jonas shook his head. He couldn't recall anyone named Edna.

"Well, they tried to make her life sound meaningful. And of course," she added primly, "all lives *are* meaningful, I don't mean that they aren't. But *Edna*. My goodness. She was a Birthmother, and then she worked in Food Production for years, until she came here. She never even had a family unit."

Larissa lifted her head and looked around to make sure no one else was listening. Then she confided, "I don't think Edna was very smart."

Jonas laughed. He rinsed her left arm, laid it back into the water, and began to wash her feet. She murmured with pleasure as he massaged her feet with the sponge.

"But Roberto's life was wonderful," Larissa went on, after a moment. "He had been an Instructor of Elevens—you now how important that is—and he'd been on the Planning Committee. And—goodness, I don't know how he found the time—he also raised two very successful children, and he was *also* the one who did the landscaping design for the Central Plaza. He didn't do the actual labor, of course."

"Now your back. Lean forward and I'll help you sit up." Jonas put his arm around her and supported her as she sat. He squeezed the sponge against her back and began to rub her sharp-boned shoulders. "Tell me about the celebration."

"Well, there was the telling of his life. That is always first. Then the toast. We all raised our glasses and cheered. We chanted the anthem. He made a lovely good-bye speech. And several of us made little speeches wishing him well. I didn't, though. I've never been fond of public speaking.

"He was thrilled. You should have seen the look on his face when they let him go."

Jonas slowed the strokes of his hand on her back thoughtfully. "Larissa," he asked, "what happens when they make the actual release? Where exactly did Roberto go?"

She lifted her bare wet shoulders in a small shrug. "I don't know. I don't think anybody does, except the committee. He just bowed to all of us and then

◀ *Who knows where those who are released go?*

walked, like they all do, through the special door in the Releasing Room. But you should have seen his look. Pure happiness, I'd call it."

Jonas grinned. "I wish I'd been there to see it."

Larissa frowned. "I don't know why they don't let children come. Not enough room, I guess. They should enlarge the Releasing Room."

"We'll have to suggest that to the committee. Maybe they'd study it," Jonas said slyly, and Larissa <u>chortled</u> with laughter.

"*Right!*" she <u>hooted</u>, and Jonas helped her from the tub.

words for everyday use

chor • tle (chōr´ tǝl) v., laugh or chuckle in satisfaction or exultation. *The waitress had been so unpleasant to us that I couldn't help but <u>chortle</u> when she dropped the dinners of the couple behind us.*

hoot (hüt´) v., shout or laugh. *The children <u>hooted</u> with laughter when the clown honked his nose.*

Respond to the Selection

From your reading of the first four chapters, do you think you would enjoy being a citizen of this community? Why, or why not? Give specific examples.

Investigate, Inquire, and Imagine

Recall: GATHERING FACTS

1a. What two responses did Jonas have to the aircraft that flew over the community? How did others in the community respond to seeing the aircraft? How did the voice through the speaker respond to the aircraft?

2a. What are most of the people on the night crew not given? Why? Why can't Jonas's family keep Gabriel as Lily suggests? How did Lily become Jonas's sister?

3a. Who decides what each citizen's Assignment, or life occupation, will be? How is this decision made?

4a. In what ceremony will Lily participate in December? In what ceremony will Jonas take part in December?

5a. What does Larissa say about "all lives"? What does she say about Edna's life? What is Lily's mother's opinion of Birthmothers?

Interpret: FINDING MEANING

1b. Why do you think Jonas and the others reacted the way they did? Why might the speaker have given the instructions he or she did?

2b. What insights do these facts provide about families in the society of *The Giver?*

3b. What might this tell you about the citizens of the community? about the community itself?

4b. In what way are citizens younger than twelve classified in the society of *The Giver?* In what way are adults categorized in the society of *The Giver?*

5b. Consider Larissa's comments about Edna and Lily's mother's comments about Birthmothers. What insights do these comments provide about adult life in the society of *The Giver?*

Analyze: TAKING THINGS APART

6a. Review your reading of the first four chapters, focusing on *one* of these two topics: language (specific words and phrases) used by citizens of the community, or specific rules of the community. As you review, make a list of all references that relate to the topic you choose.

Synthesize: BRINGING THINGS TOGETHER

6b. Look carefully at the list you've created, and think for a while about the references you've compiled. Make a comment or form a question about the role that language or specific rules appear to play in the society of *The Giver*. Share your ideas with your classmates. Take note of further development of these topics as the story progresses.

Perspective: LOOKING AT OTHER VIEWS

7a. How do Jonas's father and Jonas differ in their perspectives on the committee's granting of Assignments? In what way(s) are their perspectives similar?

Empathy: SEEING FROM INSIDE

7b. How might you feel if you were Jonas or another eleven-year-old citizen waiting to be assigned your life's occupation? Would there be disadvantages to having others decide this for you? Would there be benefits?

Understanding Literature

CHARACTERIZATION. **Characterization** is the act of creating or describing a character. Writers create character using three major techniques: by showing what characters say, do, or think; by showing what other characters say or think about them; and by describing what physical features, dress, and personality the characters display. Consider the following characters: Jonas, Asher, Lily, Jonas's mother, and Jonas's father. Go back to the first chapter, and note which technique(s) of characterization the author uses to introduce each character to the reader. Write some details about each introduction: if the first technique of characterization is used, tell what is said, done or thought; if the second technique is used, tell what one character says or thinks about another; and if the third technique is used, list the details given about the character's features, dress, and/or personality. What do these details tell you about each character's personality?

FORESHADOWING. **Foreshadowing** is the act of hinting at events that will happen later in a literary work. In reading the first four chapters, did you notice any details that seem as though they may hint at events that will take place later in the story? What effect does this foreshadowing have on the story? on you as the reader? Explain.

Chapter 5

▶ What happens at the morning ritual?

USUALLY, AT THE morning ritual when the family members told their dreams, Jonas didn't contribute much. He rarely dreamed. Sometimes he awoke with a feeling of fragments afloat in his sleep, but he couldn't seem to grasp them and put them together into something worthy of telling at the ritual.

But this morning was different. He had dreamed very vividly the night before.

His mind wandered while Lily, as usual, <u>recounted</u> a lengthy dream, this one a frightening one in which she had, against the rules, been riding her mother's bicycle and been caught by the Security Guards.

They all listened carefully and discussed with Lily the warning that the dream had given.

"Thank you for your dream, Lily." Jonas said the standard phrase automatically, and tried to pay better attention while his mother told of a dream fragment, a disquieting scene where she had been chastised for a rule infraction she didn't understand. Together they agreed that it probably resulted from her feelings when she had reluctantly dealt punishment to the citizen who had broken the major rules a second time.

Father said that he had had no dreams.

"Gabe?" Father asked, looking down at the basket where the newchild lay gurgling after his feeding, ready to be taken back to the Nurturing Center for the day.

They all laughed. Dream-telling began with Threes. If newchildren dreamed, no one knew.

"Jonas?" Mother asked. They always asked, though they knew how rarely Jonas had a dream to tell.

"I *did* dream last night," Jonas told them. He shifted in his chair, frowning.

"Good," Father said. "Tell us."

"The details aren't clear, really," Jonas explained, trying to recreate the odd dream in his mind. "I think I was in the bathing room at the House of the Old."

---

words for everyday use

re • count (ri kount´) v., relate in detail. *Once Jared was in dry clothing and settled in front of the fire with a blanket and a cup of hot tea, he began to <u>recount</u> his story of being stuck in the woods in the middle of a vicious storm.*

"That's where you were yesterday," Father pointed out.

Jonas nodded. "But it wasn't really the same. There was a tub, in the dream. But only one. And the real bathing room has rows and rows of them. But the room in the dream was warm and damp. And I had taken off my tunic, but hadn't put on the smock, so my chest was bare. I was perspiring, because it was so warm. And Fiona was there, the way she was yesterday."

"Asher, too?" Mother asked.

Jonas shook his head. "No. It was only me and Fiona, alone in the room, standing beside the tub. She was laughing. But I wasn't. I was almost a little angry at her, in the dream, because she wasn't taking me seriously."

"Seriously about what?" Lily asked.

Jonas looked at his plate. For some reason that he didn't understand, he felt slightly embarrassed. "I think I was trying to convince her that she should get into the tub of water."

◀ How does Jonas feel about his dream?

He paused. He knew he had to tell it all, that it was not only all right but necessary to tell *all* of a dream. So he forced himself to relate the part that made him uneasy.

◀ Why does Jonas tell all of his dream even though he is uncomfortable with it?

"I wanted her to take off her clothes and get into the tub," he explained quickly. "I wanted to bathe her. I had the sponge in my hand. But she wouldn't. She kept laughing and saying no."

He looked up at his parents. "That's all," he said.

"Can you describe the strongest feeling in your dream, son?" Father asked.

Jonas thought about it. The details were <u>murky</u> and <u>vague</u>. But the feelings were clear, and flooded him again now as he thought. "The *wanting*," he said. "I knew that she wouldn't. And I think I knew that

---

words for everyday use

mur • ky (mər´ kē) *adj.* hazy; veiled; not distinct. *The water in the lake was green and <u>murky</u>, not the best for swimming or finding shells.*

vague (vāg´) *adj.,* not clearly expressed, defined, grasped or understood. *I apologized to Kurt for my rude behavior at his party, but rather than forgiving me, he uttered a <u>vague</u> comment and walked away.*

she *shouldn't*. But I wanted it so terribly. I could feel the wanting all through me."

"Thank you for your dream, Jonas," Mother said after a moment. She glanced at Father.

"Lily," Father said, "it's time to leave for school. Would you walk beside me this morning and keep an eye on the newchild's basket? We want to be certain he doesn't wiggle himself loose."

▶ What surprises Jonas?

Jonas began to rise to collect his schoolbooks. He thought it surprising that they hadn't talked about his dream at length before the thank you. Perhaps they found it as confusing as he had.

"Wait, Jonas," Mother said gently. "I'll write an apology to your instructor so that you won't have to speak one for being late."

He sank back down into his chair, puzzled. He waved to Father and Lily as they left the dwelling, carrying Gabe in his basket. He watched while Mother tidied the remains of the morning meal and placed the tray by the front door for the Collection Crew.

▶ What does Jonas's mother call the feelings he experienced in his dream?

Finally she sat down beside him at the table. "Jonas," she said with a smile, "the feeling you described as the wanting? It was your first Stirrings. Father and I have been expecting it to happen to you. It happens to everyone. It happened to Father when he was your age. And it happened to me. It will happen someday to Lily.

"And very often," Mother added, "it begins with a dream."

Stirrings. He had heard the word before. He remembered that there was a <u>reference</u> to the Stirrings in the Book of Rules, though he didn't remember what it said. And now and then the Speaker mentioned it. ATTENTION. A REMINDER THAT STIRRINGS MUST BE REPORTED IN ORDER FOR TREATMENT TO TAKE PLACE.

He had always ignored that announcement because he didn't understand it and it had never

---

words for everyday use
ref • er • ence (rə´ fə rənts) *n.*, mention of. *As I skimmed Jen's essay about her best memories from the past summer, I was pleased to see a <u>reference</u> to one of our trips to the beach.*

seemed to apply to him in any way. He ignored, as most citizens did, many of the commands and reminders read by the Speaker.

"Do I have to report it?" he asked his mother.

She laughed. "You did, in the dream-telling. That's enough."

"But what about the treatment? The Speaker says that treatment must take place." Jonas felt miserable. Just when the Ceremony was about to happen, his Ceremony of Twelve, would he have to go away someplace for treatment? Just because of a stupid dream?

◄ What is the treatment for Stirrings?

But his mother laughed again in a reassuring, affectionate way. "No, no," she said. "It's just the pills. You're ready for the pills, that's all. That's the treatment for Stirrings."

Jonas brightened. He knew about the pills. His parents both took them each morning. And some of his friends did, he knew. Once he had been heading off to school with Asher, both of them on their bikes, when Asher's father had called from their dwelling doorway, "You forgot your pill, Asher!" Asher had groaned good-naturedly, turned his bike, and ridden back while Jonas waited.

It was the sort of thing one didn't ask a friend about because it might have fallen into that uncomfortable category of "being different." Asher took a pill each morning; Jonas did not. Always better, less rude, to talk about things that were the same.

Now he swallowed the small pill that his mother handed him.

"That's all?" he asked.

"That's all," she replied, returning the bottle to the cupboard. "But you mustn't forget. I'll remind you for the first weeks, but then you must do it on your own. If you forget, the Stirrings will come back. The dreams of Stirrings will come back. Sometimes the <u>dosage</u> must be adjusted."

words for everyday use   dos • age (dō´ səj) *n.*, quantity of a drug taken at one time. *The doctor administered a* <u>*dosage*</u> *of the painkiller to my sister after she broke her arm.*

▶ How long does one's treatment for Stirrings continue?

▶ How did Jonas feel about the Stirrings?

"Asher takes them," Jonas confided.

His mother nodded, unsurprised. "Many of your groupmates probably do. The males, at least. And they all will, soon. Females too."

"How long will I have to take them?"

"Until you enter the House of the Old," she explained. "All of your adult life. But it becomes routine; after a while you won't even pay much attention to it."

She looked at her watch. "If you leave right now, you won't even be late for school. Hurry along.

"And thank you again, Jonas," she added, as he went to the door, "for your dream."

Pedaling rapidly down the path, Jonas felt oddly proud to have joined those who took the pills. For a moment, though, he remembered the dream again. The dream had felt pleasurable. Though the feelings were confused, he thought that he had liked the feelings that his mother had called Stirrings. He remembered that upon waking, he had wanted to feel the Stirrings again.

Then, in the same way that his own dwelling slipped away behind him as he rounded a corner on his bicycle, the dream slipped away from his thoughts. Very briefly, a little guiltily, he tried to grasp it back. But the feelings had disappeared. The Stirrings were gone.

Chapter 6

"LILY, *PLEASE* HOLD still," Mother said again.

Lily, standing in front of her, fidgeted impatiently. "I can tie them myself," she complained. "I always have."

"I know that," Mother replied, straightening the hair ribbons on the little girl's braids. "But I also know that they constantly come loose and more often than not, they're dangling down your back by afternoon. Today, at least, we want them to be neatly tied and to *stay* neatly tied."

"I don't like hair ribbons. I'm glad I only have to wear them one more year," Lily said irritably. "Next year I get my bicycle, too," she added more cheerfully.

"There are good things each year," Jonas reminded her. "This year you get to start your volunteer hours. And remember last year, when you became a Seven, you were so happy to get your front-buttoned jacket?"

The little girl nodded and looked down at herself, at the jacket with its row of large buttons that <u>designated</u> her as a Seven. Fours, Fives, and Sixes all wore jackets that fastened down the back so that they would have to help each other dress and would learn interdependence.

◀ *What type of jacket do Fours, Fives, and Sixes wear? Why?*

The front-buttoned jacket was the first sign of independence, the first very visible symbol of growing up. The bicycle, at Nine, would be the powerful emblem of moving gradually out into the community, away from the protective family unit.

Lily grinned and wriggled away from her mother. "And this year you get your Assignment," she said to Jonas in an excited voice. "I hope you get Pilot. And that you take me flying!"

"Sure I will," said Jonas. "And I'll get a special little parachute that just fits you, and I'll take you up to, oh, maybe twenty thousand feet, and open the door, and—"

---

words for everyday use   des • ig • nate (de´ zig nāt) v., indicate and set apart for a specific purpose; denote; specify. *My sister and I decided to <u>designate</u> half the money we made from the yard sale "money for later," which we'd save until later for something we really wanted.*

"*Jonas,*" Mother warned.

"I was only joking," Jonas groaned. "I don't want Pilot, anyway. If I get Pilot I'll put in an appeal."

"Come on," Mother said. She gave Lily's ribbons a final tug. "Jonas?" Are you ready? Did you take your pill? I want to get a good seat in the Auditorium." She prodded Lily to the front door and Jonas followed.

It was a short ride to the Auditorium, Lily waving to her friends from her seat on the back of Mother's bicycle. Jonas stowed his bicycle beside Mother's and made his way through the <u>throng</u> to find his group.

The entire community attended the Ceremony each year. For the parents, it meant two days' holiday from work; they sat together in the huge hall. Children sat with their groups until they went, one by one, to the stage.

Father, though, would not join Mother in the audience right away. For the earliest ceremony, the Naming, the Nurturers brought the newchildren to the stage. Jonas, from his place in the balcony with the Elevens, searched the Auditorium for a glimpse of Father. It wasn't at all hard to spot the Nurturers' section at the front; coming from it were the wails and howls of the newchildren who sat squirming on the Nurturers' laps. At every other public ceremony, the audience was silent and attentive. But once a year, they all smiled indulgently at the commotion from the little ones waiting to receive their names and families.

Jonas finally caught his father's eye and waved. Father grinned and waved back, then held up the hand of the newchild on his lap, making it wave, too.

It wasn't Gabriel. Gabe was back at the Nurturing Center today, being cared for by the night crew. He had been given an unusual and special reprieve from the committee, and granted an additional year of nurturing before his Naming and Placement. Father had gone before the committee with a plea on behalf

▶ *What plea did Jonas's father make on behalf of Gabriel?*

words for everyday use

throng (thräŋˊ) *n.*, crowding together of many persons. *After the game, a <u>throng</u> of people requesting autographs surrounded one of the sports figures.*

of Gabriel, who had not yet gained the weight appropriate to his days of life nor begun to sleep soundly enough at night to be placed with his family unit. Normally such a newchild would be labeled Inadequate and released from the community.

Instead, as a result of Father's plea, Gabriel had been labeled Uncertain and given the additional year. He would continue to be nurtured at the Center and would spend his nights with Jonas's family unit. Each family member, including Lily, had been required to sign a pledge that they would not become attached to this little temporary guest and that they would relinquish him without protest or appeal when he was assigned to his own family unit at next year's Ceremony.

◀ *What pledge was each family member required to make in response to the committee's granting of Jonas's father's plea?*

At least, Jonas thought, after Gabriel was placed next year, they would still see him often because he would be part of the community. If he were released, they would not see him again. Ever. Those who were released—even as newchildren—were sent Elsewhere and never returned to the community.

Father had not had to release a single newchild this year, so Gabriel would have represented a real failure and sadness. Even Jonas, though he didn't hover over the little one the way Lily and his father did, was glad that Gabe had not been released.

The first Ceremony began right on time, and Jonas watched as one after another each newchild was given a name and handed by the Nurturers to its new family unit. For some, it was a first child. But many came to the stage accompanied by another child beaming with pride to receive a little brother or sister, the way Jonas had when he was about to be a Five.

Asher poked Jonas's arm. "Remember when we got Phillipa?" he asked in a loud whisper. Jonas nodded. It had only been last year. Asher's parents had waited quite a long time before applying for a second child. Maybe, Jonas suspected, they had been so exhausted by Asher's lively foolishness that they had needed a little time.

Two of their group, Fiona and another female named Thea, were missing temporarily, waiting with their parents to receive newchildren. But it was rare that there was such an age gap between children in a family unit.

When her family's ceremony was completed, Fiona took the seat that had been saved for her in the row ahead of Asher and Jonas. She turned and whispered to them, "He's cute. But I don't like his name very much." She made a face and giggled. Fiona's new brother had been named Bruno. It wasn't a *great* name, Jonas thought, like—well, like Gabriel, for example. But it was okay.

The audience applause, which was enthusiastic at each Naming, rose in an <u>exuberant</u> swell when one parental pair, glowing with pride, took a male newchild and heard him named Caleb.

▶ What happened to the first Caleb? How did the community respond?

This new Caleb was a replacement child. The couple had lost their first Caleb, a cheerful little Four. Loss of a child was very, very rare. The community was extraordinarily safe, each citizen watchful and protective of all children. But somehow the first little Caleb had wandered away unnoticed, and had fallen into the river. The entire community had performed the Ceremony of Loss together, murmuring the name Caleb throughout an entire day, less and less frequently, softer in volume, as the long and <u>somber</u> day went on, so that the little Four seemed to fade away gradually from everyone's consciousness.

▶ What ceremony does the community perform for the new Caleb?

Now, at this special Naming, the community performed the brief Murmur-of-Replacement Ceremony, repeating the name for the first time since the loss: softly and slowly at first, then faster and with greater volume, as the couple stood on the stage with the newchild sleeping in the mother's arms. It was as if the first Caleb were returning.

Another newchild was given the name Roberto, and Jonas remembered that Roberto the Old had been released only last week. But there was no

---

words for everyday use

ex • u • ber • ant (ig zü´ bə rənt) *adj.,* extreme or excessive in degree; joyously unrestrained and enthusiastic. *Mica was absolutely <u>exuberant</u> about getting accepted to the college of her choice.*

som • ber (säm´ bər) *adj.,* of a dismal or depressing character. *After the <u>somber</u> events of the day, I was in need of some cheering up and decided to rent a comedy.*

Murmur-of-Replacement Ceremony for the new little Roberto. Release was not the same as Loss.

He said politely through the ceremonies of Two and Three and Four, increasingly bored as he was each year. Then a break for midday meal—served outdoors—and back again to the seats, for the Fives, Sixes, Sevens, and finally, last of the first day's ceremonies, the Eights.

Jonas watched and cheered as Lily marched proudly to the stage, became an Eight and received the identifying jacket that she would wear this year, this one with smaller buttons and, for the first time, pockets, indicating that she was mature enough now to keep track of her own small belongings. She stood solemnly listening to the speech of firm instructions on the responsibilities of Eight and doing volunteer hours for the first time. But Jonas could see that Lily, though she seemed attentive, was looking longingly at the row of gleaming bicycles, which would be presented tomorrow morning to the Nines.

Next year, Lily-billy, Jonas thought.

It was an exhausting day, and even Gabriel, retrieved in his basket from the Nurturing Center, slept soundly that night.

Finally it was the morning of the Ceremony of Twelve.

Now Father sat beside Mother in the audience. Jonas could see them applauding dutifully as the Nines, one by one, wheeled their new bicycles, each with its gleaming nametag attached to the back, from the stage. He knew that his parents <u>cringed</u> a little, as he did, when Fritz, who lived in the dwelling next door to theirs, received his bike and almost immediately bumped into the podium with it. Fritz was a very awkward child who had been summoned for chastisement again and again. His transgressions were small ones, always: shoes on the wrong feet,

◀ What do the pockets in the Eights' jackets indicate?

◀ How do Fritz's transgressions affect his parents? the community?

words for everyday use

cringe (krinj´) v., draw in or contract one's muscles involuntarily; shrink; flinch; wince.
I try not to let them bother me, but often, I can't help but <u>cringe</u> when bees get too close to me.

schoolwork misplaced, failure to study adequately for a quiz. But each such error reflected negatively on his parents' guidance and infringed on the community's sense of order and success. Jonas and his family had not been looking forward to Fritz's bicycle, which they realized would probably too often be dropped on the front walk instead of wheeled neatly into its port.

Finally the Nines were all resettled in their seats, each having wheeled a bicycle outside where it would be waiting for its owner at the end of the day. Everyone always chuckled and made small jokes when the Nines rode home for the first time. "Want me to show you how to ride?" older friends would call. "I know you've never been on a bike before!" But invariably the grinning Nines, who in technical violation of the rule had been practicing secretly for weeks, would mount and ride off in perfect balance, training wheels never touching the ground.

▶ What happens at the Ceremony of Ten?

Then the Tens. Jonas never found the Ceremony of Ten particularly interesting—only time-consuming, as each child's hair was snipped neatly into its distinguishing cut: females lost their braids at Ten, and males, too, relinquished their long childish hair and took on the more manly short style which exposed their ears.

Laborers moved quickly to the stage with brooms and swept away the mounds of discarded hair. Jonas could see the parents of the new Tens stir and murmur, and he knew that this evening, in many dwellings, they would be snipping and straightening the hastily done haircuts, trimming them into a neater line.

Elevens. It seemed a short time ago that Jonas had undergone the Ceremony of Eleven, but he remembered that it was not one of the more interesting ones. By Eleven, one was only waiting to be Twelve. It was simply a marking of time with no meaningful changes. There was new clothing: different undergarments for the females, whose bodies were beginning to change; and longer trousers for the males, with a specially shaped pocket for the small calculator that they would use this year in school; but those were simply presented in wrapped packages without an accompanying speech.

Break for midday meal. Jonas realized he was hungry. He and his groupmates congregated by the tables in front of the Auditorium and took their packaged food. Yesterday there had been merriment at lunch, a lot of teasing and energy. But today the group stood anxiously, separate from the other children. Jonas watched the new Nines gravitate toward their waiting bicycles, each one admiring his or her nametag. He saw the Tens stroking their new shortened hair, the females shaking their heads to feel the unaccustomed lightness without the heavy braids they had worn so long.

"I heard about a guy who was absolutely certain he was going to be assigned Engineer," Asher muttered as they ate, "and instead they gave him Sanitation Laborer. He went out the next day, jumped into the river, swam across, and joined the next community he came to. Nobody ever saw him again."

Jonas laughed. "Somebody made that story up, Ash," he said. "My father said he heard that story when *he* was a Twelve."

But Asher wasn't reassured. He was eyeing the river where it was visible behind the Auditorium. "I can't even swim very well," he said. "My swimming instructor said that I don't have the right boyishness or something."

"Buoyancy," Jonas corrected him.

"Whatever. I don't have it. I sink."

"Anyway," Jonas pointed out, "have you ever once known of anyone—I mean really known for sure, Asher, not just heard a story about it—who joined another community?"

"No," Asher admitted reluctantly. "But you can. It says so in the rules. If you don't fit in, you can apply for Elsewhere and be released. My mother says that once, about ten years ago, someone applied and was gone the next day." Then he chuckled. "She told me

◄ What can one do if one doesn't fit in?

---

words for everyday use

buoy • an • cy (bŏi´ yənt sē) *n.*, the tendency of a body to float or rise when submerged in liquid. *Fishermen often choose lures that have* buoyancy *when fishing in shallow, weedy water.*

that because I was driving her crazy. She threatened to apply for Elsewhere."

"She was joking."

"I know. but it was true, what she said, that someone did that once. She said that it was really true. Here today and gone tomorrow. Never seen again. Not even a Ceremony of Release."

▶ Why does Jonas find it hard to believe that one might not fit into the community?

Jonas shrugged. It didn't worry him. How could someone not fit in? The community was so meticulously ordered, the choices so carefully made.

Even the Matching of Spouses was given such weighty consideration that sometimes an adult who applied to receive a spouse waited months or even *years* before a Match was approved and announced. All of the factors—disposition, energy level, intelligence, and interests—had to correspond and to interact perfectly. Jonas's mother, for example, had higher intelligence than his father; but his father had a calmer disposition. They balanced each other. Their Match, which like all Matches had been monitored by the Committee of Elders for three years before they could apply for children, had always been a successful one.

▶ What are four of the decisions made by the Committee of Elders for the community?

Like the Matching of Spouses and the Naming and Placement of newchildren, the Assignments were scrupulously thought through by the Committee of Elders.

He was certain that his Assignment, whatever it was to be, and Asher's too, would be the right one for them. He only wished that the midday break would conclude, that the audience would reenter the Auditorium, and the suspense would end.

As if in answer to his unspoken wish, the signal came and the crowd began to move toward the doors.

Chapter 7

NOW JONAS'S GROUP had taken a new place in the Auditorium, trading with the new Elevens, so that they sat in the very front, immediately before the stage.

They were arranged by their original numbers, the numbers they had been given at birth. The numbers were rarely used after the Naming. But each child knew his number, of course. Sometimes parents used them in irritation at a child's misbehavior, indicating that mischief made one unworthy of a name. Jonas always chuckled when he heard a parent, exasperated, call sharply to a whining toddler, "That's *enough*, Twenty-three!"

Jonas was Nineteen. He had been the nineteenth newchild born his year. It had meant that at his Naming, he had been already standing and bright-eyed, soon to walk and talk. It had given him a slight advantage the first year or two, a little more maturity than many of his groupmates who had been born in the later months of that year. But it evened out, as it always did, by Three.

After Three, the children <u>progressed</u> at much the same level, though by their first number one could always tell who was a few months older than others in his group. Technically, Jonas's full number was Eleven-nineteen, since there were other Nineteens, of course, in each age group. And today, now that the new Elevens had been advanced this morning, there were *two* Eleven-nineteens. At the midday break he had exchanged smiles with the new one, a shy female named Harriet.

But the duplication was only for these few hours. Very soon he would not be an Eleven but a Twelve, and age would no longer matter. He would be an adult, like his parents, though a new one and untrained still.

◀ What will Jonas soon be? What will no longer matter?

words for everyday use pro • gress (prə gres´) v., develop to a higher, better, or more advanced stage; move forward. *Students have to be able to tread water for three minutes in order to <u>progress</u> to the advanced swimming class.*

Asher was Four, and sat now in the row ahead of Jonas. He would receive his Assignment fourth.

Fiona, Eighteen, was on his left; on his other side sat Twenty, a male named Pierre whom Jonas didn't like much. Pierre was very serious, not much fun, and a worrier and tattletale, too. "Have you checked the rules, Jonas?" Pierre was always whispering solemnly. "I'm not sure that's within the rules." Usually it was some foolish thing that no one cared about—opening his tunic if it was a day with a breeze; taking a brief try on a friend's bicycle, just to experience the different feel of it.

The initial speech at the Ceremony of Twelve was made by the Chief Elder, the leader of the community who was elected every ten years. The speech was much the same each year: recollection of the time of childhood and the period of preparation, the coming responsibilities of adult life, the profound importance of Assignment, the seriousness of training to come.

Then the Chief Elder moved ahead in her speech.

"This is the time," she began, looking directly at them, "when we acknowledge differences. You Elevens have spent all your years till now learning to fit in, to <u>standardize</u> your behavior, to curb any impulse that might set you apart from the group.

"But today we honor your differences. They have determined your futures."

She began to describe this year's group and its variety of personalities, though she singled no one out by name. She mentioned that there was one who had singular skills at caretaking, another who loved newchildren, one with unusual scientific aptitude, and a fourth for whom physical labor was an obvious pleasure. Jonas shifted in his seat, trying to recognize each reference as one of his groupmates. The caretaking skills were no doubt those of Fiona, on his left; he remembered noticing the tenderness with which

▶ *How does the Chief Elder say the Elevens have spent their years until now?*

words
for
everyday
use

stan • dard • ize (stan´ dər dīz) v., bring into conformity or agreement with a standard. *Throughout the school, teachers have decided to <u>standardize</u> their expectations for classroom behavior and completion of assignments, so that students have only one set of guidelines to follow.*

she had bathed the Old. Probably the one with scientific aptitude was Benjamin, the male who had devised new, important equipment for the Rehabilitation Center.

He heard nothing that he recognized as himself, Jonas.

Finally the Chief Elder paid tribute to the hard work of her committee, which had performed the observations so meticulously all year. The Committee of Elders stood and was acknowledged by applause. Jonas noticed Asher yawn slightly, covering his mouth politely with his hand.

Then, at last, the Chief Elder called number One to the stage, and the Assignments began.

Each announcement was lengthy, accompanied by a speech directed at the new Twelve. Jonas tried to pay attention as One, smiling happily, received her Assignment as Fish Hatchery Attendant along with words of praise for her childhood spent doing many volunteer hours there, and her obvious interest in the important process of providing nourishment for the community.

Number One—her name was Madeline—returned, finally, amidst applause, to her seat, wearing the new badge that designated her Fish Hatchery Attendant. Jonas was certainly glad that *that* Assignment was taken; he wouldn't have wanted it. But he gave Madeline a smile of congratulation.

When Two, a female named Inger, received her Assignment as Birthmother, Jonas remembered that his mother had called it a job without honor. But he thought that the Committee had chosen well. Inger was a nice girl though somewhat lazy, and her body was strong. She would enjoy the three years of being <u>pampered</u> that would follow her brief training; she would give birth easily and well; and the task of Laborer that would follow would use her strength, keep her healthy, and impose self-discipline. Inger

◀ *What does Jonas think about the choice of Inger's Assignment? Why?*

words for everyday use **pam • per** (pam´ pər) v., treat with excessive or extreme care or attention. *I think Sunday is a good day to <u>pamper</u> yourself, sleep in late, have a great breakfast, and do things you really enjoy.*

was smiling when she resumed her seat. Birthmother was an important job, if lacking in prestige.

Jonas noticed that Asher looked nervous. He kept turning his head and glancing back at Jonas until the group leader had to give him a silent chastisement, a motion to sit still and face forward.

Three, Isaac, was given an Assignment as Instructor of Sixes, which obviously pleased him and was well deserved. Now there were three Assignments gone, none of them ones that Jonas would have liked—not that he could have been a Birthmother, anyway, he realized with amusement. He tried to sort through the list in his mind, the possible Assignments that remained. But there were so many he gave it up; and anyway, now it was Asher's turn. He paid strict attention as his friend went to the stage and stood self-consciously beside the Chief Elder.

"All of us in the community know and enjoy Asher," the Chief Elder began. Asher grinned and scratched one leg with the other foot. The audience chuckled softly.

"When the committee began to consider Asher's Assignment," she went on, "there were some possibilities that were immediately <u>discarded</u>. Some that would clearly not have been right for Asher.

"For example," she said, smiling, "we did not consider for an instant designating Asher an Instructor of Threes."

The audience howled with laughter. Asher laughed, too, looking sheepish but pleased at the special attention. The Instructors of Threes were in charge of the acquisition of correct language.

"In fact," the Chief Elder continued, chuckling a little herself, "we even gave a little thought to some <u>retroactive</u> chastisement for the one who had been *Asher's* Instructor of Threes so long ago. At the meet-

---

words for everyday use

dis • card (dis kärd´) v., get rid of because of unsuitability. *When we weren't able to get the reclining chair to recline, we decided it was time to discard it.*

ret • ro • ac • tive (re trō ak´ tiv) adj., extending in scope or effect to a prior time or to conditions that existed or originated in the past. *Kenya's boss told her that her pay raise would be retroactive because she should have received her raise two months earlier.*

ing where Asher was discussed, we retold many of the stories that we all remembered from his days of language <u>acquisition</u>.

"Especially," she said, chuckling, "the difference between snack and smack. Remember, Asher?"

Asher nodded ruefully, and the audience laughed aloud. Jonas did, too. He remembered, though he had been only a Three at the time himself.

The punishment used for small children was a regulated system of smacks with the discipline wand: a thin, flexible weapon that stung painfully when it was wielded. The Childcare specialists were trained very carefully in the discipline methods: a quick smack across the hands for a bit of minor misbehavior; three sharper smacks on the bare legs for a second offense.

◀ How are small children punished?

Poor Asher, who always talked too fast and mixed up words, even as a toddler. As a Three, eager for his juice and crackers at snacktime, he one day said "smack" instead of "snack" as he stood waiting in line for the morning treat.

Jonas remembered it clearly. He could still see little Asher, wiggling with impatience in the line. He remembered the cheerful voice calling out, "I want my smack!"

The other Threes, including Jonas, had laughed nervously. "Snack!" they corrected. "You meant snack, Asher!" But the mistake had been made. And precision of language was one of the most important tasks of small children. Asher had asked for a smack.

The discipline wand, in the hand of the Childcare worker, whistled as it came down across Asher's hands. Asher whimpered, cringed, and corrected himself instantly. "Snack," he whispered.

But the next morning he had done it again. And again the following week. He couldn't seem to stop, though for each lapse the discipline wand came again, <u>escalating</u> to a series of painful lashes that left

words for everyday use	ac • qui • si • tion (a kwə zi´ shən) n., act of obtaining. The <u>acquisition</u> of material goods is easier to accomplish than the acquisition of respect.	es • ca • late (es´ kə lāt) v., increase in extent, volume, number, amount, intensity, or scope. Tension in the room began to <u>escalate</u> as Bryan and Juan traded insults in increasingly loud voices.

▶ What did Asher do for a period of time when he was a Three?

marks on Asher's legs. Eventually, for a period of time, Asher stopped talking altogether, when he was a Three.

"For a while," the Chief Elder said, relating the story, "we had a silent Asher! But he learned."

She turned to him with a smile. "When he began to talk again, it was with greater <u>precision</u>. And now his lapses are very few. His corrections and apologies are very prompt. And his good humor is unfailing." The audience murmured in agreement. Asher's cheerful disposition was well known throughout the community.

"Asher." She lifted her voice to make the official announcement. "We have given you the Assignment of Assistant Director of Recreation."

She clipped on his new badge as he stood beside her, beaming. Then he turned and left the stage as the audience cheered. When he had taken his seat again, the Chief Elder looked down at him and said the words that she had said now four times, and would say to each new Twelve. Somehow she gave it special meaning for each of them.

▶ What words does the Chief Elder say to each new Twelve?

"Asher," she said, "thank you for your childhood."

The Assignments continued, and Jonas watched and listened, relieved now by the wonderful Assignment his best friend had been given. But he was more and more apprehensive as his own approached. Now the new Twelves in the row ahead had all received their badges. They were fingering them as they sat, and Jonas knew that each one was thinking about the training that lay ahead. For some—one studious male had been selected as Doctor, a female as Engineer, and another for Law and Justice—it would be years of hard work and study. Others, like Laborers and Birthmothers, would have a much shorter training period.

---

words for everyday use pre • ci • sion (pri si´ zhən) n., exactness. *We couldn't question the <u>precision</u> of the architect's plans, as we saw that he had taken into account even the most minuscule details.*

Eighteen, Fiona, on his left, was called. Jonas knew she must be nervous, but Fiona was a calm female. She had been sitting quietly, serenely, throughout the Ceremony.

Even the applause, though enthusiastic, seemed serene when Fiona was given the important Assignment of Caretaker of the Old. It was perfect for such a sensitive, gentle girl, and her smile was satisfied and pleased when she took her seat beside him again.

◀ What Assignment is Fiona given?

Jonas prepared himself to walk to the stage when the applause ended and the Chief Elder picked up the next folder and looked down to the group to call forward the next new Twelve. He was calm now that his turn had come. He took a deep breath and smoothed his hair with his hand.

"Twenty," he heard her voice say clearly. "Pierre."

She skipped me, Jonas thought stunned. Had he heard wrong? No. There was a sudden hush in the crowd, and he knew that the entire community realized that the Chief Elder had moved from Eighteen to Twenty, leaving a gap. On his right, Pierre, with a startled look, rose from his seat and moved to the stage.

◀ What do Jonas and the entire community realize?

A mistake. She made a mistake. But Jonas knew, even as he had the thought, that she hadn't. The Chief Elder made no mistakes. Not at the Ceremony of Twelve.

He felt dizzy, and couldn't focus his attention. He didn't hear what Assignment Pierre received, and was only dimly aware of the applause as the boy returned, wearing his new badge. Then: Twenty-one. Twenty-two.

The numbers continued in order. Jonas sat, dazed, as they moved into the Thirties and then the Forties, nearing the end. Each time, at each announcement, his heart jumped for a moment, and he thought wild thoughts. Perhaps now she would call his name. Could he have forgotten his own number? No. He had always been Nineteen. He was sitting in the seat marked Nineteen.

But she had *skipped* him. He saw the others in his group glance at him, embarrassed, and then avert their eyes quickly. He saw a worried look on the face of his group leader.

He hunched his shoulders and tried to make himself smaller in the seat. He wanted to disappear, to fade away, not to exist. He didn't dare to turn and find his parents in the crowd. He couldn't bear to see their faces darkened with shame.

Jonas bowed his head and searched through his mind. *What had he done wrong?*

Chapter 8

THE AUDIENCE WAS clearly ill at ease. They applauded at the final Assignment; but the applause was <u>piecemeal</u>, no longer a <u>crescendo</u> of united enthusiasm. There were murmurs of confusion.

Jonas moved his hands together, clapping, but it was an automatic, meaningless gesture that he wasn't even aware of. His mind had shut out all of the earlier emotions: the anticipation, excitement, pride, and even the happy <u>kinship</u> with his friends. Now he felt only humiliation and terror.

The Chief Elder waited until the uneasy applause subsided. Then she spoke again.

"I know," she said in her vibrant, gracious voice, "that you are all concerned. That you feel I have made a mistake."

She smiled. The community, relieved from its discomfort very slightly by her benign statement, seemed to breathe more easily. It was very silent.

Jonas looked up.

"I have caused you anxiety," she said. "I apologize to my community." Her voice flowed over the assembled crowd.

◀ For what does the Chief Elder apologize to the community? to Jonas?

"We accept your apology," they all uttered together.

"Jonas," she said, looking down at him, "I apologize to you in particular. I caused you <u>anguish</u>."

"I accept your apology," Jonas replied shakily.

"Please come to the stage now."

Earlier that day, dressing in his own dwelling, he had practiced the kind of <u>jaunty</u>, self-assured walk that he hoped he could make to the stage when his

---

words for everyday use

piece • meal (pēs´ mēl) *adj.,* done or made in a fragmentary way. *The <u>piecemeal</u> garden didn't look at all planned; while some spots were bare, others were overgrown.*

cre • scen • do (krə shen´ dō) *n.,* gradual increase; climax. *As the music rose to a <u>crescendo</u>, the dancers leaped in unison.*

kin • ship (kin´ ship) *n.,* the quality or state of being related. *<u>Kinship</u> can exist outside of relationships between blood relatives.*

an • guish (an´ gwish) *n.,* sorrow; extreme pain, distress, or anxiety. *Tatiana was in a state of deep <u>anguish</u> for several days after the death of her dog.*

jaun • ty (jän´ tē) *adj.,* light-hearted; relaxed; effortless. *We knew Bobby's <u>jaunty</u> walk was something he practiced, and we couldn't help but laugh when he tripped as he was making his way over to us.*

turn came. All of that was forgotten now. He simply willed himself to stand, to move his feet that felt weighted and clumsy, to go forward, up the steps and across the platform until he stood at her side.

Reassuringly she placed her arm across his tense shoulders.

"Jonas has not been assigned," she informed the crowd, and his heart sank.

Then she went on. "Jonas has been *selected.*"

He blinked. What did that mean? He felt a <u>collective</u>, questioning stir from the audience. They, too, were puzzled.

▶ *For what has Jonas been selected?*

In a firm, commanding voice she announced, "Jonas has been selected to be our next Receiver of Memory."

Then he heard the gasp—the sudden intake of breath, drawn sharply in astonishment, by each of the seated citizens. He saw their faces; the eyes widened in awe.

And still he did not understand.

"Such a selection is very, very rare," the Chief Elder told the audience. "Our community has only one Receiver. It is he who trains his successor.

"We have had our current Receiver for a very long time," she went on. Jonas followed her eyes and saw that she was looking at one of the Elders. The Committee of Elders was sitting together in a group; and the Chief Elder's eyes were now on one who sat in the midst but seemed oddly separate from them. It was a man Jonas had never noticed before, a bearded man with pale eyes. He was watching Jonas intently.

▶ *What causes the audience to be uncomfortable?*

"We failed in our last selection," the Chief Elder said solemnly. "It was ten years ago, when Jonas was just a toddler. I will not dwell on the experience because it causes us all terrible discomfort."

Jonas didn't know what she was referring to, but he could sense the discomfort of the audience. They shifted uneasily in their seats.

---

words for everyday use

col • lec • tive (kə lek´ tiv) *adj.,* involving all members of a group as distinct from its individuals; shared or assumed by all members of a group. *The audience emitted a* <u>collective</u> *gasp when the murderer appeared behind the heroine on the dark stage.*

"We have not been hasty this time," she continued. "We could not afford another failure."

"Sometimes," she went on, speaking now in a lighter tone, relaxing the tension in the Auditorium, "we are not entirely certain about the Assignments, even after the most painstaking observations. Sometimes we worry that the one assigned might not develop, through training, every attribute necessary. Elevens are still children, after all. What we observe as playfulness and patience—the requirements to become Nurturer—could, with maturity, be revealed as simply foolishness and indolence. So we continue to observe during training, and to modify behavior when necessary.

"But the Receiver-in-training cannot be observed, cannot be modified. That is stated quite clearly in the rules. He is to be alone, apart, while he is prepared by the current Receiver for the job which is the most honored in our community."

◄ Why can't the Receiver-in-training be observed?

Alone? Apart? Jonas listened with increasing unease.

"Therefore the selection must be sound. It must be a unanimous choice of the Committee. They can have no doubts, however fleeting. If, during the process, an Elder reports a dream of uncertainty, that dream has the power to set a candidate aside instantly.

"Jonas was identified as a possible Receiver many years ago. We have observed him meticulously. There were no dreams of uncertainty.

"He has shown all of the qualities that a Receiver must have."

With her hand still firmly on his shoulder, the Chief Elder listed the qualities.

"Intelligence," she said. "We are all aware that Jonas has been a top student throughout his school days.

---

words for everyday use

u • nan • i • mous (yü na´ nə məs) adj., having the agreement and consent of all. *The vote was unanimous: Seth for class president!*

me • tic • u • lous (mə ti´ kyə ləs) adj., marked by extreme or excessive care in the consideration or treatment of details. *Kara took meticulous care of her magazines; all were filed alphabetically with tabs marking the best articles.* **meticulously,** adv.

"*Integrity,*" she said next. "Jonas has, like all of us, committed minor transgressions." She smiled at him. "We expect that. We hoped, also, that he would present himself promptly for chastisement, and he has always done so.

"*Courage,*" she went on. "Only one of us here today has ever undergone the rigorous training required of a Receiver. He, of course, is the most important member of the Committee: the current Receiver. It was he who reminded us, again and again, of the courage required.

"Jonas," she said, turning to him, but speaking in a voice that the entire community could hear, "the training required of you involves pain. Physical pain."

He felt fear flutter within him.

"You have never experienced that. Yes, you have scraped your knees in falls from your bicycle. Yes, you crushed your finger in a door last year."

Jonas nodded, agreeing, as he recalled the incident, and its accompanying misery.

▶ *Why does the Receiver need to possess courage?*

"But you will be faced, now," she explained gently, "with pain of a magnitude that none of us here can comprehend because it is beyond our experience. The Receiver himself was not able to describe it, only to remind us that you would be faced with it, that you would need immense courage. We cannot prepare you for that.

"But we feel certain that you are brave," she said to him.

He did not feel brave at all. Not now.

"The fourth essential <u>attribute</u>," the Chief Elder said, "is *wisdom.* Jonas has not yet acquired that. The acquisition of wisdom will come through his training.

"We are convinced that Jonas has the ability to acquire wisdom. That is what we looked for.

"Finally, The Receiver must have one more quality, and it is one which I can only name, but not describe. I do not understand it. You members of the

---

words for everyday use **at • tri • bute** (a´ trə byüt) *n.,* an inherent characteristic or quality. *As you get older you realize that integrity and intelligence are among the most important <u>attributes</u> a person can possess.*

community will not understand it, either. Perhaps Jonas will, because the current Receiver has told us that Jonas already has this quality. He calls it the Capacity to See Beyond."

◀ What is the fifth quality needed in a Receiver?

The Chief Elder looked at Jonas with a question in her eyes. The audience watched him, too. They were silent.

For a moment he froze, consumed with despair. He *didn't* have it, the whatever-she-had-said. He didn't know what it was. Now was the moment when he would have to confess, to say, "No, I don't. I *can't*," and throw himself on their mercy, ask their forgiveness, to explain that he had been wrongly chosen, that he was not the right one at all.

But when he looked out across the crowd, the sea of faces, the thing happened again. The thing that had happened with the apple.

◀ What happens when Jonas looks out at the crowd? What does he feel for the first time?

They *changed.*

He blinked, and it was gone. His shoulders straightened slightly. Briefly he felt a tiny sliver of sureness for the first time.

She was still watching him. They all were.

"I think it's true," he told the Chief Elder and the community. "I don't understand it yet. I don't know what it is. But sometimes I see something. And maybe it's beyond."

She took her arm from his shoulders.

"Jonas," she said, speaking not to him alone but to the entire community of which he was a part, "you will be trained to be our next Receiver of Memory. We thank you for your childhood."

Then she turned and left the stage, left him there alone, standing and facing the crowd, which began spontaneously the collective murmur of his name.

"Jonas." It was a whisper at first: hushed, barely audible. "Jonas, Jonas."

Then louder, faster. "JONAS. JONAS. JONAS."

---

words for everyday use   spon • ta • ne • ous (spän tā´ nē əs) *adj.*, proceeding from natural feeling without external constraint; arising from a momentary impulse. *As our science teacher was explaining to the class the changing colors of leaves, he acted in a spontaneous manner, jumping out of his seat and whisking us outside into the fall afternoon.* **spontaneously,** *adv.*

▶ What does Jonas know?

▶ Why is Jonas filled with fear?

With the chant, Jonas knew, the community was accepting him and his new role, giving him life, the way they had given it to the newchild Caleb. His heart swelled with gratitude and pride.

But at the same time he was filled with fear. He did not know what his selection meant. He did not know what he was to become.

Or what would become of him.

Respond to the Selection

Once members of the community of *The Giver* become Twelves, they prepare for the coming responsibilities of adult life. Do you think this is wise? Why, or why not?

Investigate, Inquire, and Imagine

Recall: GATHERING FACTS

1a. Each morning, family members participate in a ritual of telling their dreams to the other members of their family. What happens after a family member shares his or her dream?

2a. Privately, Jonas's mother responds to the dream he shares with the family by telling him he has experienced his first Stirrings. What are Stirrings, and how does the community of *The Giver* deal with Stirrings?

3a. Jonas's father makes a plea on behalf of Gabriel. What would have happened if his father had not done this?

4a. What happens during the Ceremony of Loss? What happens during the Murmur-of-Replacement Ceremony?

Interpret: FINDING MEANING

1b. Why do you think members of all families in the community of *The Giver* practice this ritual?

2b. What motivations might the community of *The Giver* have for treating Stirrings as they do?

3b. How does the society of *The Giver* regard children who develop at a slower than average pace?

4b. What is the desired result of each of these ceremonies?

Analyze: TAKING THINGS APART

5a. Chapter 1 describes the evening ritual of telling one's feelings. Chapter 2 tells of the increasing observation that all Elevens undergo by the Committee of Elders. Chapter 3 tells of the public announcement chastising Jonas for taking an apple home. Chapter 5 describes the morning ritual of sharing one's dreams and also about Stirrings and the treatment for them. In Chapter 6, the reader learns that each member of Jonas's family had to sign a pledge not to become attached to Gabriel. In this chapter, the reader also learns how the Matching of Spouses is conducted. Consider each of these specific details from the story, and decide which relate to the way the society of *The Giver* deals with emotions, and which tell something about an individual's right to privacy in the society of *The Giver.* Note that some details may reveal how the society deals with emotions and also tell something about the individual right to privacy within the society.

Synthesize: BRINGING THINGS TOGETHER

5b. Based on your analysis in questions 5a, state how the society in *The Giver* chooses to deal with human emotion. Make a comment also about the individual's right to privacy in the society of *The Giver.* Does the way society deals with human emotion affect the right of individuals to have privacy, or vice versa? Explain.

Perspective: LOOKING AT OTHER VIEWS

6a. In Chapter 6, Asher tells Jonas that if a person doesn't fit into the community, he or she can "apply for Elsewhere and be released." Why does Asher say this? Does he think this is a good plan?

Empathy: SEEING FROM INSIDE

6b. How would you feel if you were asked to "apply for Elsewhere"? What would your thoughts about Elsewhere by? If yourself thought you didn't fit into the community, would you be hopeful or fearful about Elsewhere?

Understanding Literature

POINT OF VIEW. **Point of view** is the vantage point from which a story is told. If a story is told from the *first-person point of view,* the narrator uses the pronouns *I* and *we* and is a part of or a witness to the action. When a story is told from a *third-person point of view,* the narrator is outside the action, uses words such as *he, she, it,* and *they;* and the narrator avoids the use of *I* and *we.* In a literary work written from a *limited point of view,* everything is seen through the eyes of a single character. In a work written from an *omniscient point of view,* the narrator or storyteller knows everything and can see into the minds of all the characters. Is *The Giver* told from a first-person or third-person point of view? Is the point of view limited or omniscient? Explain. Why do you think the author might have chosen to use this point of view to tell the story of *The Giver?*

Point of view	Pronouns commonly used	Examples
first-person point of view	I, we, me, us, my, our	**I** read *The Giver* last year after **my** teacher told **me** it was her favorite book. **We** wrote a letter to Lois Lowry, asking her to come speak at **our** school.
third-person point of view	he, she, it, they, him, her, them	Lois Lowry never forgot **her** experiences in Japan; they will remain with **her** forever. **They** argued for hours about which novel was better: *The Giver* or *Number the Stars.*

SYMBOL. A **symbol** is a thing that stands for, or represents, both itself and something else. Some well-known symbols are the dove to represent peace, light and dark to represent good and evil, and the season of spring to represent life or rebirth. Identify two symbols from Chapter 6 and tell what each symbolizes.

ANECDOTE. An **anecdote** is a usually short narrative of an interesting, amusing, or biographical incident. Although anecdotes are often the basis for short stories, an anecdote differs from a short story in that it lacks a complicated plot and relates a single episode. What anecdote does Asher relate in Chapter 6? Why might the author have chosen to have Asher relate this anecdote? What does it reveal about the citizens of the community in *The Giver?*

Chapter 9

NOW, FOR THE first time in his twelve years of life, Jonas felt separate, different. He remembered what the Chief Elder had said: that his training would be alone and apart.

But his training had not yet begun and already, upon leaving the Auditorium, he felt the apartness. Holding the folder she had given him, he made his way through the throng, looking for his family unit and for Asher. People moved aside for him. They watched him. He thought he could hear whispers.

◀ Upon leaving the Auditorium, what does Jonas already feel?

"Ash!" he called, spotting his friend near the rows of bicycles. "Ride back with me?"

"Sure." Asher smiled, his usual smile, friendly and familiar. But Jonas felt a moment of hesitation from his friend, an uncertainty.

"Congratulations," Asher said.

"You, too," Jonas replied. "It was really funny, when she told about the smacks. You got more applause than almost anybody else."

The other new Twelves clustered nearby, placing their folders carefully into the carrying containers on the backs of the bikes. In each dwelling tonight they would be studying the instructions for the beginning of their training. Each night for years the children had memorized the required lessons for school, often yawning with boredom. Tonight they would all begin eagerly to memorize the rules for their adult Assignments.

"Congratulations, Asher!" someone called. Then that hesitation again. "You too, Jonas!"

◀ What does Jonas sense from Asher and others?

Asher and Jonas responded with congratulations to their groupmates. Jonas saw his parents watching him from the place where their own bicycles were waiting. Lily had already been strapped into her seat.

He waved. They waved back, smiling, but he noticed that Lily was watching him solemnly, her thumb in her mouth.

He rode directly to his dwelling, exchanging only small jokes and unimportant remarks with Asher.

"See you in the morning, Recreation Director!" he called, dismounting by his door as Asher continued on.

"Right! See you!" Asher called back. Once again, there was just a moment when things weren't quite the same, weren't quite as they had always been through the long friendship. Perhaps he had imagined it. Things couldn't change, with Asher.

The evening meal was quieter than usual. Lily chattered about her plans for volunteer work; she would begin, she said, at the Nurturing Center, since she was already an expert at feeding Gabriel.

"I know," she added quickly, when her father gave her a warning glance, "I won't mention his name. I know I'm not supposed to know his name.

"I can't wait for tomorrow to come," she said happily.

Jonas sighed uneasily. "I can," he muttered.

▶ What do Jonas's parents say about his selection?

"You've been greatly honored," his mother said. "Your father and I are very proud."

"It's the most important job in the community," Father said.

"But just the other night, you said that the job of making Assignments was the most important!"

Mother nodded. "This is different. It's not a *job*, really. I never thought, never expected—" She paused. "There's only one Receiver."

"But the Chief Elder said that they had made a selection before, and that it failed. What was she talking about?"

Both of his parents hesitated. Finally his father described the previous selection. "It was very much as it was today, Jonas—the same suspense, as one Eleven had been passed over when the Assignments were given. Then the announcement, when they singled out the one—"

Jonas interrupted. "What was his name?"

His mother replied, "Her, not his. It was a female. But we are never to speak the name, or to use it again for a newchild."

Jonas was shocked. A name designated Not-to-Be-Spoken indicated the highest degree of disgrace.

"What happened to her?" he asked nervously.

▶ What happened to the last Eleven chosen to be Receiver?

But his parents looked blank. "We don't know," his father said uncomfortably. "We never saw her again."

A silence fell over the room. They looked at each other. Finally his mother, rising from the table, said, "You've been greatly honored Jonas. Greatly honored."

Alone in his sleepingroom, prepared for bed, Jonas opened his folder at last. Some of the other Twelves, he had noticed, had been given folders thick with printed pages. He imagined Benjamin, the scientific male in his group, beginning to read pages of rules and instructions with relish. He pictured Fiona smiling her gentle smile as she bent over the lists of duties and methods that she would be required to learn in the days to come.

But his own folder was startlingly close to empty. Inside there was only a single printed sheet. He read it twice:

JONAS

RECEIVER OF MEMORY

1. Go immediately at the end of school hours each day to the Annex entrance behind the House of the Old and present yourself to the attendant.
2. Go immediately to your dwelling at the conclusion of Training Hours each day.
3. From this moment you are exempted from rules governing rudeness. You may ask any question of any citizen and you will receive answers.

◀ From what is Jonas now exempt?

4. Do not discuss your training with any other member of the community, including parents and Elders.
5. From this moment you are prohibited from dream-telling.

◀ From what is Jonas now prohibited?

6. Except for illness or injury unrelated to your training, do not apply for any medication.
7. You are not permitted to apply for release.
8. You may lie.

Jonas was stunned. What would happen to his friendships? His mindless hours playing ball, or riding his bike along the river? Those had been happy and vital times for him. Were they to be completely taken from him, now? The simple <u>logistic</u> instructions—

---

words for everyday use

lo • gis • tic (lō jis´ tik) *adj.,* relating to symbolic logic; relating to the handling of the details of an operation. *Planning a wedding involves a great deal of logistic preparation.*

where to go, and when—were expected. Every Twelve had to be told, of course, where and how and when to report for training. But he was a little dismayed that his schedule left no time, apparently, for recreation.

The exemption from rudeness startled him. Reading it again, however, he realized that it didn't compel him to be rude; it simply allowed him the option. He was quite certain he would never take advantage of it. He was so completely, so thoroughly accustomed to courtesy within the community that the thought of asking another citizen an intimate question, of calling someone's attention to an area of awkwardness, was unnerving.

▶ Of what is Jonas quite certain? Why?

The <u>prohibition</u> of dream-telling, he thought, would not be a real problem. He dreamed so rarely that the dream-telling did not come easily to him anyway, and he was glad to be excused from it. He wondered briefly, though, how to deal with it at the morning meal. What if he *did* dream—should he simply tell his family unit, as he did so often, anyway, that he hadn't? That would be a lie. Still, the final rule said . . . well, he wasn't quite ready to think about the final rule on the page.

The restriction of medication unnerved him. Medication was always available to citizens, even to children, through their parents. When he had crushed his finger in the door, he had quickly, gasping into the speaker, notified his mother; she had hastily <u>requisitioned</u> relief-of-pain medication which had promptly been delivered to his dwelling. Almost instantly the excruciating pain in his hand had diminished to the throb which was, now, all he could recall of the experience.

Re-reading rule number 6, he realized that a crushed finger fell into the category of "unrelated to training." So if it ever happened again—and he was

---

words for everyday use

pro • hi • bi • tion (prō ə bi´ shən) *n.*, act of forbidding the doing of something. *The prohibition of food and drinks in the museum was necessary to prevent damage to the artifacts.*

req • ui • si • tion (re kwə zi´ shən) *v.*, request or require that something be provided. *The head of the department told the new employees to go ahead and requisition any supplies they would need to do their jobs.*

quite certain it wouldn't; he had been very careful near heavy doors since the accident!—he could still receive medication.

The pill he took now, each morning, was also unrelated to training. So he would continue to receive the pill.

But he remembered uneasily what the Chief Elder had said about the pain that would come with his training. She had called it indescribable.

Jonas swallowed hard, trying without success to imagine what such pain might be like, with no medication at all. But it was beyond his comprehension.

He felt no reaction to rule number 7 at all. It had never occurred to him that under any circumstances, ever, he might apply for release.

Finally he <u>steeled</u> himself to read the final rule again. He had been trained since earliest childhood, since his earliest learning of language, never to lie. It was an integral part of the learning of precise speech. Once, when he had been a Four, he had said, just prior to the midday meal at school, "I'm starving."

◀ *What has Jonas been trained not to do since earliest childhood?*

Immediately he had been taken aside for a brief private lesson in language precision. He was not starving, it was pointed out. He was *hungry.* No one in the community was starving, had ever been starving, would ever be starving. To say "starving" was to speak a lie. An unintentional lie, of course. But the reason for precision of language was to ensure that unintentional lies were never uttered. Did he understand that? they asked him. And he had.

◀ *What is the reason for precision of language?*

He had never, within his memory, been tempted to lie. Asher did not lie. Lily did not lie. His parents did not lie. No one did. Unless . . .

Now Jonas had a thought that he had never had before. This new thought was frightening. What if *others—adults—*had, upon becoming Twelves, received in *their* instructions the same terrifying sentence?

◀ *What thought terrifies Jonas?*

---

words for everyday use

steel (stēl´) v., fill with resolution or determination. *Listening to the words of great leaders from the past can often give us comfort and <u>steel</u> us to face the future bravely.*

What if they had all been instructed: *You may lie?*

His mind reeled. Now, <u>empowered</u> to ask questions of utmost rudeness—and promised answers—he *could,* <u>conceivably</u> (though it was almost unimaginable), ask someone, some adult, his father perhaps: "Do you lie?"

But he would have no way of knowing if the answer he received was true.

words for everyday use

em • pow • er (im pou´ ər) *v.*, give official authority or legal power to. *Our teacher <u>empowered</u> Wayne, as hall monitor, to request a pass from any student wandering the corridors during class time.*

con • ceiv • able (kən sē´ və bəl) *adj.*, imaginable; thinkable; possible. *Before Roger Bannister did it in 1954, hardly anyone believed it was <u>conceivable</u> to run a mile in under four minutes.* **conceivably,** *adv.*

Chapter 10

"I GO IN HERE, Jonas," Fiona told him when they reached the front door of the House of the Old after parking their bicycles in the designated area.

"I don't know why I'm nervous," she confessed. "I've been here so often before." She turned her folder over in her hands.

"Well, everything's different now," Jonas reminded her.

"Even the nameplates on our bikes," Fiona laughed. During the night the nameplate of each new Twelve had been removed by the Maintenance Crew and replaced with the style that indicated citizen-in-training.

"I don't want to be late," she said hastily, and started up the steps. "If we finish at the same time, I'll ride home with you."

Jonas nodded, waved to her, and headed around the building toward the Annex, a small wing attached to the back. He certainly didn't want to be late for his first day of training, either.

The Annex was very ordinary, its door unremarkable. He reached for the heavy handle, then noticed a buzzer on the wall. So he buzzed instead.

"Yes?" The voice came through a small speaker above the buzzer.

"It's, uh, Jonas. I'm the new—I mean—"

"Come in." A click indicated that the door had been unlatched.

The lobby was very small and contained only a desk at which a female Attendant sat working on some papers. She looked up when he entered; then, to his surprise, she stood. It was a small thing, the standing; but no one had ever stood automatically to acknowledge Jonas's presence before.

◀ What does the Attendant do when Jonas enters?

"Welcome, Receiver of Memory," she said respectfully.

"Oh, please," he replied uncomfortably. "Call me Jonas."

She smiled, pushed a button, and he heard a click that unlocked the door to her left. "You may go right on in," she told him.

▶ *What makes Jonas uncomfortable? Why?*

Then she seemed to notice his discomfort and to realize its origin. No doors in the community were locked, ever. None that Jonas knew of, anyway.

"The locks are simply to insure The Receiver's privacy because he needs concentration," she explained. "It would be difficult if citizens wandered in, looking for the Department of Bicycle Repair, or something."

Jonas laughed, relaxing a little. The woman seemed very friendly, and it was true—in fact it was a joke throughout the community—that the Department of Bicycle Repair, an unimportant little office, was relocated so often that no one ever knew where it was.

"There is nothing dangerous here," she told him.

"But," she added, glancing at the wall clock, "he doesn't like to be kept waiting."

Jonas hurried through the door and found himself in a comfortably furnished living area. It was not unlike his own family unit's dwelling. Furniture was standard throughout the community: practical, sturdy, the function of each piece clearly defined. A bed for sleeping. A table for eating. A desk for studying.

All of those things were in this spacious room, though each was slightly different from those in his own dwelling. The fabrics on the upholstered chairs and sofa were slightly thicker and more luxurious; the table legs were not straight like those at home, but slender and curved, with a small carved decoration at the foot. The bed, in an alcove at the far end of the room, was draped with a splendid cloth embroidered over its entire surface with <u>intricate</u> designs.

But the most <u>conspicuous</u> difference was the books. In his own dwelling, there were the necessary reference volumes that each household contained: a dictionary, and the thick community volume which

---

words for everyday use

in • tri • cate (in´ tri kət) *adj.,* having many complexly interrelating parts. *The blanket was handmade by her great grandmother and featured a beautiful and <u>intricate</u> pattern.*

con • spic • u • ous (kən spi´ kyə wəs) *adj.,* obvious to the eye or mind; striking; noticeable. *It is always easy to spot Colleen in a crowd as her bright red hair is so <u>conspicuous</u>.*

contained descriptions of every office, factory, building, and committee. And the Book of Rules, of course.

The books in his own dwelling were the only books that Jonas had ever seen. He had never known that other books existed.

◀ What had Jonas never known?

But this room's walls were completely covered by bookcases, filled, which reached to the ceiling. There must have been hundreds—perhaps thousands—of books, their titles <u>embossed</u> in shiny letters.

Jonas stared at them. He couldn't imagine what the thousands of pages contained. Could there be rules beyond the rules that governed the community? Could there be more descriptions of offices and factories and committees?

◀ What can't Jonas imagine?

He had only a second to look around because he was aware that the man sitting in a chair beside the table was watching him. Hastily he moved forward, stood before the man, bowed slightly, and said, "I'm Jonas."

"I know. Welcome, Receiver of Memory."

Jonas recognized the man. He was the Elder who had seemed separate from the others at the Ceremony, though he was dressed in the same special clothing that only Elders wore.

Jonas looked self-consciously into the pale eyes that mirrored his own.

"Sir, I apologize for my lack of understanding. . . ."

He waited, but the man did not give the standard accepting-of-apology response.

◀ For what does Jonas wait but not get?

After a moment, Jonas went on, "But I thought—I mean I *think*," he corrected, reminding himself that if precision of language were ever to be important, it was certainly important *now*, in the presence of this man, "that *you* are the Receiver of Memory. I'm only, well, I was only assigned, I mean selected, yesterday. I'm not anything at all. Not yet."

---

words for everyday use   em • boss (im bäs´) v., to ornament with raised work; raise in relief from a surface. *The printer will <u>emboss</u> the invitations, giving them a very formal look.*

The man looked at him thoughtfully, silently. It was a look that combined interest, curiosity, concern, and perhaps a little sympathy as well.

Finally he spoke. "Beginning today, this moment, at least to me, you are The Receiver.

"I have been The Receiver for a long time. A very, very long time. You can see that, can't you?"

Jonas nodded. The man was wrinkled, and his eyes, though piercing in their unusual lightness, seemed tired. The flesh around them was darkened into shadowed circles.

"I can see that you are very old," Jonas responded with respect. The Old were always given the highest respect.

The man smiled. He touched the sagging flesh on his own face with amusement. "I am not, actually, as old as I look," he told Jonas. "This job has aged me. I know I look as if I should be scheduled for release very soon. But actually I have a good deal of time left.

"I was pleased, though, when you were selected. It took them a long time. The failure of the previous selection was ten years ago, and my energy is starting to diminish. I need what strength I have remaining for your training. We have hard and painful work to do, you and I.

"Please sit down," he said, and gestured toward the nearby chair. Jonas lowered himself onto the soft cushioned seat.

The man closed his eyes and continued speaking. "When I became a Twelve, I was selected, as you were. I was frightened, as I'm sure you are." He opened his eyes for a moment and peered at Jonas, who nodded.

The eyes closed again. "I came to this very room to begin my training. It was such a long time ago.

"The previous Receiver seemed just as old to me as I do to you. He was just as tired as I am today."

He sat forward suddenly, opened his eyes, and said, "You may ask questions. I have so little experience in describing this process. It is forbidden to talk of it."

"I know, sir. I have read the instructions," Jonas said.

"So I may neglect to make things as clear as I should." The man chuckled. "My job is important

▶ *Why does the previous Receiver encourage Jonas to ask questions?*

and has enormous honor. But that does not mean I am perfect, and when I tried before to train a successor, I failed. Please ask any questions that will help you."

In his mind, Jonas had questions. A thousand. A *million* questions. As many questions as there were books lining the walls. But he did not ask one, not yet.

The man sighed, seeming to put his thoughts in order. Then he spoke again. "Simply stated," he said, "although it's not really simple at all, my job is to <u>transmit</u> to you all the memories I have within me. Memories of the past."

◄ *Put simply, what is the previous Receiver's job?*

"Sir," Jonas said <u>tentatively</u>, "I would be very interested to hear the story of your life, and to listen to your memories.

"I apologize for interrupting," he added quickly.

The man waved his hand impatiently. "No apologies in this room. We haven't time."

"Well," Jonas went on, uncomfortably aware that he might be interrupting again, "I am really interested, I don't mean that I'm not. But I don't exactly understand why it's so important. I could do some adult job in the community, and in my recreation time I could come and listen to the stories from your childhood. I'd like that. Actually," he added, "I've done that already, in the House of the Old. The Old like to tell about their childhoods, and it's always fun to listen."

The man shook his head. "No, no," he said. "I'm not being clear. It's not my past, not my childhood that I must transmit to you."

◄ *What must the previous Receiver transmit to Jonas?*

He leaned back, resting his head against the back of the upholstered chair. "It's the memories of the whole world," he said with a sigh. "Before you, before me, before the previous Receiver, and <u>generations</u> before him."

---

words for everyday use

trans • mit (tranz mit´) v., send or convey from one person or place to another; cause to pass or be conveyed through space or a medium. *The Internet makes it possible for people to <u>transmit</u> information across the world in matter of seconds.*

ten • ta • tive (ten´ tə tiv) adj., hesitant; uncertain. *Helen made a <u>tentative</u> motion to shake my hand to say goodbye, but then she saw me smile and gave me a hug instead.* tentatively, adv.

gen • er • a • tion (je nə rā´ shən) n., average span of time between the birth of parents and that of their offspring; a group of individuals born and living during the same period of time. *At the party, we took a picture of great grandmother, grandmother, mother, and granddaughter: four <u>generations</u> of women in our family.*

▶ What doesn't
Jonas understand?

Jonas frowned. "The whole world?" he asked. "I don't understand. Do you mean not just us? Not just the community? Do you mean Elsewhere, too?" He tried, in his mind, to grasp the concept. "I'm sorry, sir. I don't understand exactly. Maybe I'm not smart enough. I don't know what you mean when you say 'the whole world' or 'generations before him.' I thought there was only us. I thought there was only now."

"There's much more. There's all that goes beyond—all that is Elsewhere—and all that goes back, and back, and back. I received all of those when I was selected. And here in this room, all alone, I re-experience them again and again. It is how wisdom comes. And how we shape our future."

He rested for a moment, breathing deeply. "I am so *weighted* with them," he said.

Jonas felt a terrible concern for the man, suddenly.

"It's as if . . ." The man paused, seeming to search his mind for the right words of description. "It's like going downhill through deep snow on a sled," he said, finally. "At first it's <u>exhilarating</u>: the speed; the sharp, clear air; but then the snow accumulates, builds up on the runners, and you slow, you have to push hard to keep going, and—"

He shook his head suddenly, and peered at Jonas. "That meant nothing to you, did it?" he asked.

Jonas was confused. "I didn't understand it, sir."

▶ What terms
doesn't Jonas know?

"Of course you didn't. You don't know what snow is, do you?"

Jonas shook his head.

"Or a sled? Runners?"

"No, sir," Jonas said.

"Downhill? The term means nothing to you?"

"Nothing, sir."

"Well, it's a place to start. I'd been wondering how to begin. Move to the bed, and lie face down. Remove your tunic first."

---

words for everyday use ex • hil • a • rat • ing (ig ziˊ lə rā tiŋ) *adj.*, enlivening; refreshing; exciting; stimulating.
I think that flying a kite, when you've got plenty of open space to run, is an <u>exhilarating</u> experience.

Jonas did so, a little apprehensively. Beneath his bare chest, he felt the soft folds of the magnificent cloth that covered the bed. He watched as the man rose and moved first to the wall where the speaker was. It was the same sort of speaker that occupied a place in every dwelling, but one thing about it was different. This one had a switch, which the man deftly snapped to the end that said OFF.

◀ What astonishes Jonas?

Jonas almost gasped aloud. To have the power to turn the speaker *off*? It was an astonishing thing.

Then the man moved with surprising quickness to the corner where the bed was. He sat on a chair beside Jonas, who was motionless, waiting for what would happen next.

"Close your eyes. Relax. This will not be painful."

Jonas remembered that he was allowed, that he had even been encouraged, to ask questions. "What are you going to do, sir?" he asked, hoping that his voice didn't betray his nervousness.

"I am going to transmit the memory of snow," the old man said, and placed his hands on Jonas's bare back.

---

words for everyday use   **deft** (deft´) *adj.,* handy; dexterous; characterized by facility and skill. *I love to watch my sister play the piano; I am always amazed at her* deft *hands flying over the keys.* **deftly,** *adv.*

Chapter 11

Jonas felt nothing unusual at first. He felt only the light touch of the old man's hands on his back.

He tried to relax, to breathe evenly. The room was absolutely silent, and for a moment Jonas feared that he might disgrace himself now, on the first day of his training, by falling asleep.

Then he shivered. He realized that the touch of the hands felt, suddenly, cold. At the same instant, breathing in, he felt the air change, and his very breath was cold. He licked his lips, and in doing so, his tongue touched the suddenly chilled air.

It was very startling; but he was not at all frightened, now. He was filled with energy, and he breathed again, feeling the sharp intake of <u>frigid</u> air. Now, too, he could feel cold air swirling around his entire body. He felt it blow against his hands where they lay at his sides, and over his back.

The touch of the man's hands seemed to have disappeared.

Now he became aware of an entirely new sensation: pinpricks? No, because they were soft and without pain. Tiny, cold, featherlike feelings peppered his body and face. He put out his tongue again, and caught one of the dots of cold upon it. It disappeared from his awareness instantly; but he caught another, and another. The sensation made him smile.

▶ *Where is one part of Jonas's consciousness? Where is the other part?*

One part of his consciousness knew that he was still lying there, on the bed, in the Annex room. Yet another, separate part of his being was upright now, in a sitting position, and beneath him he could feel that he was not on the soft decorated bedcovering at all, but rather seated on a flat, hard surface. His hands now held (though at the same time they were still motionless at his sides) a rough, damp rope.

And he could *see*, though his eyes were closed. He could see a bright, whirling torrent of crystals in the air around him, and he could see them gather on the backs of his hands, like cold fur.

His breath was visible.

Beyond, through the swirl of what he now, somehow, perceived was the thing the old man had spoken of—*snow*—he could look out and down a great distance. He was up high someplace. The ground was thick with the furry snow, but he sat slightly above it on a hard, flat object.

Sled, he knew abruptly. He was sitting on a thing called *sled*. And the sled itself seemed to be poised at the top of a long, extended mound that rose from the very land where he was. Even as he thought the word "mound," his new consciousness told him *hill*.

Then the sled, with Jonas himself upon it, began to move through the snowfall, and he understood instantly that now he was going downhill. No voice made an explanation. The experience explained itself to him.

His face cut through the frigid air as he began the descent, moving through the substance called snow on the <u>vehicle</u> called sled, which propelled itself on what he now knew without doubt to be *runners*.

Comprehending all of those things as he sped downward, he was free to enjoy the breathless glee that overwhelmed him: the speed, the clear cold air, the total silence, the feeling of balance and excitement and peace.

Then, as the angle of incline lessened, as the mound—the *hill*—flattened, nearing the bottom, the sled's forward motion slowed. The snow was piled now around it, and he pushed with his body, moving it forward, not wanting the exhilarating ride to end.

Finally the <u>obstruction</u> of the piled snow was too much for the thin runners of the sled, and he came to a stop. He sat there for a moment, panting, holding the rope in his cold hands. Tentatively he opened his eyes—not his snow-hill-sled eyes, for they had

---

words for everyday use

ve • hi • cle (vē´ ə kəl) *n.*, a means of carrying or transporting something; a conveyance. *Malik drove us all to the game because he has the largest <u>vehicle</u>.*

ob • struc • tion (äb strək´ shən) *n.*, condition of being clogged or blocked. *A tree root proved to be the <u>obstruction</u> that was causing our main plumbing line to clog.*

been open throughout the strange ride. He opened his ordinary eyes, and saw that he was still on the bed, that he had not moved at all.

The old man, still beside the bed, was watching him. "How do you feel?" he asked.

Jonas sat up and tried to answer honestly. "Surprised," he said, after a moment.

The old man wiped his forehead with his sleeve. "Whew," he said. "It was exhausting. But you know, even transmitting that tiny memory to you—I think it lightened me just a little."

"Do you mean—you did say I could ask questions?"

The man nodded, encouraging his question.

▶ What happens to the memory the old man transmits to Jonas?

"Do you mean that now you don't have the memory of it—of that ride on the sled—anymore?"

"That's right. A little weight off this old body."

"But it was such fun! And now you don't have it anymore! I *took* it from you!"

But the old man laughed. "All I gave you was one ride, on one sled, in one snow, on one hill. I have a whole world of them in my memory. I could give them to you one by one, a thousand times, and there would still be more."

"Are you saying that I—I mean we—could do it again?" Jonas asked. "I'd really like to. I think I could steer, by pulling the rope. I didn't try this time, because it was so new."

The old man, laughing, shook his head. "Maybe another day, for a treat. But there's no time, really, just to play. I only wanted to begin by showing you how it works.

"Now," he said, turning businesslike, "lie back down. I want to—"

Jonas did. He was eager for whatever experience would come next. But he had, suddenly, so many questions.

"Why don't we have snow, and sleds, and hills?" he asked. "And when did we, in the past? Did my parents have sleds when they were young? Did you?"

The old man shrugged and gave a short laugh. "No," he told Jonas. "It's a very distant memory. That's why it was so exhausting—I had to tug it forward from many generations back. It was given to me when I was a new Receiver, and the previous Receiver had to pull it through a long time period, too."

"But what happened to those things? Snow, and the rest of it?"

◀ Why doesn't snow exist anymore?

"<u>Climate</u> Control. Snow made growing food difficult, limited the agricultural periods. And unpredictable weather made transportation almost impossible at times. It wasn't a practical thing, so it became <u>obsolete</u> when we went to Sameness.

"And hills, too," he added. "They made <u>conveyance</u> of goods <u>unwieldy</u>. Trucks; buses. Slowed them down. So—" He waved his hand, as if a gesture had caused hills to disappear. "Sameness," he concluded.

◀ Why don't hills exist anymore?

Jonas frowned. "I wish we had those things, still. Just now and then."

The old man smiled. "So do I," he said. "But that choice is not ours."

"But sir," Jonas suggested, "since you have so much power—"

The man corrected him. "Honor," he said firmly. "I have great honor. So will you. But you will find that that is not the same as power.

◀ What two things does the old man tell Jonas are not the same?

"Lie quietly now. Since we've entered into the topic of climate, let me give you something else. And this time I'm not going to tell you the name of it, because I want to test the receiving. You should be able to perceive the name without being told. I gave away snow and sled and downhill and runners by telling them to you in advance."

Without being instructed, Jonas closed his eyes again. He felt the hands on his back again. He waited.

Now it came more quickly, the feelings. This time the hands didn't become cold, but instead began to

---

words for everyday use

cli • mate (klī´ mət) n., average course or condition of the weather of a specific location. *Many people base where they want to live on the climate of the area.*

ob • so • lete (äb sə lēt´) adj., no longer in use or no longer useful. *Because we all have cars, some people seem to think walking has become an obsolete activity; this thinking contributes both to weight gain and pollution.*

con • vey • ance (kən vā´ ənts) n., the act of transferring or delivering. *The conveyance of goods around the world is accomplished by the use of trucks, ships, and planes.*

un • wield • y (ən wēəl´ dē) adj., not easily managed, handled, or used; awkward; cumbersome. *She decided to purchase the picture last, as otherwise, it would be an unwieldy package that she'd have to lug around the mall all day.*

feel warm on his body. They moistened a little. The warmth spread, extending across his shoulders, up his neck, onto the side of his face. He could feel it through his clothed parts, too: a pleasant, all-over sensation; and when he licked his lips this time, the air was hot and heavy.

He didn't move. There was no sled. His posture didn't change. He was simply alone someplace, out of doors, lying down, and the warmth came from far above. It was not as exciting as the ride through the snowy air; but it was pleasurable and comforting.

Suddenly he perceived the word for it: *sunshine*. He perceived that it came from the sky.

Then it ended.

"Sunshine," he said aloud, opening his eyes.

"Good. You did get the word. That makes my job easier. Not so much explaining."

"And it came from the sky."

"That's right," the old man said. "Just the way it used to."

"Before Sameness. Before Climate Control," Jonas added.

The man laughed. "You receive well, and learn quickly. I'm very pleased with you. That's enough for today, I think. We're off to a good start."

There was a question bothering Jonas. "Sir," he said, "The Chief Elder told me—she told everyone—and you told me, too, that it would be painful. So I was a little scared. But it didn't hurt at all. I really enjoyed it." He looked quizzically at the old man.

The man sighed. "I started you with memories of pleasure. My previous failure gave me the wisdom to do that." He took a few deep breaths. "Jonas," he said, "it *will* be painful. But it need not be painful yet."

"I'm brave. I really am." Jonas sat up a little straighter.

The old man looked at him for a moment. He smiled. "I can see that," he said. "Well, since you asked the question—I think I have enough energy for one more transmission.

"Lie down once more. This will be the last today."

Jonas obeyed cheerfully. He closed his eyes, waiting, and felt the hands again; then he felt the warmth again, the sunshine again, coming from the sky of this other consciousness that was so new to him. This time, as he lay basking in the wonderful warmth, he felt the passage of time. His real self was aware that it was only a minute or two; but his other, memory-receiving self felt hours pass in the sun. His skin began to sting. Restlessly he moved one arm, bending it, and felt a sharp pain in the crease of his inner arm at the elbow.

"Ouch," he said loudly, and shifted on the bed. "Owwww," he said, wincing at the shift, and even moving his mouth to speak made his face hurt.

He knew there was a word, but the pain kept him from grasping it.

Then it ended. He opened his eyes, wincing with discomfort. "It hurt," he told the man, "and I couldn't get the word for it."

"It was sunburn," the old man told him.

"It hurt a *lot*," Jonas said, "but I'm glad you gave it to me. It was interesting. And now I understand better, what it meant, that there would be pain."

The man didn't respond. He sat silently for a second. Finally he said, "Get up, now. It's time for you to go home."

They both walked to the center of the room. Jonas put his tunic back on. "Goodbye, sir," he said. "Thank you for my first day."

The old man nodded to him. He looked drained, and a little sad.

"Sir?" Jonas said shyly.

"Yes? Do you have a question?"

"It's just that I don't know your name. I thought you were The Receiver, but you say that now *I'm* The Receiver. So I don't know what to call you."

The man had sat back down in the comfortable upholstered chair. He moved his shoulders around as if to ease away an aching sensation. He seemed terribly weary.

"Call me The Giver," he told Jonas.

◀ What does the old man tell Jonas to call him?

Respond to the Selection

In a short paragraph, answer one of the following questions: What is the difference between honor and power? How can knowledge change a person's view of the world around him or her?

Investigate, Inquire, and Imagine

Recall: GATHERING FACTS

1a. Whose name has been designated Not-to-Be-Spoken? What does a name designated Not-to-Be-Spoken indicate?

2a. List the ways in which Jonas's selection as Receiver of Memory set him apart from others in the community.

3a. How does Jonas respond when The Giver tells him: "It's not my past, not my childhood that I must transmit to you. . . . It's the memories of the whole world, . . . Before you, before me, before the previous Receiver, and generations before him."

Interpret: FINDING MEANING

➤ 1b. What possible motivation might the community of The Giver have for mandating that a name never again be spoken?

➤ 2b. What freedoms does Jonas gain by becoming Receiver of Memory? What freedoms must Jonas surrender?

➤ 3b. What does Jonas's response reveal about Jonas and the entire community?

Analyze: TAKING THINGS APART

4a. During Jonas's first meeting with The Giver, the reader learns of several things that do not exist in the world in which Jonas lives. Identify these things.

Synthesize: BRINGING THINGS TOGETHER

➤ 4b. Consider your list of things that do not exist in the world of The Giver, and consider the reasons The Giver provides for why they no longer exist. Based on these, make a statement about what members of the society of The Giver value.

Perspective: LOOKING AT OTHER VIEWS

5a. Provide a few specific examples that reveal how Jonas views the society in which he lives before he meets with The Giver for the first time. Next, identify specific things of which Jonas becomes aware during his meeting with The Giver that hold the power to alter his perspective, and explain why they hold this power.

Empathy: SEEING FROM INSIDE

→ 5b. Imagine that you are Jonas and that you have returned home from your first meeting with The Giver. Alone in your room that evening, what thoughts and feelings might you have?

Understanding Literature

CONFLICT. A **conflict** is a struggle between two people or things in a literary work. A *plot* is formed around conflict. A conflict can be internal or external. A struggle that takes place between a character and some outside force such as another character, society, or nature is called an *external conflict.* A struggle that takes place within a character is called an *internal conflict.* Based on your reading so far, attempt to predict a conflict that will take place further in the story. Will it be an internal or external conflict? Provide reasons for your answer.

DESCRIPTION. **Description** is a type of writing that portrays a character, object, or scene. Descriptions make use of sensory details—words and phrases that describe how things look, sound, smell, taste, or feel. Think carefully about the eleven chapters you've read and about whether the author has chosen to describe how things look, sound, smell, taste, or feel. Comment on the author's use of description in the first half of *The Giver.*

SETTING. The **setting** of a literary work is the time and place in which it happens. Writers create settings in many different ways. In fiction, setting is most often revealed by means of descriptions of landscape, scenery, buildings, furniture, clothing, the weather, and the season. It can also be revealed by how characters talk and behave. What do the author's descriptions of landscape, scenery, buildings, furniture, clothing, weather, and/or season reveal about the setting of *The Giver?* Comment on the role that setting plays in the first half of the book.

Chapter 12

"YOU SLEPT SOUNDLY, Jonas?" his mother asked at the morning meal. "No dreams?"

Jonas simply smiled and nodded, not ready to lie, not willing to tell the truth. "I slept very soundly," he said.

"I wish this one would," his father said, leaning down from his chair to touch Gabriel's waving fist. The basket was on the floor beside him; in its corner, beside Gabriel's head, the stuffed hippo sat staring with its blank eyes.

"So do I," Mother said, rolling her eyes. "He's so fretful at night."

Jonas had not heard the newchild during the night because as always, he *had* slept soundly. But it was not true that he had no dreams.

Again and again, as he slept, he had slid down that snow-covered hill. Always, in the dream, it seemed as if there were a <u>destination</u>: a *something*—he could not grasp what—that lay beyond the place where the thickness of snow brought the sled to a stop.

◄ *What does Jonas repeatedly dream about? How does he feel upon waking?*

He was left, upon awakening, with the feeling that he wanted, even somehow needed, to reach the something that waited in the distance. The feeling that it was good. That it was welcoming. That it was significant.

But he did not know how to get there.

He tried to shed the leftover dream, gathering his schoolwork and preparing for the day.

School seemed a little different today. The classes were the same: language and communications; <u>commerce</u> and <u>industry</u>; science and technology; <u>civil</u> procedures and government. But during the breaks

---

words for everyday use

des • ti • na • tion (des tə nā´ shən) *n.,* place to which one is journeying. *We took two weeks off and just headed West, with no particular <u>destination</u> in mind.*

com • merce (kä´ mərs) *n.,* exchange or buying and selling of commodities on a large scale involving transportation from place to place; business. *International <u>commerce</u> insures that people in one part of the world can enjoy goods from other countries around the world.*

in • dus • try (in´ dəs trē) *n.,* systematic labor for a useful purpose or the creation of something of value; manufacturing activity as a whole. *The success of various <u>industries</u> often depends on events taking place around the world.*

civ • il (si´ vəl) *adj.,* relating to the state or its citizens. *When my mother was called for jury duty, she didn't try to get out of it; she said it was her <u>civil</u> responsibility.*

for recreation periods and the midday meal, the other new Twelves were abuzz with descriptions of their first day of training. All of them talked at once, interrupting each other, hastily making the required apology for interrupting, then forgetting again in the excitement of describing the new experiences.

Jonas listened. He was very aware of his own <u>admonition</u> not to discuss his training. But it would have been impossible, anyway. There was no way to describe to his friends what he had experienced there in the Annex room. How could you describe a sled without describing a hill and snow; and how could you describe a hill and snow to someone who had never felt height or wind or that feathery, magical cold?

Even trained for years as they all had been in precision of language, what words could you use which would give another the experience of sunshine?

So it was easy for Jonas to be still and to listen.

After school hours he rode again beside Fiona to the House of the Old.

"I looked for you yesterday," she told him, "so we could ride home together. Your bike was still there, and I waited for a little while. But it was getting late, so I went on home."

"I apologize for making you wait," Jonas said.

"I accept your apology," she replied automatically.

"I stayed a little longer than I expected," Jonas explained.

She pedaled forward silently, and he knew that she expected him to tell her why. She expected him to describe his first day of training. But to ask would have fallen into the category of rudeness.

"You've been doing so many volunteer hours with the Old," Jonas said, changing the subject. "There won't be much that you don't already know."

"Oh, there's lots to learn," Fiona replied. "There's <u>administrative</u> work, and the dietary rules, and

words for everyday use

ad • mo • ni • tion (ad mə ni´ shən) n., warning; advice. *We listened impatiently to our mother's <u>admonition</u> to dress warmly.*

ad • min • is • tra • tive (əd mi´ nə strā tiv) adj., managerial. *At first, Maxwell was happy when he was promoted to head of the department, but as his <u>administrative</u> responsibilities mounted, he realized he'd preferred his old job better.*

punishment for disobedience—did you know that they use a discipline wand on the Old, the same as for small children? And there's occupational therapy, and recreational activities, and medications, and—"

They reached the building and braked their bikes.

"I really think I'll like it better than school," Fiona confessed.

"Me too," Jonas agreed, wheeling his bike into its place.

She waited for a second, as if, again, she expected him to go on. Then she looked at her watch, waved, and hurried toward the entrance.

Jonas stood for a moment beside his bike, startled. It had happened again: the thing that he thought of now as "seeing beyond." This time it had been Fiona who had undergone that fleeting indescribable change. As he looked up and toward her going through the door, it happened; she changed. Actually, Jonas thought, trying to recreate it in his mind, it wasn't Fiona in her entirety. It seemed to be just her hair. And just for that flickering instant.

He ran through it in his mind. It was clearly beginning to happen more often. First, the apple a few weeks before. The next time had been the faces in the audience at the Auditorium, just two days ago. Now, today, Fiona's hair.

Frowning, Jonas walked toward the Annex. I will ask The Giver, he decided.

The old man looked up, smiling, when Jonas entered the room. He was already seated beside the bed, and he seemed more energetic today, slightly renewed, and glad to see Jonas.

"Welcome," he said. "We must get started. You're one minute late."

"I apologi—" Jonas began, and then stopped, flustered, remembering there were to be no apologies.

He removed his tunic and went to the bed. "I'm one minute late because something happened," he explained. "And I'd like to ask you about it, if you don't mind."

"You may ask me anything."

Jonas tried to sort it out in his mind so that he could explain it clearly. "I think it's what you call seeing-beyond," he said.

The Giver nodded. "Describe it," he said.

Jonas told him about the experience with the apple. Then the moment on the stage, when he had looked out and seen the same phenomenon in the faces of the crowd.

"Then today, just now, outside, it happened with my friend Fiona. She herself didn't change, exactly. But something about her changed for a second. Her hair looked different; but not in its shape, not in its length. I can't quite—" Jonas paused, frustrated by his inability to grasp and describe exactly what *had* occurred.

Finally he simply said, "It changed. I don't know how, or why.

"That's why I was one minute late," he concluded, and looked questioningly at The Giver.

▶ Why was Jonas one minute late?

To his surprise, the old man asked him a question which seemed unrelated to the seeing-beyond. "When I gave you the memory yesterday, the first one, the ride on the sled, did you look around?"

Jonas nodded. "Yes," he said, "but the stuff—I mean the snow—in the air made it hard to see any-thing."

"Did you look at the sled?"

Jonas thought back. "No. I only felt it under me. I dreamed of it last night, too. But I don't remember *seeing* the sled in my dream, either. Just feeling it."

The Giver seemed to be thinking.

"When I was observing you, before the selection, I perceived that you probably had the capacity, and what you describe <u>confirms</u> that. It happened some-what differently to me," The Giver told him. "When I was just your age—about to become the new Receiver—I began to experience it, though it took a

---

words for everyday use   con • firm (kən fərm´) v., verify; give new assurance of the correctness or accuracy of. *The fact that we haven't lost a game in five weeks seems to <u>confirm</u> our coach's motto that each win builds confidence and the path to the next win.*

different form. With me it was . . . well, I won't describe that now; you wouldn't understand it yet.

"But I think I can guess how it's happening with you. Let me just make a little test, to confirm my guess. Lie down."

Jonas lay on the bed again with his hands at his sides. He felt comfortable here now. He closed his eyes and waited for the familiar feel of The Giver's hands on his back.

But it didn't come. Instead, The Giver instructed him, "Call back the memory of the ride on the sled. Just the *beginning* of it, where you're at the top of the hill, before the slide starts. And this time, look down at the sled."

Jonas was puzzled. He opened his eyes. "Excuse me," he asked politely, "but don't *you* have to give me the memory?"

"It's your memory, now. It's not mine to experience any longer. I gave it away."

"But how can I call it back?"

"You can remember last year, or the year that you were a Seven, or a Five, can't you?"

"Of course."

"It's much the same. Everyone in the community has one-generation memories like those. But now you will be able to go back farther. Try. Just concentrate."

Jonas closed his eyes again. He took a deep breath and sought the sled and the hill and the snow in his consciousness.

There they were, with no effort. He was again sitting in that whirling world of snowflakes, atop the hill.

Jonas grinned with delight, and blew his own steamy breath into view. Then, as he had been instructed, he looked down. He saw his own hands, furred again with snow, holding the rope. He saw his legs, and moved them aside for a glimpse of the sled beneath.

Dumbfounded, he stared at it. This time it was not a fleeting impression. This time the sled had—and continued to have, as he blinked, and stared at it again—that same mysterious quality that the apple had had so briefly. And Fiona's hair. The sled did not change. It simply was—whatever the thing was.

Jonas opened his eyes and was still on the bed. The Giver was watching him curiously.

"Yes," Jonas said slowly. "I saw it, in the sled."

"Let me try one more thing. Look over there, to the bookcase. Do you see the very top row of books, the ones behind the table, on the top shelf?"

Jonas sought them with his eyes. He stared at them, and they changed. But the change was fleeting. It slipped away the next instant.

"It happened," Jonas said. "It happened to the books, but it went away again."

▶ What is Jonas beginning to see?

"I'm right, then," The Giver said. "You're beginning to see the color red."

"The what?"

The Giver sighed. "How to explain this? Once, back in the time of the memories, everything had a shape and size, the way things still do, but they also had a quality called *color*.

"There were a lot of colors, and one of them was called red. That's the one you are starting to see. Your friend Fiona has red hair—quite <u>distinctive</u>, actually; I've noticed it before. When you mentioned Fiona's hair, it was the clue that told me you were probably beginning to see the color red."

"And the faces of people? The ones I saw at the Ceremony?"

▶ What does The Giver tell Jonas about skin tones before Sameness?

The Giver shook his head. "No, flesh isn't red. But it has red tones in it. There was a time, actually— you'll see this in the memories later—when flesh was many different colors. That was before we went to Sameness. Today flesh is all the same, and what you saw was the red tones. Probably when you saw the faces take on color it wasn't as deep or <u>vibrant</u> as the apple, or your friend's hair."

The Giver chuckled, suddenly. "We've never completely mastered Sameness. I suppose the <u>genetic</u> sci-

---

words for everyday use

dis • tinc • tive (di stiŋk´ tiv) *adj.*, unusual; uncommon; remarkable. *The color of Rivka's eyes is quite <u>distinctive</u>, an unusual shade of blue-green with flecks of yellow.*

vi • brant (vī´ brənt) *adj.*, filled with life, vigor, or activity. *The young boy was*

<u>vibrant</u> *and cheerful and full of energy; he made his mother happy and very, very tired.*

ge • net • ic (jə ne´ tik) *adj.*, relating to the branch of biology that deals with the heredity and variation of organisms. *The <u>genetic</u> engineering of the seeds of plants that we eat is a highly controversial issue.*

---

entists are still hard at work trying to work the kinks out. Hair like Fiona's must drive them crazy."

Jonas listened, trying hard to comprehend. "And the sled?" he said. "It had the same thing: the color red. But it didn't *change*, Giver. It just *was*."

◀ Why doesn't the sled "change" like the other red objects Jonas has seen?

"Because it's a memory from the time when color *was*."

"It was so—oh, I wish language were more precise! The red was so beautiful!"

The Giver nodded. "It is."

"Do you see it all the time?"

"I see all of them. All the colors."

"Will I?"

"Of course. When you receive the memories. You have the capacity to see beyond. You'll gain wisdom, then, along with colors. And lots more."

Jonas wasn't interested, just then, in wisdom. It was the colors that fascinated him. "Why can't everyone see them? Why did colors disappear?"

The Giver shrugged. "Our people made that choice, the choice to go to Sameness. Before my time, before the previous time, back and back and back. We relinquished color when we relinquished sunshine and did away with differences." He thought for a moment. "We gained control of many things. But we had to let go of others."

"We shouldn't have!" Jonas said fiercely.

◀ How does Jonas feel about the community's choice to relinquish color and sunshine and differences?

The Giver looked startled at the certainty of Jonas's reaction. Then he smiled wryly. "You've come very quickly to that conclusion," he said. "It took me many years. Maybe your wisdom will come much more quickly than mine."

He glanced at the wall clock. "Lie back down, now. We have so much to do."

"Giver," Jonas asked as he arranged himself again on the bed, "how did it happen to you when you were becoming The Receiver? You said that the seeing-beyond happened to you, but not the same way."

---

words for everyday use   re • lin • quish (ri liŋ´ kwish) v., give up. *Grace was very happy to have a new baby sister, but not so happy to have to relinquish having a room of her own.*

The hands came to his back. "Another day," The Giver said gently. "I'll tell you another day. Now we must work. And I've thought of a way to help you with the concept of color.

"Close your eyes and be still, now. I'm going to give you a memory of a rainbow."

Chapter 13

DAYS WENT BY, and weeks. Jonas learned, through the memories, the names of colors; and now he began to see them all, in his ordinary life (though he knew it was ordinary no longer, and would never be again). But they didn't last. There would be a glimpse of green—the landscaped lawn around the Central Plaza; a bush on the riverbank. The bright orange of pumpkins being trucked in from the agricultural fields beyond the community boundary—seen in an instant, the flash of brilliant color, but gone again, returning to their flat and hueless shade.

The Giver told him that it would be a very long time before he had the colors to keep.

"But I want them!" Jonas said angrily. "It isn't fair that nothing has color!"

"Not fair?" The Giver looked at Jonas curiously. "Explain what you mean."

"Well . . ." Jonas had to stop and think it through. "If everything's the same, then there aren't any choices! I want to wake up in the morning and *decide* things! A blue tunic, or a red one?"

He looked down at himself, at the colorless fabric of his clothing. "But it's all the same, always."

Then he laughed a little. "I know it's not important, what you wear. It doesn't matter. But—"

"It's the choosing that's important, isn't it?" The Giver asked him.

Jonas nodded. "My little brother—" he began, and then corrected himself. "No, that's <u>inaccurate</u>. He's not my brother, not really. But this newchild that my family takes care of—his name's Gabriel?"

"Yes, I know about Gabriel."

"Well, he's right at the age where he's learning so much. He grabs toys when we hold them in front of him—my father says he's learning small-muscle control. And he's really cute."

◀ What does Jonas realize about everything being the same? What does Jonas realize he wants?

---

words for everyday use

in • ac • cu • rate (in a′ kyə rət) *adj.,* inexact; imprecise; incorrect. *Sasha believed that Greg's interpretation of the play was <u>inaccurate</u>; she interpreted it differently.*

The Giver nodded.

"But now that I can see colors, at least sometimes, I was just thinking: what if we could hold up things that were bright red, or bright yellow, and he could *choose?* Instead of the Sameness."

"He might make wrong choices."

"Oh." Jonas was silent for a minute. "Oh, I see what you mean. It wouldn't matter for a newchild's toy. But later it *does* matter, doesn't it? We don't dare to let people make choices of their own."

"Not safe?" The Giver suggested.

"Definitely not safe," Jonas said with certainty. "What if they were allowed to choose their own mate? And chose *wrong?*

"Or what if," he went on, almost laughing at the absurdity, "they chose their own *jobs?*"

"Frightening, isn't it?" The Giver said.

Jonas chuckled. "Very frightening. I can't even imagine it. We really have to protect people from wrong choices."

"It's safer."

"Yes," Jonas agreed. "Much safer."

But when the conversation turned to other things, Jonas was left, still, with a feeling of frustration that he didn't understand.

He found that he was often angry, now: irrationally angry at his groupmates, that they were satisfied with their lives which had none of the vibrance his own was taking on. And he was angry at himself, that he could not change that for them.

He tried. Without asking permission from The Giver, because he feared—or knew—that it would be denied, he tried to give his new awareness to his friends.

"Asher," Jonas said one morning, "look at those flowers very carefully." They were standing beside a bed of geraniums planted near the Hall of Open Records. He put his hands on Asher's shoulders, and concentrated on the red of the petals, trying to hold it as long as he could, and trying at the same time to transmit the awareness of red to his friend.

"What's the matter?" Asher asked uneasily. "Is something wrong?" He moved away from Jonas's

▶ What does Jonas conclude about people making their own choices? Why?

▶ Without permission, what does Jonas try to do? Why?

hands. It was extremely rude for one citizen to touch another outside of family units.

"No, nothing. I thought for a minute that they were wilting, and we should let the Gardening Crew know they needed more watering." Jonas sighed, and turned away.

One evening he came home from his training weighted with new knowledge. The Giver had chosen a startling and disturbing memory that day. Under the touch of his hands, Jonas had found himself suddenly in a place that was completely alien: hot and windswept under a vast blue sky. There were <u>tufts</u> of sparse grass, a few bushes and rocks, and nearby he could see an area of thicker vegetation: broad, low trees outlined against the sky. He could hear noises: the sharp crack of weapons—he perceived the word *guns*— and then shouts, and an immense crashing thud as something fell, tearing branches from the trees.

He heard voices calling to one another. Peering from the place where he stood hidden behind some shrubbery, he was reminded of what The Giver had told him, that there had been a time when flesh had different colors. Two of these men had dark brown skin; the others were light. Going closer, he watched them hack the tusks from a motionless elephant on the ground and haul them away, spattered with blood. He felt himself overwhelmed with a new perception of the color he knew as red.

◀ *What are the men doing?*

Then the men were gone, speeding toward the horizon in a vehicle that spit pebbles from its whirling tires. One hit his forehead and stung him there. But the memory continued, though Jonas ached now for it to end.

Now he saw another elephant emerge from the place where it had stood hidden in the trees. Very slowly it walked to the mutilated body and looked down. With its <u>sinuous</u> trunk it stroked the huge

---

words for everyday use

tuft (təft´) *n.*, clump; cluster; a small cluster of elongated flexible outgrowths attached at the base and free at the opposite ends. *A <u>tuft</u> of Joey's hair always stood up on his head instead of lying flat.*

sin • u • ous (sin´ yə wəs) *adj.*, of a serpentine or wavy form; winding; marked by strong, lithe movements. *The snake's <u>sinuous</u> body wound through the garden and over the road.*

corpse; then it reached up, broke some leafy branches with a snap, and draped them over the mass of torn thick flesh.

Finally it tilted its massive head, raised its trunk, and roared into the empty landscape. Jonas had never heard such a sound. It was a sound of rage and grief and it seemed never to end.

He could still hear it when he opened his eyes and lay anguished on the bed where he received the memories. It continued to roar into his consciousness as he pedaled slowly home.

"Lily," he asked that evening when his sister took her comfort object, the stuffed elephant, from the shelf, "did you know that once there really were elephants? Live ones?"

She glanced down at the ragged comfort object and grinned. "Right," she said, <u>skeptically</u>. "Sure, Jonas."

Jonas went and sat beside them while his father untied Lily's hair ribbons and combed her hair. He placed one hand on each of their shoulders. With all of his being he tried to give each of them a piece of the memory: not of the tortured cry of the elephant, but of the *being* of the elephant, of the towering, immense creature and the meticulous touch with which it had tended its friend at the end.

But his father had continued to comb Lily's long hair, and Lily, impatient, had finally wiggled under her brother's touch. "Jonas," she said, "you're *hurting* me with your hand."

"I apologize for hurting you, Lily," Jonas mumbled, and took his hand away.

"'Ccept your apology," Lily responded <u>indifferently</u>, stroking the lifeless elephant.

"Giver," Jonas asked once, as they prepared for the day's work, "don't you have a spouse? Aren't you allowed to apply for one?" Although he was exempted

---

words for everyday use

skep • ti • cal (skep´tə kəl) *adj.*, unbelieving. *Kara cast a <u>skeptical</u> look my way as I told the tall tale about my ancestors.* **skeptically**, *adv.*

in • dif • fer • ent (in di´ fərnt) *adj.*, of no importance or value one way or the other. *You may choose whether we go to the movies or the mall, because I am <u>indifferent</u>.* **indifferently**, *adv.*

from the rules against rudeness, he was aware that this was a rude question. But The Giver had encouraged all of his questions, not seeming to be embarrassed or offended by even the most personal.

The Giver chuckled. "No, there's no rule against it. And I did have a spouse. You're forgetting how old I am, Jonas. My former spouse lives now with the Childless Adults."

"Oh, of course." Jonas *had* forgotten The Giver's obvious age. When adults of the community became older, their lives became different. They were no longer needed to create family units. Jonas's own parents, when he and Lily were grown, would go to live with the Childless Adults.

"You'll be able to apply for a spouse, Jonas, if you want to. I'll warn you, though, that it will be difficult. Your living arrangements will have to be different from those of most family units, because the books are forbidden to citizens. You and I are the only ones with access to the books."

◀ Why does the Receiver of Memory need to have a different living arrangement?

Jonas glanced around at the astonishing array of volumes. From time to time, now, he could see their colors. With their hours together, his and The Giver's, consumed by conversation and by the transmission of memories, Jonas had not yet opened any of the books. But he read the titles here and there, and knew that they contained all of the knowledge of centuries, and that one day they would belong to him.

"So if I have a spouse, and maybe children, I will have to hide the books from them?"

The Giver nodded. "I wasn't permitted to share the books with my spouse, that's correct. And there are other difficulties, too. You remember the rule that says the new Receiver can't talk about his training?"

Jonas nodded. Of course he remembered. It had turned out, by far, to be the most frustrating of the rules he was required to obey.

"When you become the official Receiver, when we're finished here, you'll be given a whole new set of rules. Those are the rules that I obey. And it won't surprise you that I am forbidden to talk about my work to anyone except the new Receiver. That's you, of course.

▶ Why is it so difficult for the Receiver of Memory to have a spouse? What does The Giver tell Jonas is his life?

"So there will be a whole part of your life which you won't be able to share with a family. It's hard, Jonas. It was hard for me.

"You do understand, don't you, that this *is* my life? The memories?"

Jonas nodded again, but he was puzzled. Didn't life consist of the things you did each day? There wasn't anything else, really. "I've seen you taking walks," he said.

The Giver sighed. "I walk. I eat at mealtime. And when I am called by the Committee of Elders, I appear before them, to give them counsel and advice."

"Do you advise them often?" Jonas was a little frightened at the thought that one day he would be the one to advise the ruling body.

But the Giver said no. "Rarely. Only when they are faced with something that they have not experienced before. Then they call upon me to use the memories and advise them. But it very seldom happens. Sometimes I wish they'd ask for my wisdom more often—there are so many things I could tell them; things I wish they would change. But they don't want change. Life here is so orderly, so predictable—so painless. It's what they've chosen."

▶ What does The Giver sometimes wish? Why does he know it won't happen?

"I don't know why they even *need* a Receiver, then, if they never call upon him," Jonas commented.

"They need me. And you," The Giver said, but didn't explain. "They were reminded of that ten years ago."

"What happened ten years ago?" Jonas asked. "Oh, I know. You tried to train a successor and it failed. Why? Why did that remind them?"

The Giver smiled grimly. "When the new Receiver failed, the memories that she had received were released. They didn't come back to me. They went . . ."

He paused, and seemed to be struggling with the concept. "I don't know, exactly. They went to the place where memories once existed before Receivers were created. Someplace out *there*—" He gestured vaguely with his arm. "And then the people had access to them. Apparently that's the way it was, once. Everyone had access to memories.

▶ What happened when the previous Receiver failed? Why does the community need a Receiver?

"It was <u>chaos</u>," he said. "They really suffered for a while. Finally it subsided as the memories were <u>assimilated</u>. But it certainly made them aware of how they need a Receiver to contain all that pain. And knowledge."

"But you have to suffer like that all the time," Jonas pointed out.

The Giver nodded. "And you will. It's my life. It will be yours."

◀ What does The Giver tell Jonas his life will be?

Jonas thought about it, about what it would be like for him. "Along with walking and eating and—" He looked around the walls of books. "Reading? That's it?"

The Giver shook his head. "Those are simply the things that I do. My *life* is here."

"In this room?"

The Giver shook his head. He put his hands to his own face, to his chest. "No. Here, in my being. Where the memories are."

"My Instructors in science and technology have taught us about how the brain works," Jonas told him eagerly. "It's full of electrical impulses. It's like a computer. If you stimulate one part of the brain with an electrode,[1] it—" He stopped talking. He could see an odd look on The Giver's face.

"They know nothing," The Giver said bitterly.

Jonas was shocked. Since the first day in the Annex room, they had together disregarded the rules about rudeness, and Jonas felt comfortable with that now. But this was different, and far beyond rude. This was a terrible accusation. What if someone had heard?

He glanced quickly at the wall speaker, terrified that the Committee might be listening as they could at any time. But, as always during their sessions together, the switch had been turned to OFF.

---

1. **electrode.** A conductor used to establish electrical contact with a non-metallic part of a circuit

words for everyday use

cha • os (kā´ äs) *n.*, a state of utter confusion. *After the school festival, <u>chaos</u> reigned in many of the classrooms.*

as • sim • i • late (ə si´ mə lāt) *v.*, absorb into the culture of a population; take into the mind and thoroughly comprehend. *After living in Spain for several months, Gina began to <u>assimilate</u> many aspects of the Spanish way of life.*

"Nothing?" Jonas whispered nervously. "But my instructors—"

The Giver flicked his hand as if brushing something aside. "Oh, your instructors are well trained. They know their scientific facts. *Everyone* is well trained for his job.

"It's just that . . . without the memories it's all meaningless. They gave that burden to me. And to the previous Receiver. And the one before him."

"And back and back and back," Jonas said, knowing the phrase that always came.

The Giver smiled, though his smile was oddly harsh. "That's right. And next it will be you. A great honor."

"Yes, sir. They told me that at the Ceremony. The very highest honor."

Some afternoons The Giver sent him away without training. Jonas knew, on days when he arrived to find The Giver hunched over, rocking his body slightly back and forth, his face pale, that he would be sent away.

"Go," The Giver would tell him tensely. "I'm in pain today. Come back tomorrow."

On those days, worried and disappointed, Jonas would walk alone beside the river. The paths were empty of people except for the few Delivery Crews and Landscape Workers here and there. Small children were all at the Childcare Center after school, and the older ones busy with volunteer hours or training.

By himself, he tested his own developing memory. He watched the landscape for glimpses of the green that he knew was <u>embedded</u> in the shrubbery; when it came flickering into his consciousness, he focused upon it, keeping it there, darkening it, holding it in his vision as long as possible until his head hurt and he let it fade away.

---

words for everyday use   em • bed (im bed´) *v.*, make something an integral part of. *Mr. Aaronson embedded a lot of writing in the science curriculum for his eighth grade students.*

He stared at the flat, colorless sky, bringing blue from it, and remembered sunshine until finally, for an instant, he could feel warmth.

He stood at the foot of the bridge that spanned the river, the bridge that citizens were allowed to cross only on official business. Jonas had crossed it on school trips, visiting the outlying communities, and he knew that the land beyond the bridge was much the same, flat and well ordered, with fields for agriculture. The other communities he had seen on visits were essentially the same as his own, the only differences were slightly altered styles of dwellings, slightly different schedules in the schools.

He wondered what lay in the far distance where he had never gone. The land didn't *end* beyond those nearby communities. Were there *hills* Elsewhere? Were there vast wind-torn areas like the place he had seen in memory, the place where the elephant died?

◀ *What does Jonas wonder?*

"Giver," he asked one afternoon following a day when he had been sent away, "what causes you pain?"

When The Giver was silent, Jonas continued. "The Chief Elder told me, at the beginning, that the receiving of memory causes terrible pain. And you described for me that the failure of the last new Receiver released painful memories to the community.

"But I haven't suffered, Giver. Not really." Jonas smiled. "Oh, I remember the sunburn you gave me on the very first day. But that wasn't so terrible. What is it that makes you suffer so much? If you gave some of it to me, maybe your pain would be less."

The Giver nodded. "Lie down," he said. "It's time, I suppose. I can't shield you forever. You'll have to take it all on eventually.

"Let me think," he went on, when Jonas was on the bed, waiting, a little fearful.

"All right," The Giver said after a moment, "I've decided. We'll start with something familiar. Let's go once again to a hill, and a sled."

He placed his hands on Jonas's back.

Chapter 14

IT WAS MUCH the same, this memory, though the hill seemed to be a different one, steeper, and the snow was not falling as thickly as it had before.

It was colder, also, Jonas perceived. He could see, as he sat waiting at the top of the hill, that the snow beneath the sled was not thick and soft as it had been before, but hard, and coated with bluish ice.

The sled moved forward, and Jonas grinned with delight, looking forward to the breathtaking slide down through the <u>invigorating</u> air.

But the runners, this time, couldn't slice through the frozen expanse as they had on the other, snow-cushioned hill. They skittered sideways and the sled gathered speed. Jonas pulled at the rope, trying to steer, but the steepness and speed took control from his hands and he was no longer enjoying the feeling of freedom but instead, terrified, was at the mercy of the wild <u>acceleration</u> downward over the ice.

Sideways, spinning, the sled hit a bump in the hill and Jonas was jarred loose and thrown violently into the air. He fell with his leg twisted under him, and could hear the crack of bone. His face scraped along jagged edges of ice and when he came, at last, to a stop, he lay shocked and still, feeling nothing at first but fear.

Then, the first wave of pain. He gasped. It was as if a hatchet lay lodged in his leg, slicing through each nerve with a hot blade. In his agony he perceived the word "fire" and felt flames licking at the torn bone and flesh. He tried to move, and could not. The pain grew.

He screamed. There was no answer.

Sobbing, he turned his head and vomited onto the frozen snow. Blood dripped from his face into the vomit.

"Nooooo!" he cried, and the sound disappeared into the empty landscape, into the wind.

---

words for everyday use

in • vig • o • rat • ing (in vi´ gə rā tiŋ) *adj.,* stimulating; energizing. *After a morning of lazing in the sun, I needed an <u>invigorating</u> shower to wake up.*

ac • cel • er • a • tion (ik se lə rā´ shən) *n.,* the act or process of gaining speed. *As the roller coaster turned the corner and moved downhill, the <u>acceleration</u> became intense.*

Then, suddenly, he was in the Annex room again, writhing on the bed. His face was wet with tears.

Able to move now, he rocked his own body back and forth, breathing deeply to release the remembered pain.

He sat, and looked at his own leg, where it lay straight on the bed, unbroken. The brutal slice of pain was gone. But the leg ached horribly, still, and his face felt raw.

"May I have relief-of-pain, please?" he begged. It was always provided in his everyday life for the bruises and wounds, or a mashed finger, a stomach ache, a skinned knee from a fall from a bike. There was always a daub of <u>anesthetic</u> ointment, or a pill; or in severe instances, an injection that brought complete and instantaneous deliverance.

But The Giver said no, and looked away.

Limping, Jonas walked home, pushing his bicycle, that evening. The sunburn pain had been so small, in comparison, and had not stayed with him. But this ache lingered.

It was not <u>unendurable</u>, as the pain on the hill had been. Jonas tried to be brave. He remembered that the Chief Elder had said he was brave.

"Is something wrong, Jonas?" his father asked at the evening meal. "You're so quiet tonight. Aren't you feeling well? Would you like some medication?"

But Jonas remembered the rules. No medication for anything related to his training.

And no discussion of his training. At the time for sharing-of-feelings, he simply said that he felt tired, that his school lessons had been unusually demanding that day.

He went to his sleepingroom early, and from behind the closed door he could hear his parents and sister laughing as they gave Gabriel his evening bath.

---

words for everyday use an • es • thet • ic (a nəs the´ tik) *adj.,* capable of producing loss of sensation with or without consciousness. *The dentist provided several types of <u>anesthetic</u> treatments for patients undergoing painful procedures.*

un • en • dur • a • ble (ən in dyür´ ə bəl) *adj.,* unbearable; unable to be tolerated or withstood. *As Ralph was running in the marathon, the pain in his legs became almost <u>unendurable</u>.*

▶ What does Jonas realize about his parents and Lily? How does his realization make him feel?

They have never known pain, he thought. The realization made him feel desperately lonely, and he rubbed his throbbing leg. He eventually slept. Again and again he dreamed of the anguish and the isolation on the forsaken hill.

The daily training continued, and now it always included pain. The agony of the fractured leg began to seem no more than a mild discomfort as The Giver led Jonas firmly, little by little, into the deep and terrible suffering of the past. Each time, in his kindness, The Giver ended the afternoon with a color-filled memory of pleasure: a brisk sail on a blue-green lake; a meadow dotted with yellow wildflowers; an orange sunset behind mountains.

▶ How does The Giver end each afternoon's training?

It was not enough to assuage the pain that Jonas was beginning, now, to know.

"*Why?*" Jonas asked him after he had received a torturous memory in which he had been neglected and unfed; the hunger had caused <u>excruciating spasms</u> in his empty, distended stomach. He lay on the bed, aching. "Why do you and I have to hold these memories?"

"It gives us wisdom," The Giver replied. "Without wisdom I could not fulfill my function of advising the Committee of Elders when they call upon me."

▶ Why do The Giver and Jonas have to hold the memories?

"But what wisdom do you get from hunger?" Jonas groaned. His stomach still hurt, though the memory had ended.

"Some years ago," The Giver told him, "before your birth, a lot of citizens <u>petitioned</u> the Committee of Elders. They wanted to increase the rate of births. They wanted each Birthmother to be assigned four births instead of three, so that the population would increase and there would be more Laborers available."

Jonas nodded, listening. "That makes sense."

---

words for everyday use

ex • cru • ci • at • ing (ik skrü′ shē ā tin) *adj.,* agonizing; causing great pain or anguish. *Happy fell out of the tree, causing an <u>excruciating</u> pain to shoot through his ankle.*

spasm (spa′ zəm) *n.,* an involuntary and abnormal muscle contraction. *After a difficult gymnastics practice, Mia sometimes experiences muscle <u>spasms</u> in her arms and legs.*

pe • ti • tion (pə ti′ shən) *v.,* make a formal request. *Jerod must <u>petition</u> the court for a retrial based on the new evidence.*

"The idea was that certain family units could accommodate an additional child."

Jonas nodded again. "Mine could," he pointed out. "We have Gabriel this year, and it's fun, having a third child."

"The Committee of Elders sought my advice," The Giver said. "It made sense to them, too, but it was a new idea, and they came to me for wisdom."

"And you used your memories?"

The Giver said yes. "And the strongest memory that came was hunger. It came from many generations back. *Centuries* back. The population had gotten so big that hunger was everywhere. Excruciating hunger and starvation. It was followed by warfare."

◀ *Why does The Giver advise the Committee of Elders against increasing the population?*

Warfare? It was a concept Jonas did not know. But hunger was familiar to him now. Unconsciously he rubbed his own abdomen, recalling the pain of its unfulfilled needs. "So you described that to them?"

"They don't want to hear about pain. They just seek the advice. I simply advised them against increasing the population."

"But you said that that was before my birth. They hardly ever come to you for advice. Only when they— what was it you said? When they have a problem they've never faced before. When did it happen last?"

"Do you remember the day when the plane flew over the community?"

"Yes. I was scared."

"So were they. They prepared to shoot it down. But they sought my advice. I told them to wait."

◀ *Why did The Giver advise the committee to wait rather than immediately shoot the plane down?*

"But how did you know? How did you know the pilot was lost?"

"I didn't. I used my wisdom, from the memories. I knew that there had been times in the past—terrible times—when people had destroyed others in haste, in fear, and had brought about their own destruction."

Jonas realized something. "That means," he said slowly, "that you have memories of destruction. And you have to give them to me, too, because I have to get the wisdom."

The Giver nodded.

"But it will hurt," Jonas said. It wasn't a question.

"It will hurt terribly," The Giver agreed.

▶ Why does Jonas think the memories should be shared?

▶ Why is the Receiver of Memory so vital to the community?

"But why can't *everyone* have the memories? I think it would seem a little easier if the memories were shared. You and I wouldn't have to bear so much by ourselves, if everybody took a part."

The Giver sighed. "You're right," he said. "But then everyone would be burdened and pained. They don't want that. And that's the real reason The Receiver is so vital to them, and so honored. They selected me—and you—to lift that burden from themselves."

"When did they decide that?" Jonas asked angrily. "It wasn't fair. Let's change it!"

"How do you suggest we do that? I've never been able to think of a way, and I'm supposed to be the one with all the wisdom."

"But there are two of us now," Jonas said eagerly. "*Together* we can think of something!"

The Giver watched him with a wry smile.

"Why can't we just apply for a change of rules?" Jonas suggested.

The Giver laughed; then Jonas, too, chuckled reluctantly.

"The decision was made long before my time or yours," The Giver said, "and before the previous Receiver, and—" He waited.

"Back and back and back." Jonas repeated the familiar phrase. Sometimes it had seemed humorous to him. Sometimes it had seemed meaningful and important.

▶ What does the phrase "back and back and back" suddenly cause Jonas to realize?

Now it was <u>ominous</u>. It meant, he knew, that nothing could be changed.

The newchild, Gabriel, was growing, and successfully passed the tests of maturity that the Nurturers gave each month; he could sit alone, now, could reach for and grasp small play objects, and he had six teeth. During the daytime hours, Father reported, he was cheerful and seemed of normal intelligence. But he

---

words for everyday use

om • i • nous (äʹ mə nəs) *adj.,* threatening; menacing, boding of bad things to come. *The <u>ominous</u> clouds signaled the coming storm.*

remained fretful at night, whimpering often, needing frequent attention.

"After all this extra time I've put in with him," Father said one evening after Gabriel had been bathed and was lying, for the moment, hugging his hippo placidly in the small crib that had replaced the basket, "I hope they're not going to decide to release him."

◀ What does Jonas's father hope? How does his mother respond?

"Maybe it would be for the best," Mother suggested. "I know you don't mind getting up with him at night. But the lack of sleep is awfully hard for me."

"If they release Gabriel, can we get another new-child as a visitor?" asked Lily. She was kneeling beside the crib, making funny faces at the little one, who was smiling back at her.

Jonas's mother rolled her eyes in dismay.

"No," Father said, smiling. He ruffled Lily's hair. "It's very rare, anyway, that a newchild's <u>status</u> is as uncertain as Gabriel's. It probably won't happen again, for a long time.

"Anyway," he sighed, "they won't make the decision for a while. Right now we're all preparing for a release we'll probably have to make very soon. There's a Birthmother who's expecting twin males next month."

"Oh, dear," Mother said, shaking her head. "If they're identical, I hope you're not the one assigned—"

"I am. I'm next on the list. I'll have to select the one to be nurtured, and the one to be released. It's usually not hard, though. Usually it's just a matter of birthweight. We release the smaller of the two."

◀ What decision will Jonas's father have to make regarding the identical twins? On what will he base his decision?

Jonas, listening, thought suddenly about the bridge and how, standing there, he had wondered what lay Elsewhere. Was there someone there, waiting, who would receive the tiny released twin? Would it grow up Elsewhere, not knowing, ever, that in this community lived a being who looked exactly the same?

---

words for everyday use   sta • tus (stā´ təs) *n.,* the condition of a person or thing in the eyes of the law. *Lena's status as a middle school student will change when she enters the ninth grade.*

For a moment he felt a tiny, fluttering hope that he knew was quite foolish. He hoped that it would be Larissa, waiting. Larissa, the old woman he had bathed. He remembered her sparkling eyes, her soft voice, her low chuckle. Fiona had told him recently that Larissa had been released at a wonderful ceremony.

But he knew that the Old were not given children to raise. Larissa's life Elsewhere would be quiet and serene as befit the Old; she would not welcome the responsibility of nurturing a newchild who needed feeding and care, and would likely cry at night.

"Mother? Father?" he said, the idea coming to him unexpectedly, "why don't we put Gabriel's crib in my room tonight? I know how to feed and comfort him, and it would let you and Father get some sleep."

Father looked doubtful. "You sleep so soundly, Jonas. What if his restlessness didn't wake you?"

It was Lily who answered that. "If no one goes to tend Gabriel," she pointed out, "he gets very loud. He'd wake *all* of us, if Jonas slept through it."

Father laughed. "You're right, Lily-billy. All right, Jonas, let's try it, just for tonight. I'll take the night off and we'll let Mother get some sleep, too."

Gabriel slept soundly for the earliest part of the night. Jonas, in his bed, lay awake for a while; from time to time he raised himself on one elbow, looking over at the crib. The newchild was on his stomach, his arms relaxed beside his head, his eyes closed, and his breathing regular and undisturbed. Finally Jonas slept too.

Then, as the middle hours of the night approached, the noise of Gabe's restlessness woke Jonas. The newchild was turning under his cover, flailing his arms, and beginning to whimper.

Jonas rose and went to him. Gently he patted Gabriel's back. Sometimes that was all it took to lull him back to sleep. But the newchild still squirmed fretfully under his hand.

Still patting rhythmically, Jonas began to remember the wonderful sail that The Giver had given him not long before: a bright, breezy day on a clear turquoise lake, and above him the white sail of the boat billowing as he moved along in the brisk wind.

He was not aware of giving the memory; but suddenly he realized that it was becoming dimmer, that it was sliding through his hand into the being of the newchild. Gabriel became quiet. Startled, Jonas pulled back what was left of the memory with a burst of will. He removed his hand from the little back and stood quietly beside the crib.

To himself, he called the memory of the sail forward again. It was still there, but the sky was less blue, the gentle motion of the boat slower, the water of the lake more murky and clouded. He kept it for a while, soothing his own nervousness at what had occurred, then let it go and returned to his bed.

Once more, toward dawn, the newchild woke and cried out. Again Jonas went to him. This time he quite deliberately placed his hand firmly on Gabriel's back, and released the rest of the calming day on the lake. Again Gabriel slept.

But now Jonas lay awake, thinking. He no longer had any more than a wisp of the memory, and he felt a small lack where it had been. He could ask The Giver for another sail, he knew. A sail perhaps on ocean, next time, for Jonas had a memory of ocean, now, and knew what it was; he knew that there were sailboats there, too, in memories yet to be acquired.

He wondered, though, if he should confess to The Giver that he had given a memory away. He was not yet qualified to be a Giver himself; nor had Gabriel been selected to be a Receiver.

That he had this power frightened him. He decided not to tell.

◀ What does Jonas suddenly realize? How does he react?

Chapter 15

JONAS ENTERED THE Annex room and realized immediately that it was a day when he would be sent away. The Giver was rigid in his chair, his face in his hands.

"I'll come back tomorrow, sir," he said quickly. Then he hesitated. "Unless maybe there's something I can do to help."

The Giver looked up at him, his face <u>contorted</u> with suffering. "Please," he gasped, "take some of the pain."

▶ What does The Giver ask Jonas to do?

Jonas helped him to his chair at the side of the bed. Then he quickly removed his tunic and lay face down. "Put your hands on me," he directed, aware that in such anguish The Giver might need reminding.

The hands came, and the pain came with them and through them. Jonas braced himself and entered the memory which was torturing The Giver.

He was in a confused, noisy, foul-smelling place. It was daylight, early morning, and the air was thick with smoke that hung, yellow and brown, above the ground. Around him, everywhere, far across the expanse of what seemed to be a field, lay groaning men. A wild-eyed horse, its bridle[1] torn and dangling, trotted frantically through the mounds of men, tossing its head, whinnying in panic. It stumbled, finally, then fell, and did not rise.

Jonas heard a voice next to him. "Water," the voice said in a parched, croaking whisper.

He turned his head toward the voice and looked into the half-closed eyes of a boy who seemed not much older than himself. Dirt streaked the boy's face and his matted blond hair. He lay sprawled, his gray uniform glistening with wet, fresh blood.

The colors of the <u>carnage</u> were grotesquely bright: the crimson wetness on the rough and dusty fabric,

---

1. **bridle.** The headgear with which a horse is governed and which carries a bit and reins

words for everyday use

con • tort (kən tôrt´) v., twist in a violent manner; twist into a strained expression. *Julian's face <u>contorted</u> into a wicked smile when he learned that his evil prank had worked.*

car • nage (kär´ nij) n., flesh of slain animals or men; great and bloody slaughter (as in battle). *The <u>carnage</u> on the newly discovered planet was horrible after the Martians attacked.*

the ripped shreds of grass, startlingly green, in the boy's yellow hair.

The boy stared at him. "Water," he begged again. When he spoke, a new spurt of blood drenched the coarse cloth across his chest and sleeve.

One of Jonas's arms was immobilized with pain, and he could see through his own torn sleeve something that looked like ragged flesh and splintery bone. He tried his remaining arm and felt it move. Slowly he reached to his side, felt the metal container there, and removed its cap, stopping the small motion of his hand now and then to wait for the surging pain to ease. Finally, when the container was open, he extended his arm slowly across the blood-soaked earth, inch by inch, and held it to the lips of the boy. Water trickled into the <u>imploring</u> mouth and down the grimy chin.

The boy sighed. His head fell back, his lower jaw dropping as if he had been surprised by something. A dull blankness slid slowly across his eyes. He was silent.

But the noise continued all around: the cries of the wounded men, the cries begging for water and for Mother and for death. Horses lying on the ground shrieked, raised their heads, and stabbed randomly toward the sky with their hooves.

From the distance, Jonas could hear the thud of cannons. Overwhelmed by pain, he lay there in the fearsome stench for hours, listened to the men and animals die, and learned what warfare meant.

◀ *What does Jonas learn?*

Finally, when he knew that he could bear it no longer and would welcome death himself, he opened his eyes and was once again on the bed.

The Giver looked away, as if he could not bear to see what he had done to Jonas. "Forgive me," he said.

words for everyday use   im • plor • ing (im plōr iŋ) *adj.,* begging; pleading. *The <u>imploring</u> look on Susie's face showed how much she wanted the doll.*

Respond to the Selection

If you were in Jonas's situation, would you, as Jonas does, try to make your friends aware of your newfound knowledge? Why, or why not?

Investigate, Inquire, and Imagine

Recall: GATHERING FACTS

1a. What does The Giver tell Jonas about the change he saw in the audience during the Ceremony of Twelve? What does The Giver tell Jonas about Fiona's hair?

2a. Jonas now finds he is often angry with his groupmates. Why does he feel anger toward them? Why is he angry with himself?

3a. When does the Committee of Elders ask the Receiver of Memory for advice?

4a. Jonas tells The Giver about what his Instructors in science and technology have taught him about how the brain works. How does The Giver respond? What does The Giver say about scientific facts and the training of Jonas's instructors?

5a. What memory came back strongly to The Giver when the Committee of Elders came to him for advice about assigning each Birthmother to have four children instead of three? Why?

6a. After The Giver has transmitted a memory of warfare to Jonas, what does he say to Jonas?

Interpret: FINDING MEANING

1b. What is one of the goals of genetic scientists in the society of *The Giver?* Why must Fiona's hair drive genetic scientists crazy?

2b. What do you think Jonas is starting to realize? What is causing him to have the feelings he is having?

3b. Why does the community need a Receiver of Memory?

4b. Why might this be true?

5b. Why might hunger lead to warfare?

6b. Why do you think The Giver says this?

Analyze: TAKING THINGS APART

7a. Look back to chapters 12 through 15, and compile a list of all the things that Jonas gains knowledge of but that are kept from all other citizens of the community.

Synthesize: BRINGING THINGS TOGETHER

7b. Contrast the life that the Receiver of Memory leads with the lives of the other citizens in the community.

Evaluate: MAKING JUDGMENTS

8a. At the beginning of Chapter 13, Jonas tells The Giver that he wants to be able to make decisions. But when he thinks more carefully about it, he comes to this conclusion: "We don't dare to let people make choices of their own. . . . Very frightening. I can't even imagine it. We really have to protect people from wrong choices." Evaluate the wisdom of this statement by considering it from both sides. What consequences can result from people making wrong choices? What consequences result from people not being able to make their own choices? Based on your consideration of the consequences of each, do you agree or disagree with Jonas?

Extend: CONNECTING IDEAS

8b. What choices do you make on a daily basis? What choices do others make for you? What is the most difficult decision you ever had to make on your own? What was the outcome? Would you rather have had someone make that decision for you? Why, or why not?

Understanding Literature

SCIENCE FICTION. **Science fiction** is imaginative literature based on scientific principles, discoveries, or laws. It is similar to fantasy in that it deals with imaginary worlds, but differs from fantasy in having a scientific basis. Often science fiction deals with the future, the distant past, or with worlds other than our own. Science fiction stories often take place on distant planets, in parallel universes, or in worlds beneath the ground or sea. Lois Lowry's *The Giver* is a work of science fiction, even though it isn't set on a distant planet, in a parallel universe, or worlds beneath the ground or sea. What aspects of the world of *The Giver* are based on possible scientific accomplishments? Do you think *The Giver* takes place in the future? Why, or why not?

CENTRAL CONFLICT. A **central conflict** is the main problem or struggle in the plot of a poem, story, or play. A conflict can be internal or external. An *internal conflict* is a struggle that takes place inside the mind of a character. An *external conflict* is a struggle that takes place between a character and an outside force such as another character, society, or nature. Identify the central conflict in *The Giver.* Is the conflict internal or external? In the Understanding Literature section for chapters 9 through 11, you predicted a conflict that would take place later in the story. How does the prediction you made relate to the conflict you have identified as the central conflict?

Chapter 16

JONAS DID NOT want to go back. He didn't want the memories, didn't want the honor, didn't want the wisdom, didn't want the pain. He wanted his childhood again, his scraped knees and ball games. He sat in his dwelling alone, watching through the window, seeing children at play, citizens bicycling home from <u>uneventful</u> days at work, ordinary lives free of anguish because he had been selected, as others before him had, to bear their burden.

◀ What doesn't Jonas want? What does he want?

But the choice was not his. He returned each day to the Annex room.

The Giver was gentle with him for many days following the terrible shared memory of war.

"There are so many good memories," The Giver reminded Jonas. And it was true. By now Jonas had experienced countless bits of happiness, things he had never known of before.

◀ What does The Giver remind Jonas?

He had seen a birthday party, with one child singled out and celebrated on his day, so that now he understood the joy of being an individual, special and unique and proud.

He had visited museums and seen paintings filled with all the colors he could now recognize and name.

In one <u>ecstatic</u> memory he had ridden a gleaming brown horse across a field that smelled of damp grass, and had <u>dismounted</u> beside a small stream from which both he and the horse drank cold, clear water. Now he understood about animals; and in the moment that the horse turned from the stream and nudged Jonas's shoulder affectionately with its head, he perceived the bonds between animal and human.

---

words for everyday use

un • e • vent • ful (ən i vent´ fəl) *adj.,* marked by no noteworthy events; routine; unchanging. *The convention was* <u>uneventful</u>; *nothing out of the ordinary occurred.*

ec • stat • ic (ek sta´ tik) *adj.,* marked by or relating to a state of overwhelming emotion, especially rapturous delight; blissful; overjoyed; elated. *Jerry and Joy* were <u>ecstatic</u> to learn that they had both been selected for the debate team.

dis • mount (dis mount´) *v.,* to come down from an elevated position (as on a horse). *The rider* <u>dismounted</u> *from her horse, grabbed her hat off the ground, and got back up.*

He had walked through woods, and sat at night beside a campfire. Although he had through the memories learned about the pain of loss and loneliness, now he gained, too, an understanding of <u>solitude</u> and its joy.

"What is your favorite?" Jonas asked The Giver. "You don't have to give it away yet," he added quickly. "Just tell me about it, so I can look forward to it, because I'll have to receive it when your job is done."

The Giver smiled. "Lie down," he said. "I'm happy to give it to you."

Jonas felt the joy of it as soon as the memory began. Sometimes it took a while for him to get his bearings, to find his place. But this time he fit right in and felt the happiness that <u>pervaded</u> the memory.

He was in a room filled with people, and it was warm, with firelight glowing on a hearth. He could see through a window that outside it was night, and snowing. There were colored lights: red and green and yellow, twinkling from a tree which was, oddly, inside the room. On a table, lighted candles stood in a polished golden holder and cast a soft, flickering glow. He could smell things cooking, and he heard soft laughter. A golden-haired dog lay sleeping on the floor.

On the floor there were packages wrapped in brightly colored paper and tied with gleaming ribbons. As Jonas watched, a small child began to pick up the packages and pass them around the room: to other children, to adults who were obviously parents, and to an older, quiet couple, man and woman, who sat smiling together on a couch.

While Jonas watched, the people began one by one to untie the ribbons on the packages, to unwrap the bright papers, open the boxes and reveal toys and clothing and books. There were cries of delight. They hugged one another.

---

words for everyday use

sol • i • tude (sä´ lə tüd) *n.*, the quality or state of being alone or remote from society. *I like to be around my friends and family, but I also enjoy <u>solitude</u>.*

per • vade (pər vād´) *v.*, to become diffused throughout every part of; permeate; saturate. *A feeling of unease <u>pervaded</u> the fairgoers as lightning cracked in the distance.*

The small child went and sat on the lap of the old woman, and she rocked him and rubbed her cheek against his.

Jonas opened his eyes and lay contentedly on the bed, still luxuriating in the warm and comforting memory. It had all been there, all the things he had learned to treasure.

"What did you perceive?" The Giver asked.

"Warmth," Jonas replied, "and happiness. And— let me think. *Family.* That it was a celebration of some sort, a holiday. And something else—I can't quite get the word for it."

◀ What does Jonas perceive from the memory?

"It will come to you."

"Who were the old people? Why were they there?" It had puzzled Jonas, seeing them in the room. The Old of the community did not ever leave their special place, the House of the Old, where they were so well cared for and respected.

◀ Why does it puzzle Jonas to see the older man and woman in the memory?

"They were called Grandparents."

"Grand parents?"

"Grandparents. It meant parents-of-the-parents, long ago."

"Back and back and back?" Jonas began to laugh. "So actually, there could be parents-of-the-parents-of-the-parents-of-the-parents?"

◀ What idea makes Jonas laugh?

The Giver laughed, too. "That's right. It's a little like looking at yourself looking in a mirror looking at yourself looking in a mirror."

Jonas frowned. "But my parents must have had parents! I never thought about it before. Who are my parents-of-the-parents? *Where* are they?"

"You could go look in the Hall of Open Records. You'd find the names. But think, son. If you apply for children, then who will be their parents-of-the-parents? Who will be their grandparents?"

"My mother and father, of course."

"And where will they be?"

Jonas thought. "Oh," he said slowly. "When I finish my training and become a full adult, I'll be given my own dwelling. And then when Lily does, a few years later, she'll get *her* own dwelling, and maybe a spouse, and children if she applies for them, and then Mother and Father—"

▶ Where will Jonas's parents go once Lily and Jonas get their own dwellings?

"That's right."

"As long as they're still working and contributing to the community, they'll go and live with the other Childless Adults. And they won't be part of my life anymore.

"And after that, when the time comes, they'll go to the House of the Old," Jonas went on. He was thinking aloud. "And they'll be well cared for, and respected, and when they're released, there will be a celebration."

"Which you won't attend," The Giver pointed out.

"No, of course not, because I won't even know about it. By then I'll be so busy with my own life. And Lily will, too. So our children, if we have them, won't know who their parents-of-parents are, either.

"It seems to work pretty well that way, doesn't it? The way we do it in our community?" Jonas asked. "I just didn't realize there was any other way, until I received that memory."

"It works," The Giver agreed.

Jonas hesitated. I certainly liked the memory, though, I can see why it's your favorite. I couldn't quite get the word for the whole feeling of it, the feeling that was so strong in the room."

▶ What is the feeling that Jonas felt so strongly in the memory?

"Love," The Giver told him.

Jonas repeated it. "Love." It was a word and concept new to him.

They were both silent for a minute. Then Jonas said, "Giver?"

"Yes?"

"I feel very foolish saying this. Very, very foolish."

"No need. Nothing is foolish here. Trust the memories and how they make you feel."

"Well," Jonas said, looking at the floor, "I know you don't have the memory anymore, because you gave it to me, so maybe you won't understand this—"

"I will. I am left with a vague wisp of that one; and I have many other memories of families, and holidays, and happiness. Of love."

Jonas blurred out what he was feeling. "I was thinking that . . . well, I can see that it wasn't a very practical way to live, with the Old right there in the same place, where maybe they wouldn't be well taken care of, the way they are now, and that we have a better-arranged way of doing things. But anyway, I was thinking, I mean feeling, actually, that it was kind of nice, then. And that I wish we could be that way, and that you could be my grandparent. The family in the memory seemed a little more—" He faltered, not able to find the word he wanted.

"A little more complete," The Giver suggested.

Jonas nodded. "I liked the feeling of love," he confessed. He glanced nervously at the speaker on the wall, reassuring himself that no one was listening. "I wish we still had that," he whispered. "Of course," he added quickly, "I do understand that it wouldn't work very well. And that it's much better to be organized the way we are now. I can see that it was a *dangerous* way to live."

"What do you mean?"

Jonas hesitated. He wasn't certain, really, what he had meant. He could feel that there was *risk* involved, though he wasn't sure how. "Well," he said finally, grasping for an explanation, "they had *fire* right there in that room. There was a fire burning in the fireplace. And there were candles on a table. I can certainly see why those things were <u>outlawed</u>.

"Still," he said slowly, almost to himself, "I did like the light they made. And the warmth."

"Father? Mother?" Jonas asked tentatively after the evening meal. "I have a question I want to ask you."

"What is it, Jonas?" his father asked.

He made himself say the words, though he felt flushed with embarrassment. He had rehearsed them in his mind all the way home from the Annex.

"Do you love me?"

There was an awkward silence for a moment. Then Father gave a little chuckle. "*Jonas.* You of all people. Precision of language, *please!*"

---

words for everyday use   **out • law** (aŭt´ lä) *adj.*, make illegal. *In the Wild West, many sheriffs <u>outlawed</u> dueling and fighting.*

▶ What does Jonas's mother say about the word love?

"What do you mean?" Jonas asked. Amusement was not at all what he had anticipated.

"Your father means that you used a very generalized word, so meaningless that it's become almost obsolete," his mother explained carefully.

Jonas stared at them. Meaningless? He had never before felt anything as meaningful as the memory.

"And of course our community can't function smoothly if people don't use precise language. You could ask, 'Do you enjoy me?' The answer is 'Yes,'" his mother said.

"Or," his father suggested, " 'Do you take pride in my accomplishments?' And the answer is wholeheartedly 'Yes.'"

"Do you understand why it's inappropriate to use a word like 'love'?" Mother asked.

Jonas nodded. "Yes, thank you, I do," he replied slowly.

It was his first lie to his parents.

"Gabriel?" Jonas whispered that night to the newchild. The crib was in his room again. After Gabe had slept soundly in Jonas's room for four nights, his parents had pronounced the experiment a success and Jonas a hero. Gabriel was growing rapidly, now crawling and giggling across the room and pulling himself up to stand. He could be upgraded in the Nurturing Center, Father said happily, now that he slept; he could be officially named and given to his family in December, which was only two months away.

But when he was taken away, he stopped sleeping again, and cried in the night.

So he was back in Jonas's sleepingroom. They would give it a little more time, they decided. Since Gabe seemed to like it in Jonas's room, he would sleep there at night a little longer, until the habit of sound sleep was fully formed. The Nurturers were very <u>optimistic</u> about Gabriel's future.

---

words for everyday use op • ti • mis • tic (äp tə mis´ tik) *adj.*, hopeful; tending toward the habit of anticipating the best possible outcome. *The vet could not guarantee that Spot would be fine after surgery, but he was quite <u>optimistic</u> about the dog's well-being.*

There was no answer to Jonas's whisper. Gabriel was sound asleep.

"Things could change, Gabe," Jonas went on. "Things could be different. I don't know how, but there must be some way for things to be different. There could be colors.

"And grandparents," he added, staring through the dimness toward the ceiling of his sleepingroom. "And everybody would have the memories.

"You know about memories," he whispered, turning toward the crib.

Gabriel's breathing was even and deep. Jonas liked having him there, though he felt guilty about the secret. Each night he gave memories to Gabriel: memories of boat rides and picnics in the sun; memories of soft rainfall against windowpanes; memories of dancing barefoot on a damp lawn.

"Gabe?"

The newchild stirred slightly in his sleep. Jonas looked over at him.

"There could be love," Jonas whispered.

The next morning, for the first time, Jonas did not take his pill. Something within him, something that had grown there through the memories, told him to throw the pill away.

◄ What does Jonas do for the first time?

Chapter 17

TODAY IS DECLARED AN UNSCHEDULED HOLIDAY. Jonas, his parents, and Lily all turned in surprise and looked at the wall speaker from which the announcement had come. It happened so rarely, and was such a treat for the entire community when it did. Adults were exempted from the day's work, children from school and training and volunteer hours. The substitute Laborers, who would be given a different holiday, took over all the necessary tasks: nurturing, food delivery, and care of the Old; and the community was free.

Jonas cheered, and put his homework folder down. He had been about to leave for school. School was less important to him now; and before much more time passed, his formal schooling would end. But still, for Twelves, though they had begun their adult training, there were the endless lists of rules to be memorized and the newest technology to be mastered.

He wished his parents, sister, and Gabe a happy day, and rode down the bicycle path, looking for Asher.

He had not taken the pills, now, for four weeks. The Stirrings had returned, and he felt a little guilty and embarrassed about the pleasurable dreams that came to him as he slept. But he knew he couldn't go back to the world of no feelings that he had lived in so long.

And his new, heightened feelings <u>permeated</u> a greater <u>realm</u> than simply his sleep. Though he knew that his failure to take the pills accounted for some of it, he thought that the feelings came also from the memories. Now he could see all of the colors; and he could *keep* them, too, so that the trees and grass and bushes stayed green in his vision. Gabriel's rosy

---

words for everyday use

per • me • ate (pər´ mē āt) *v.*, diffuse through or penetrate something; to pass through the pores of; seep through; spread throughout. *The scent of sautéing onions <u>permeated</u> my shirt as I cooked the omelet ingredients.*

realm (relm´) *n.*, domain; region; arena. *The library is Ms. Hubbard's <u>realm</u>; as the librarian, she knows it better than anyone else.*

cheeks stayed pink, even when he slept. And apples were always, always red.

Now, through the memories, he had seen oceans and mountain lakes and streams that gurgled through woods; and now he saw the familiar wide river beside the path differently. He saw all of the light and color and history it contained and carried in its slow-moving water; and he knew that there was an Elsewhere from which it came, and an Elsewhere to which it was going.

◄ What has changed about the way Jonas sees the river? What does he now know about it?

On this unexpected, casual holiday he felt happy, as he always had on holidays; but with a deeper happiness than ever before. Thinking, as he always did, about precision of language, Jonas realized that it was a new *depth* of feelings that he was experiencing. Somehow they were not at all the same as the feelings that every evening, in every dwelling, every citizen analyzed with endless talk.

"I felt angry because someone broke the play area rules," Lily had said once, making a fist with her small hand to indicate her fury. Her family—Jonas among them—had talked about the possible reasons for rule-breaking, and the need for understanding and patience, until Lily's fist had relaxed and her anger was gone.

But Lily had not felt anger, Jonas realized now. Shallow impatience and exasperation, that was all Lily had felt. He knew that with certainty because now he knew what anger was. Now he had, in the memories, experienced injustice and cruelty, and he had reacted with rage that welled up so passionately inside him that the thought of discussing it calmly at the evening meal was unthinkable.

◄ What does Jonas realize about the anger Lily said she felt?

"I felt sad today," he had heard his mother say, and they had comforted her.

But now Jonas had experienced real sadness. He had felt grief. He knew that there was no quick comfort for emotions like those.

These were deeper and they did not need to be told. They were *felt*.

Today, he felt happiness.

"Asher!" He spied his friend's bicycle leaning against a tree at the edge of the playing field. Nearby, other bikes were strewn about on the ground. On a holiday the usual rules of order could be disregarded.

He skidded to a stop and dropped his own bike beside the others. "Hey, Ash!" he shouted, looking around. There seemed to be no one in the play area. "Where are you?"

"Psssheeewwww!" A child's voice coming from behind a nearby bush, made the sound. "Pow! Pow! Pow!"

A female Eleven named Tanya staggered forward from where she had been hiding. Dramatically she clutched her stomach and stumbled about in a zig-zag pattern, groaning. "You got me!" she called, and fell to the ground, grinning.

"Blam!"

Jonas, standing on the side of the playing field, recognized Asher's voice. He saw his friend aiming an imaginary weapon in his hand, dart from behind one tree to another. "Blam! You're in my line of <u>ambush</u>, Jonas! Watch out!"

Jonas stepped back. He moved behind Asher's bike and knelt so that he was out of sight. It was a game he had often played with the other children, a game of good guys and bad guys, a harmless pasttime that used up their contained energy and ended only when they all lay posed in freakish postures on the ground.

He had never recognized it before as a game of war.

"Attack!" The shout came from behind the small storehouse where play equipment was kept. Three children dashed forward, their imaginary weapons in firing position.

From the opposite side of the field came an oppos-ing shout: "Counter-attack!" From their hiding places a <u>horde</u> of children—Jonas recognized Fiona in the group—emerged, running in a crouched posi-tion, firing across the field. Several of them stopped, grabbed their own shoulders and chests with exag-

words for everyday use

am • bush (am´ bush) *n.*, surprise attack. *I sat reading in the living room when all of a sudden I was surprised by a sudden <u>ambush</u> as my baby brother attacked from the other side of the couch.*

horde (hōrd´) *n.*, crowd or throng; swarm. *Every time I walked out into the water, a <u>horde</u> of minnows came up and bit my ankles.*

gerated gestures, and pretended to be hit. They dropped to the ground and lay suppressing giggles.

Feelings surged within Jonas. He found himself walking forward into the field.

"You're hit, Jonas!" Asher yelled from behind the tree. "Pow! You're hit again!"

Jonas stood alone in the center of the field. Several of the children raised their heads and looked at him uneasily. The attacking armies slowed, emerged from their crouched positions, and watched to see what he was doing.

In his mind, Jonas saw again the face of the boy who had lain dying on a field and had begged him for water. He had a sudden choking feeling, as if it were difficult to breathe.

◀ In his mind, what does Jonas see?

One of the children raised an imaginary rifle and made an attempt to destroy him with a firing noise. "Pssheeew!" Then they were all silent, standing, awkwardly, and the only sound was the sound of Jonas's shuddering breaths. He was struggling not to cry.

Gradually, when nothing happened, nothing changed, the children looked at each other nervously and went away. He heard the sounds as they righted their bicycles and began to ride down the path that led from the field.

Only Asher and Fiona remained.

"What's wrong, Jonas? It was only a game." Fiona said.

"You ruined it," Asher said in an irritated voice.

"Don't play it anymore," Jonas pleaded.

"I'm the one who's training for Assistant Recreation Director," Asher pointed out angrily. "Games aren't *your* area of expertness."

◀ What does Jonas ask Asher not to do? How does Asher respond?

"Expertise," Jonas corrected him automatically.

"Whatever. You can't say what we play, even if you *are* going to be the new Receiver." Asher looked warily at him. "I apologize for not paying you the respect you deserve," he mumbled.

---

words for everyday use   ex • per • tise (ek spər tēz´) *n.,* expert opinion or commentary; special skill, knowledge, or mastery. *Drew's* expertise *at fixing computers was well known in the school and in great demand.*

"Asher," Jonas said. He was trying to speak carefully, and with kindness, to say exactly what he wanted to say. "You had no way of knowing this. I didn't know it myself until recently. But it's a cruel game. In the past, there have—"

"I said I *apologize*, Jonas."

Jonas sighed. It was no use. Of course Asher couldn't understand. "I accept your apology, Asher," he said wearily.

"Do you want to go for a ride along the river, Jonas?" Fiona asked, biting her lip with nervousness.

Jonas looked at her. She was so lovely. For a fleeting instant he thought he would like nothing better than to ride peacefully along the river path, laughing and talking with his gentle female friend. But he knew that such times had been taken from him now. He shook his head. After a moment his two friends turned and went to their bikes. He watched as they rode away.

Jonas trudged to the bench beside the Storehouse and sat down, overwhelmed with feelings of loss. His childhood, his friendships, his carefree sense of security—all of these things seemed to be slipping away. With his new, heightened feelings, he was overwhelmed by sadness at the way the others had laughed and shouted, playing at war. But he knew that they could not understand why, without the memories. He felt such love for Asher and for Fiona. But they could not feel it back, without the memories. And he could not give them those. Jonas knew with certainty that he could change nothing.

Back in their dwelling, that evening, Lily chattered merrily about the wonderful holiday she had had, playing with her friends, having her midday meal out of doors, and (she confessed) sneaking a very short try on her father's bicycle.

"I can't wait till I get my very own bicycle next month. Father's is too big for me. I fell," she explained matter-of-factly. "Good thing Gabe wasn't in the child seat!"

"A very good thing," Mother agreed, frowning at the idea of it. Gabriel waved his arms at the mention of himself. He had begun to walk just the week before. The first steps of a newchild were always the occasion for celebration at the Nurturing Center, Father said, but also for the introduction of a discipline wand. Now Father brought the slender instrument home with him each night, in case Gabriel misbehaved.

But he was a happy and easygoing toddler. Now he moved unsteadily across the room, laughing. "Gay!" he chirped. "Gay!" It was the way he said his own name.

Jonas brightened. It had been a depressing day for him, after such a bright start. But he set his glum thoughts aside. He thought about starting to teach Lily to ride so that she could speed off proudly after her Ceremony of Nine, which would be coming soon. It was hard to believe that it was almost December again, that almost a year had passed since he had become a Twelve.

He smiled as he watched the newchild plant one small foot carefully before the other, grinning with glee at his own steps as he tried them out.

"I want to get to sleep early tonight," Father said. "Tomorrow's a busy day for me. The twins are being born tomorrow, and the test results show that they're identical."

"One for here, one for Elsewhere," Lily chanted. "One for here, one for Else—"

"Do you actually *take* it Elsewhere, Father?" Jonas asked.

"No, I just have to make the selection. I weigh them, hand the larger over to a Nurturer who's standing by, waiting, and then I get the smaller one all cleaned up and comfy. Then I perform a small Ceremony of Release and—" He glanced down, grinning at Gabriel. "Then I wave bye-bye," he said, in a special sweet voice he used when he spoke to the newchild. He waved his hand in the familiar gesture.

Gabriel giggled and waved bye-bye back to him.

"And somebody else comes to get him? Somebody from Elsewhere?"

"That's right, Jonas-bonus."

Jonas rolled his eyes in embarrassment that his father had used the silly pet name.

◀ What part does Jonas's father play in the release of a twin to Elsewhere?

Lily was deep in thought. "What if they give the little twin a name Elsewhere, a name like, oh, maybe Jonathan? And here, in our community, at his naming, the twin that we kept here is given the name Jonathan, and then there would be two children with the same name, and they would *look* exactly the same, and someday, maybe when they were a Six, one group of Sixes would go to visit another community on a bus, and there in the other community, in the *other* group of Sixes, would be a Jonathan who was exactly the same as the *other* Jonathan, and then maybe they would get mixed up and take the wrong Jonathan home, and maybe his parents wouldn't notice, and then—"

She paused for breath.

"Lily," Mother said, "I have a wonderful idea. Maybe when you become a Twelve, they'll give you the Assignment of Storyteller! I don't think we've had a Storyteller in the community for a long time. But if I were on the Committee, I would definitely choose you for that job!"

Lily grinned. "I have a *better* idea for one more story," she announced. "What if actually we were *all* twins and didn't know it, and so Elsewhere there would be another Lily, and another Jonas, and another Father, and another Asher, and another Chief Elder, and another—"

Father groaned. "Lily," he said. "It's bedtime."

▶ *What Assignment does Lily's mother say would be perfect for Lily?*

Chapter 18

"GIVER," JONAS ASKED the next afternoon, "Do you ever think about release?"

"Do you mean my own release, or just the general topic of release?"

"Both, I guess. I apologi—I mean I should have been more precise. But I don't know exactly what I meant."

"Sit back up. No need to lie down while we're talking." Jonas, who had already been stretched out on the bed when the question came to his mind, sat back up.

"I guess I do think about it occasionally," The Giver said. "I think about my own release when I'm in an awful lot of pain. I wish I could put in a request for it, sometimes. But I'm not permitted to do that until the new Receiver is trained."

"Me," Jonas said in a <u>dejected</u> voice. He was not looking forward to the end of the training, when he would become the new Receiver. It was clear to him what a terribly difficult and lonely life it was, despite the honor.

◀ *What is Jonas not looking forward to? Why?*

"I can't request release either," Jonas pointed out. "It was in my rules."

The Giver laughed harshly. "I know that. They hammered out those rules after the failure ten years ago."

Jonas had heard again and again now, reference to the previous failure. But he still did not know what had happened ten years before. "Giver," he said, "tell me what happened. Please."

The Giver shrugged. "On the surface, it was quite simple. A Receiver-to-be was selected, the way you were. The selection went smoothly enough. The Ceremony was held, and the selection was made. The crowd cheered, as they did for you. The new Receiver was puzzled and a little frightened, as you were."

"My parents told me it was a female."

---

words for everyday use   **de • ject • ed** (di jek´ təd) *adj.*, cast down in spirits; depressed. *Dylan felt <u>dejected</u> after getting cut from the baseball team.*

The Giver nodded.

Jonas thought of his favorite female, Fiona, and shivered. He wouldn't want his gentle friend to suffer the way he had, taking on the memories. "What was she like?" he asked The Giver.

The Giver looked sad, thinking about it. "She was a remarkable young woman. Very <u>self-possessed</u> and serene. Intelligent, eager to learn." He shook his head and drew a deep breath. "You know, Jonas, when she came to me in this room, when she presented herself to begin her training—"

Jonas interrupted him with a question. "Can you tell me her name? My parents said that it wasn't to be spoken again in the community. But couldn't you say it just to me?"

The Giver hesitated painfully, as if saying the name aloud might be excruciating. "Her name was Rosemary," he told Jonas, finally.

"Rosemary. I like that name."

The Giver went on. "When she came to me for the first time, she sat there in the chair where you sat on your first day. She was eager and excited and a little scared. We talked. I tried to explain things as well as I could."

"The way you did to me."

The Giver chuckled ruefully. "The explanations are difficult. The whole thing is so beyond one's experience. But I tried. And she listened carefully. Her eyes were very <u>luminous</u>, I remember."

He looked up suddenly. "Jonas, I gave you a memory that I told you was my favorite. I still have a shred of it left. The room, with the family, and grandparents?"

Jonas nodded. Of course he remembered. "Yes," he said. "It had that wonderful feeling with it. You told me it was love."

---

words for everyday use

self-pos • sessed (self´ pə zest´) *adj.,* composed in mind or manner; calm. *Vickie's <u>self-possessed</u> nature helped her to remain calm in even the most uncomfortable situations.*

lu • mi • nous (lü´ mə nəs) *adj.,* bright; shining; radiant. *The <u>luminous</u> lights from the castle shone brightly for miles.*

"You can understand, then, that that's what I felt for Rosemary," The Giver explained. "I loved her.

"I feel it for you, too," he added.

"What happened to her?" Jonas asked.

"Her training began. She received well, as you do. She was so enthusiastic. So delighted to experience new things. I remember her laughter . . ."

His voice <u>faltered</u> and trailed off.

"What happened?" Jonas asked again, after a moment. "Please tell me."

The Giver closed his eyes. "It broke my heart, Jonas, to transfer pain to her. But it was my job. It was what I had to do, the way I've had to do it to you."

The room was silent. Jonas waited. Finally The Giver continued.

"Five weeks. That was all. I gave her happy memories: a ride on a merry-go-round; a kitten to play with; a picnic. Sometimes I chose one just because I knew it would make her laugh, and I so treasured the sound of that laughter in this room that had always been so silent.

"But she was like you, Jonas. She wanted to experience everything. She knew that it was her responsibility. And so she asked me for more difficult memories."

Jonas held his breath for a moment. "You didn't give her *war*, did you? Not after just five weeks?"

The Giver shook his head and sighed. "No. And I didn't give her physical pain. But I gave her loneliness. And I gave her loss. I transferred a memory of a child taken from its parents. That was the first one. She appeared stunned at its end."

Jonas swallowed. Rosemary, and her laughter, had begun to seem real to him, and he pictured her looking up from the bed of memories, shocked.

The Giver continued. "I backed off, gave her more little delights. But everything changed, once she knew about pain. I could see it in her eyes."

"She wasn't brave enough?" Jonas suggested.

◀ What did The Giver feel for Rosemary? What does he feel for Jonas?

◀ What painful memory did The Giver transfer to Rosemary?

words for everyday use

fal • ter (fôl´ tər) v., hesitate in purpose or action; speak brokenly or weakly; stammer. *We gave Jamie a pep talk, encouraging her so that she wouldn't <u>falter</u> during her presentation.*

The Giver didn't respond to the question. "She insisted that I continue, that I not spare her. She said it was her duty. And I knew, of course, that she was correct.

▶ What couldn't The Giver bring himself to do?

"I couldn't bring myself to inflict physical pain on her. But I gave her anguish of many kinds. Poverty, and hunger, and terror.

"I *had* to, Jonas. It was my job. And she had been chosen." The Giver looked at him imploringly. Jonas stroked his hand.

"Finally one afternoon, we finished for the day. It had been a hard session. I tried to finish—as I do with you—by transferring something happy and cheerful. But the times of laughter were gone by then. She stood up very silently, frowning, as if she were making a decision. Then she came over to me and put her arms around me. She kissed my cheek." As Jonas watched, The Giver stroked his own cheek, recalling the touch of Rosemary's lips ten years before.

▶ For what had Rosemary asked?

"She left here that day, left this room, and did not go back to her dwelling. I was notified by the Speaker that she had gone directly to the Chief Elder and asked to be released."

"But it's against the rules! The Receiver-in-training can't apply for rel—"

"It's in your rules, Jonas. But it wasn't in hers. She asked for release, and they had to give it to her. I never saw her again."

So that was the failure, Jonas thought. It was obvious that it saddened The Giver very deeply. But it didn't seem such a terrible thing, after all. And he, Jonas, would never have done it—never have requested release, no matter how difficult his training became. The Giver needed a successor, and he had been chosen.

A thought occurred to Jonas. Rosemary had been released very early in her training. What if something happened to him, Jonas? He had a whole year's worth of memories now.

"Giver," he asked, "I can't request release, I know that. But what if something happened: an accident? What if I fell into the river like the little Four, Caleb, did? Well, that doesn't make sense because I'm a good swimmer. But what if I couldn't swim, and fell into the river and was lost? Then there wouldn't be a new Receiver, but you would already have given away an awful lot of important memories, so even though they would select a new Receiver, the memories would be gone except for the shreds that you have left of them? And then what if—"

He started to laugh, suddenly. "I sound like my sister, Lily," he said, amused at himself.

The Giver looked at him <u>gravely</u>. "You just stay away from the river, my friend," he said. "The community lost Rosemary after five weeks and it was a disaster for them. I don't know *what* the community would do if they lost you."

"Why was it a disaster?"

"I think I mentioned to you once," The Giver reminded him, "That when she was gone, the memories came back to the people. If you were to be lost in the river, Jonas, your memories would not be lost with you. Memories are *forever.*

"Rosemary had only those five weeks' worth, and most of them were good ones. But there were those few terrible memories, the ones that had overwhelmed her. For a while they overwhelmed the community. All those *feelings!* They'd never experienced that before.

"I was so devastated by my own grief at her loss, and my own feeling of failure, that I didn't even try to help them through it. I was angry, too."

The Giver was quiet for a moment, obviously thinking. "You know," he said, finally, "if they lost *you,* with all the training you've had now, they'd have all those memories again themselves."

Jonas made a face. "They'd hate that."

"They certainly would. They wouldn't know how to deal with it at all."

"The only way *I* deal with it is by having you there to help me," Jonas pointed out with a sigh.

◄ What happened to the memories The Giver had transmitted to Rosemary? If the community were to lose Jonas, what would happen to the memories he has received?

---

words for everyday use grave (grāv´) *adj.*, serious; somber; grim. *My mother's face was <u>grave</u> when she opened the door to see me being escorted home by a police officer.* **gravely,** *adv.*

▶ What does The Giver need to think some more about?

The Giver nodded. "I suppose," he said slowly, "that I could—"

"You could what?"

The Giver was still deep in thought. After a moment, he said, "If you floated off in the river, I suppose I could help the whole community the way I've helped you. It's an interesting concept. I need to think about it some more. Maybe we'll talk about it again sometime. But not now.

"I'm glad you're a good swimmer, Jonas. But stay away from the river." He laughed a little, but the laughter was not <u>lighthearted</u>. His thoughts seemed to be elsewhere, and his eyes were very troubled.

---

words for everyday use light • heart • ed (līt´ här təd) *adj.,* free from care; hopeful; easy going. *The day before summer vacation, the school was filled with <u>lighthearted</u> conversation and little serious studying.*

Respond to the Selection

At the beginning of Chapter 16, the narrator tells us that Jonas has learned about the following things: "the joy of being an individual, special and unique and proud"; the bonds between an animal and human; and the joy of solitude. Choose one of these three things and give your thoughts on it in a few short paragraphs.

Investigate, Inquire, and Imagine

Recall: GATHERING FACTS

1a. Where do parents go once their children get their own dwellings? At that point, what part will they play in their children's lives?

2a. What feeling that Jonas has never before experienced is strongly present in The Giver's favorite memory?

3a. How do Jonas's parents respond when he asks them if they love him?

Interpret: FINDING MEANING

1b. What reasons might the community have for organizing the family unit to work this way?

2b. What do you think Jonas really means when he says: "I can see that it was a *dangerous* way to live"? Do you think he is really talking about the fire and the candles, or about something else? Explain.

3b. Why do you think Jonas lies to them, telling them he understands their answer?

Analyze: TAKING THINGS APART

4a. Look carefully through chapters 16, 17, and 18 and identify as many examples as you can of the way the memories have changed Jonas and his life.

Synthesize: BRINGING THINGS TOGETHER

4b. Based on your answer to question 4a, comment on the following: how receiving the memories has given Jonas a broader, more true view of the world; and how receiving the memories has isolated Jonas.

Evaluate: MAKING JUDGMENTS

5a. Based on your answers to questions 4a and 4b, is it a sacrifice or a reward to be selected Receiver of Memory for the community? Thoroughly explain your answer.

Extend: CONNECTING IDEAS

5b. What is one of your most cherished memories? Try to explain it in a letter to one of the characters in the book other than Jonas or The Giver.

Understanding Literature

MOTIVATION. A **motivation** is a force that moves a character to think, feel, or behave in a certain way. At the end of Chapter 16, the reader learns that for the first time, Jonas is not taking his pill for Stirrings: "Something within him, something that had grown there through the memories, told him to throw the pill away." What do you think is "the something within him" that is his motivation for throwing the pill away? Do you think motivation plays a role in the lives of other citizens in the community?

IMAGE. An **image** is the concrete representation of an object or an experience created through the use of language. An image is also the vivid mental picture created in the reader's mind by that language. The images in a literary work are referred to, when considered altogether, as the work's *imagery.* Identify some of the images Lowry uses to create The Giver's favorite memory. Think about your own family gatherings. Use imagery to convey a few of your favorite things about the gatherings.

Chapter 19

JONAS GLANCED AT the clock. There was so much work to be done, always, that he and The Giver seldom simply sat and talked, the way they just had.

"I'm sorry that I wasted so much time with my questions," Jonas said. "I was only asking about release because my father is releasing a newchild today. A twin. He has to select one and release the other one. They do it by weight." Jonas glanced at the clock. "Actually, I suppose he's already finished. I think it was this morning."

The Giver's face took on a solemn look. "I wish they wouldn't do that," he said quietly, almost to himself.

"Well, they can't have two identical people around. Think how confusing it would be!" Jonas chuckled.

"I wish I could watch," he added, as an **afterthought**. He liked the thought of seeing his father perform the ceremony, and making the little twin clean and comfy. His father was such a gentle man.

◀ Why does Jonas wish that he could watch the release of the smaller twin?

"You can watch," The Giver said.

"No," Jonas told him. "They never let children watch. It's very private."

"Jonas," The Giver told him, "I know that you read your training instructions very carefully. Don't you remember that you are allowed to ask anyone anything?"

Jonas nodded. "Yes, but—"

"Jonas, when you and I have finished our time together, you will be the new Receiver. You can read the books; you'll have the memories. You have access to *everything*. It's part of your training. If you want to watch a release, you have simply to ask."

Jonas shrugged. "Well, maybe I will, then. But it's too late for this one. I'm sure it was this morning."

---

words for everyday use   **af • ter • thought** (af´ tər thät) *n.*, idea occurring later. *Tilly thought she was invited to Bob's party as an afterthought because everyone else got their invitations days earlier.*

The Giver told him, then, something he had not known. "All private ceremonies are recorded. They're in the Hall of Closed Records. *Do you want to see this morning's release?"*

▶ Why does Jonas hesitate? Of what is he afraid?

Jonas hesitated. He was afraid that his father wouldn't like it, if he watched something so private.

"I think you should," The Giver told him firmly.

"All right, then," Jonas said. "Tell me how."

The Giver rose from his chair, went to the speaker on the wall, and clicked the switch from OFF to ON.

The voice spoke immediately. "Yes, Receiver. How may I help you?"

"I would like to see this morning's release of the twin."

"One moment, Receiver. Thank you for your instructions."

Jonas watched the video screen above the row of switches. Its blank face began to flicker with zig-zag lines; then some numbers appeared, followed by the date and time. He was astonished and delighted that this was available to him, and surprised that he had not known.

Suddenly he could see a small windowless room, empty except for a bed, a table with some equipment on it—Jonas recognized a scale; he had seen them before, when he'd been doing volunteer hours at the Nurturing Center—and a cupboard. He could see pale carpeting on the floor.

"It's just an ordinary room," he commented. "I thought maybe they'd have it in the Auditorium, so that everybody could come. All the Old go to Ceremonies of Release. But I suppose that when it's just a newborn, they don't—"

"Shhh," The Giver said, his eyes on the screen.

Jonas's father, wearing his nurturing uniform, entered the room, cradling a tiny newchild wrapped in a soft blanket in his arms. A uniformed woman followed through the door, carrying a second new-child wrapped in a similar blanket.

"That's my father." Jonas found himself whispering, as if he might wake the little ones if he spoke aloud. "And the other Nurturer is his assistant. She's still in training, but she'll be finished soon."

The two Nurturers unwrapped the blankets and laid the identical newborns on the bed. They were naked. Jonas could see that they were males.

He watched, fascinated, as his father gently lifted one and then the other to the scale and weighed them.

He heard his father laugh. "Good," his father said to the woman. "I thought for a moment that they might both be exactly the same. *Then* we'd have a problem. But this one"—he handed one, after rewrapping it, to his assistant—"is six pounds even. So you can clean him up and dress him and take him over to the Center."

The woman took the newchild and left through the door she had entered.

Jonas watched as his father bent over the squirming newchild on the bed. "And you, little guy, you're only five pounds ten ounces. A *shrimp!*"

"That's the special voice he uses with Gabriel," Jonas remarked, smiling.

"Watch," The Giver said.

"Now he cleans him up and makes him comfy," Jonas told him. "He told me."

"Be quiet, Jonas," The Giver commanded in a strange voice. *"Watch."*

Obediently Jonas concentrated on the screen, waiting for what would happen next. He was especially curious about the ceremony part.

His father turned and opened the cupboard. He took out a syringe[1] and a small bottle. Very carefully he inserted the needle into the bottle and began to fill the syringe with a clear liquid.

Jonas winced sympathetically. He had forgotten that newchildren had to get shots. He hated shots himself, though he knew that they were necessary.

To his surprise, his father began very carefully to direct the needle into the top of the newchild's forehead, puncturing the place where the fragile skin pulsed. The newborn squirmed, and wailed faintly.

"Why's he—"

◀ What does Jonas watch his father do?

---

1. **syringe.** Device used to inject fluids into or withdraw them from something

"Shhh," The Giver said sharply.

His father was talking, and Jonas realized that he was hearing the answer to the question he had started to ask. Still in the special voice, his father was saying, "I know, I know. It hurts, little guy. But I have to use a vein, and the veins in your arms are still too teeny-weeny."

He pushed the plunger very slowly, injecting the liquid into the scalp vein until the syringe was empty.

"All done. That wasn't so bad, was it?" Jonas heard his father say cheerfully. He turned aside and dropped the syringe into a waste receptacle.

Now he cleans him up and makes him comfy, Jonas said to himself, aware that The Giver didn't want to talk during the little ceremony.

▶ As Jonas continues to watch, what happens to the newchild?

As he continued to watch, the newchild, no longer crying, moved his arms and legs in a jerking motion. Then he went limp. His head fell to the side, his eyes half open. Then he was still.

With an odd, shocked feeling, Jonas recognized the gestures and posture and expression. They were familiar. He had seen them before. But he couldn't remember where.

Jonas stared at the screen, waiting for something to happen. But nothing did. The little twin lay motionless. His father was putting things away. Folding the blanket. Closing the cupboard.

Once again, as he had on the playing field, he felt the choking sensation. Once again he saw the face of the light-haired, bloodied soldier as life left his eyes. The memory came back.

▶ What does Jonas realize?

He killed it! My father killed it! Jonas said to himself, stunned at what he was realizing. He continued to stare at the screen <u>numbly</u>.

His father tidied the room. Then he picked up a small carton that lay waiting on the floor, set it on the bed, and lifted the limp body into it. He placed the lid on tightly.

**words
for
everyday
use**   **numb** (nəm´) *adj.*, without sensation or feeling. *The people's faces were numb when they heard the shocking news.* **numbly,** *adv.*

He picked up the carton and carried it to the other side of the room. He opened a small door in the wall; Jonas could see darkness behind the door. It seemed to be the same sort of <u>chute</u> into which trash was deposited at school.

His father loaded the carton containing the body into the chute and gave it a shove.

◀ What does his father do with the newchild?

"Bye-bye, little guy," Jonas heard his father say before he left the room. Then the screen went blank.

The Giver turned to him. Quite calmly, he related, "When the Speaker notified me that Rosemary had applied for release, they turned on the tape to show me the process. There she was—my last glimpse of that beautiful child—waiting. They brought in the syringe and asked her to roll up her sleeve.

"You suggested, Jonas, that perhaps she wasn't brave enough? I don't know about bravery: what it is, what it means. I do know that I sat here numb with horror. <u>Wretched</u> with helplessness. And I listened as Rosemary told them that she would prefer to inject herself.

◀ What did Rosemary prefer to do herself?

"Then she did so. I didn't watch. I looked away."

The Giver turned to him. "Well, there you are, Jonas. You were wondering about release," he said in a bitter voice.

Jonas felt a ripping sensation inside himself, the feeling of terrible pain clawing its way forward to emerge in a cry.

---

words for everyday use

chute (shüt´) *n.,* Passage down which or through which things may pass or slide. *We have a laundry <u>chute</u> in the bathroom, so I toss my dirty clothes down it before taking a shower.*

wretch • ed (re´ chəd) *adj.,* deeply dejected or distressed in body or mind. *I felt <u>wretched</u> after lying to my grandmother.*

Chapter 20

"I won't! I won't go home! You can't make me!" Jonas sobbed and shouted and pounded the bed with his fists.

"Sit up, Jonas," The Giver told him firmly.

Jonas obeyed him. Weeping, <u>shuddering</u>, he sat on the edge of the bed. He would not look at The Giver.

"You may stay here tonight. I want to talk to you. But you must be quiet now, while I notify your family unit. No one must hear you cry."

Jonas looked up wildly. "No one heard that little twin cry, either! No one but my father!" He collapsed in sobs again.

The Giver waited silently. Finally Jonas was able to quiet himself and he sat huddled, his shoulders shaking.

The Giver went to the wall speaker and clicked the switch to ON.

"Yes, Receiver. How may I help you?"

"Notify the new Receiver's family unit that he will be staying with me tonight, for additional training."

"I will take care of that, sir. Thank you for your instructions," the voice said.

"I will take care of that, sir. I will take care of that, sir," Jonas <u>mimicked</u> in a cruel, <u>sarcastic</u> voice. "I will do whatever you like, sir. I will kill people, sir. Old people? Small newborn people? I'd be happy to kill them, sir. Thank you for your instructions, sir. How may I help y—" He couldn't seem to stop.

The Giver grasped his shoulders firmly. Jonas fell silent and stared at him.

"Listen to me, Jonas. They can't help it. *They know nothing.*"

"You said that to me once before."

"I said it because it's true. It's the way they live. It's the life that was created for them. It's the same life

---

words for everyday use

shud • der (shə´ dər) v., tremble convulsively; shiver. *As winter approaches, I <u>shudder</u> when I think about how cold it will soon be.*

mim • ic (mi´ mik) v., copy, imitate, often to ridicule. *Raul <u>mimics</u> his sister's temper tantrums, which causes her to become even more upset.*

sar • cas • tic (sär kas´ tik) adj., having ironic or bitter characteristics intended to cause pain. *Portia's <u>sarcastic</u> jokes aren't very funny; they make people uncomfortable.*

that you would have, if you had not been chosen as my successor."

"But he *lied* to me!" Jonas wept.

"It's what he was told to do, and he knows nothing else."

"What about you? Do *you* lie to me, too?" Jonas almost spat the question at The Giver.

"I am empowered to lie. But I have never lied to you."

Jonas stared at him. "Release is always like that? For people who break the rules three times? For the *Old?* Do they kill the Old, too?"

"Yes, it's true."

"And what about Fiona? She loves the Old! She's in training to care for them. Does she know yet? What will she do when she finds out? How will she feel?" Jonas brushed wetness from his face with the back of one hand.

"Fiona is already being trained in the fine art of release," The Giver told him. "She's very efficient at her work, your red-haired friend. Feelings are not part of the life she's learned."

◄ What does The Giver tell Jonas about Fiona?

Jonas wrapped his arms around himself and rocked his own body back and forth. "What should I do? I can't go back! I can't!"

The Giver stood up. "First, I will order our evening meal. Then we will eat."

Jonas found himself using the nasty, sarcastic voice again. "Then we'll have a sharing of feelings?"

The Giver gave a rueful, anguished, empty laugh, "Jonas, you and I are the only ones who *have* feelings. We've been sharing them now for almost a year."

"I'm sorry, Giver," Jonas said miserably. "I don't mean to be so hateful. Not to you."

The Giver rubbed Jonas's hunched shoulders. "And after we eat," he went on, "we'll make a plan."

Jonas looked up, puzzled. "A plan for what? There's nothing. There's nothing we can do. It's

---

words for everyday use   **suc • ces • sor** (sək se´ sər) *n.*, one who comes after another in office or position. *Last year, Gail was the class president; soon we will vote to see who will be her successor.*

always been this way. Before me, before you, before the ones who came before you. Back and back and back." His voice trailed the familiar phrase.

"Jonas," The Giver said, after a moment, "it's true that it has been this way for what seems forever. But the memories tell us that it has not *always* been. People felt things once. You and I have been part of that, so we know. We know that they once felt things like pride, and sorrow, and—"

"And love," Jonas added, remembering the family scene that had so affected him. "And pain." He thought again of the soldier.

"The worst part of holding the memories is not the pain. It's the loneliness of it. Memories need to be shared."

"I've started to share them with you," Jonas said, trying to cheer him.

"That's true. And having you here with me over the past year has made me realize that things must change. For years I've felt that they should, but it seemed so hopeless.

"Now for the first time I think there might be a way," The Giver said slowly. "And you brought it to my attention, barely"—he glanced at the clock— "two hours ago."

Jonas watched him, and listened.

It was late at night, now. They had talked and talked. Jonas sat wrapped in a robe belonging to The Giver, the long robe that only Elders wore.

It was possible, what they had planned. Barely possible. If it failed, he would very likely be killed.

But what did that matter? If he stayed, his life was no longer worth living.

"Yes," he told The Giver. "I'll do it. I think I can do it. I'll try anyway. But I want you to come with me."

The Giver shook his head. "Jonas," he said, "the community has depended, all these generations, back and back and back, on a resident Receiver to hold their memories for them. I've turned over many of them to you in the past year. And I can't take them back. There's no way for me to get them back if I have given them.

▶ What do the memories tell The Giver and Jonas?

▶ What is the worst part of holding the memories?

"So if you escape, once you are gone—and, Jonas, you know that you can never return—"

Jonas nodded solemnly. It was the terrifying part. "Yes," he said, "I know. But if you come with me—"

The Giver shook his head and made a gesture to silence him. He continued. "If you get away, if you get beyond, if you get to Elsewhere, it will mean that the community has to bear the burden themselves, of the memories you had been holding for them.

"I think that they can, and that they will acquire some wisdom. But it will be desperately hard for them. When we lost Rosemary ten years ago, and her memories returned to the people, they panicked. And those were such few memories, compared to yours. When your memories return, they'll need help. Remember how I helped you in the beginning, when the receiving of memories was new to you?"

Jonas nodded. "It was scary at first. And it hurt a lot."

"You needed me then. And now they will."

"It's no use. They'll find someone to take my place. They'll choose a new Receiver."

"There's no one ready for training, not right away. Oh, they'll speed up the selection, of course. But I can't think of another child who has the right qualities—"

"There's a little female with pale eyes. But she's only a Six."

"That's correct. I know the one you mean. Her name is Katharine. But she's too young. So they will be *forced* to bear those memories."

"I want you to come, Giver," Jonas pleaded.

"No. I have to stay here," The Giver said firmly. "I want to, Jonas. If I go with you, and together we take away *all* their protection from the memories, Jonas, the community will be left with no one to help them. They'll be thrown into chaos. They'll destroy themselves. I can't go."

"Giver," Jonas suggested, "you and I don't need to *care* about the rest of them."

The Giver looked at him with a questioning smile. Jonas hung his head. Of course they needed to care. It was the meaning of everything.

◀ *Why must The Giver stay?*

"And in any case, Jonas," The Giver sighed, "I wouldn't make it. I'm very weakened now. Do you know that I no longer see colors?"

Jonas's heart broke. He reached for The Giver's hand.

"You have the colors," The Giver told him. "And you have the courage. I will help you to have the strength."

"A year ago," Jonas reminded him, "when I had just become a Twelve, when I began to see the first color, you told me that the beginning had been different for you. But that I wouldn't understand."

The Giver brightened. "That's true. And do you know, Jonas that with all your knowledge now, with all you memories, with all you've learned—*still* you won't understand? Because I've been a little selfish. I haven't given any of it to you. I wanted to keep it for myself to the last."

"Keep what?"

▶ When The Giver was a young boy, what did he experience?

"When I was just a boy, younger than you, it began to come to me. But it wasn't the seeing-beyond for me. It was different. For me, it was *hearing*-beyond."

Jonas frowned, trying to figure that out. "What did you hear?" he asked.

"Music," The Giver said, smiling. "I began to hear something truly remarkable, and it is called music. I'll give you some before I go."

Jonas shook his head <u>emphatically</u>. "No, Giver," he said. "I want you to keep that, to have with you, when I'm gone."

Jonas went home the next morning, cheerfully greeted his parents, and lied easily about what a busy, pleasant night he had had.

His father smiled and lied easily, too, about his busy and pleasant day the day before.

Throughout the school day, as he did his lessons, Jonas went over the plan in his head. It seemed star-

---

words for everyday use em • phat • ic (em fa´ tik) *adj.*, forceful; decisive. *Mother was very <u>emphatic</u> when she said that we had to attend the neighborhood meeting.* **emphatically,** *adv.*

tlingly simple. Jonas and The Giver had gone over it and over it, late into the night hours.

For the next two weeks, as the time for the December Ceremony approached, The Giver would transfer every memory of courage and strength that he could to Jonas. He would need those to help him find the Elsewhere that they were both sure existed. They knew it would be a very difficult journey.

Then, in the middle of the night before the Ceremony, Jonas would secretly leave his dwelling. This was probably the most dangerous part, because it was a violation of a major rule for any citizen not on official business to leave a dwelling at night.

◄ What will Jonas do in the middle of the night before the Ceremony?

"I'll leave at midnight," Jonas said. "The Food Collectors will be finished picking up the evening-meal remains by then, and the Path-Maintenance Crews don't start their work that early. So there won't be anyone to see me, unless of course someone is out on emergency business."

"I don't know what you should do if you are seen, Jonas," The Giver had said. "I have memories, of course, of all kinds of escapes. People fleeing from terrible things throughout history. But every situation is individual. There is no memory of one like this."

"I'll be careful," Jonas said. "No one will see me."

"As Receiver-in-training, you're held in very high respect already. So I think you wouldn't be questioned very forcefully."

"I'd just say I was on some important errand for the Receiver. I'd say it was all your fault that I was out after hours," Jonas teased.

They both laughed a little nervously. But Jonas was certain that he could slip away, unseen, from his house, carrying an extra set of clothing. Silently he would take his bicycle to the riverbank and leave it there hidden in bushes with the clothing folded beside it.

Then he would make his way through the darkness, on foot, silently, to the Annex.

"There's no nighttime attendant," The Giver explained. "I'll leave the door unlocked. You simply slip into the room. I'll be waiting for you."

▶ What will Jonas's parents find in the morning?

His parents would discover, when they woke, that he was gone. They would also find a cheerful note from Jonas on his bed, telling them that he was going for an early-morning ride along the river; that he would be back for the Ceremony.

His parents would be irritated but not alarmed. They would think him inconsiderate and they would plan to chastise him, later.

They would wait, with mounting anger, for him; finally they would be forced to go, taking Lily to the Ceremony without him.

▶ Why is Jonas certain his parents won't mention his absence to anyone?

"They won't say anything to anyone, though," Jonas said, quite certain. "They won't call attention to my rudeness because it would reflect on their parenting. And anyway, everyone is so involved in the Ceremony that they probably won't notice that I'm not there. Now that I'm a Twelve and in training, I don't have to sit with my age group any more. So Asher will think I'm with my parents, or with you—"

"And your parents will assume you're with Asher, or with me—"

Jonas shrugged. "It will take everyone a while to realize that I'm not there at all."

"And you and I will be long on our way by then."

In the early morning, The Giver would order a vehicle and driver from the Speaker. He visited the other communities frequently, meeting with their Elders; his responsibilities extend over all the surrounding areas. So this would not be an unusual undertaking.

Ordinarily The Giver did not attend the December Ceremony. Last year he had been present because of the occasion of Jonas's selection, in which he was so involved. But his life was usually quite separate from that of the community. No one would comment on his absence, or on the fact that he had chosen this day to be away.

▶ What will The Giver do during the driver's absence?

When the driver and vehicle arrived, The Giver would send the driver on some brief errand. During his absence, The Giver would help Jonas hide in the storage area of the vehicle. He would have with him a bundle of food which The Giver would save from his own meals during the next two weeks.

The Ceremony would begin, with all the community there, and by then Jonas and The Giver would be on their way.

By midday Jonas's absence would become apparent, and would be a cause for serious concern. The Ceremony would not be disrupted—such a disruption would be unthinkable. But searchers would be sent out into the community.

By the time his bicycle and clothing were found, The Giver would be returning. Jonas, by then, would be on his own, making his journey Elsewhere.

The Giver, on his return, would find the community in a state of confusion and panic. Confronted by a situation which they had never faced before, and having no memories from which to find either <u>solace</u> or wisdom, they would not know what to do and would seek his advice.

◀ On hearing of Jonas's absence, in what state will the community find itself? What will they do?

He would go to the Auditorium where the people would be gathered, still. He would stride to the stage and command their attention.

He would make the solemn announcement that Jonas had been lost in the river. He would immediately begin the Ceremony of Loss.

◀ After making the solemn announcement that Jonas has been lost, what ceremony will The Giver begin?

"Jonas, Jonas," they would say loudly, as they had once said the name of Caleb. The Giver would lead the chant. Together they would let Jonas's presence in their lives fade away as they said his name in unison more slowly, softer and softer, until he was disappearing from them, until he was no more than an occasional murmur and then, by the end of the long day, gone forever, not to be mentioned again.

Their attention would turn to the overwhelming task of bearing the memories themselves. The Giver would help them.

◀ To what will the community turn their attention after the ceremony?

"Yes, I understand that they'll need you," Jonas had said at the end of the lengthy discussion and planning.

words for everyday use so • lace (säl´ əs) *n.*, relief from grief. *After Aunt Beth died, Jeremy took <u>solace</u> in visiting her favorite spot along the river.*

"But I'll need you, too. Please come with me." He knew the answer even as he made the final <u>plea</u>.

"My work will be finished," The Giver had replied gently, "when I have helped the community to change and become whole.

▶ Why is The Giver grateful to Jonas?

"I'm grateful to you, Jonas, because without you I would never have figured out a way to bring about the change. But your role now is to escape. And my role is to stay."

"But don't you *want* to be with me, Giver?" Jonas asked sadly.

The Giver hugged him. "I love you, Jonas," he said. "But I have another place to go. When my work here is finished, I want to be with my daughter."

Jonas had been staring <u>glumly</u> at the floor. Now he looked up, startled. "I didn't know you had a daughter, Giver! You told me that you'd had a spouse. But I never knew about your daughter."

The Giver smiled, and nodded. For the first time in their long months together, Jonas saw him look truly happy.

▶ What was The Giver's daughter's name?

"Her name was Rosemary," The Giver said.

---

words for everyday use

plea (plē´) *n.*, an earnest request or appeal. *Peter uttered a soft <u>plea</u> for help before he collapsed on the ground.*

glum (gləm´) *adj.*, gloomy; dismal; sullen. *Paula's usually cheery face became <u>glum</u> when she learned that her best friend was moving.* **glumly,** *adv.*

Chapter 21

IT WOULD WORK. They could make it work, Jonas told himself again and again throughout the day.

But that evening everything changed. All of it—all the things they had thought through so meticulously—fell apart.

That night, Jonas was forced to flee. He left the dwelling shortly after the sky became dark and the community still. It was terribly dangerous because some of the work crews were still about, but he moved <u>stealthily</u> and silently, staying in the shadows, making his way past the darkened dwellings and the empty Central Plaza, toward the river. Beyond the Plaza he could see the House of the Old, with the Annex behind it, outlined against the night sky. But he could not stop there. There was no time. Every minute counted now, and every minute must take him farther from the community.

Now he was on the bridge, hunched over on the bicycle, pedaling steadily. He could see the dark, churning water far below.

He felt, surprisingly, no fear, nor any regret at leaving the community behind. But he felt a very deep sadness that he had left his closest friend behind. He knew that in the danger of his escape he must be absolutely silent; but with his heart and mind, he called back and hoped that with his capacity for hearing-beyond, The Giver would know that Jonas had said goodbye.

◀ *What does Jonas not feel as he leaves the Community behind? What does he feel? Why?*

It had happened at the evening meal. The family unit was eating together as always: Lily chattering away, Mother and Father making their customary comments (and lies, Jonas knew) about the day. Nearby, Gabriel played happily on the floor, babbling his baby talk, looking with glee now and then toward

---

words for everyday use

steal • thy (stel´ thē) *adj.*, slow, deliberate, and secret in action or character. *The cat's stealthy movements got it all the way across the room before the mouse noticed and ran away.* **stealthily,** *adv.*

Jonas, obviously delighted to have him back after the unexpected night away from the dwelling.

Father glanced down toward the toddler. "Enjoy it, little guy," he said. "This is your last night as visitor."

"What do you mean?" Jonas asked him.

Father sighed with disappointment. "Well, you know he wasn't here when you got home this morning because we had him stay overnight at the Nurturing Center. It seemed like a good opportunity, with you gone, to give it a try. He'd been sleeping so soundly."

"Didn't it go well?" Mother asked sympathetically.

Father gave a rueful laugh. "That's an understatement. It was a disaster. He cried all night, apparently. The night crew couldn't handle it. They were *really* frazzled by the time I got to work."

"Gabe, you naughty thing," Lily said, with a scolding little cluck toward the grinning toddler on the floor.

▶ What does Jonas's father tell him about Gabriel?

"So," Father went on, "we obviously had to make the decision. Even *I* voted for Gabriel's release when we had the meeting this afternoon."

Jonas put down his fork and stared at his father. "Release?" he asked.

Father nodded. "We certainly gave it our best try, didn't we?"

"Yes, we did," Mother agreed emphatically.

Lily nodded in agreement, too.

Jonas worked at keeping his voice absolutely calm. "When?" he asked. "When will he be released?"

"First thing tomorrow morning. We have to start our preparations for the Naming Ceremony, so we thought we'd get this taken care of right away.

"It's bye-bye to you, Gabe, in the morning," Father had said, in his sweet, sing-song voice.

Jonas reached the opposite side of the river, stopped briefly, and looked back. The community where his

---

words for everyday use

fraz • zle (fra´ zəl) v., put in a state of extreme physical or nervous fatigue. *The rowdy kids managed to frazzle the substitute teacher and earn the entire class an hour of detention.*

entire life had been lived lay behind him now, sleeping. At dawn, the orderly, disciplined life he had always known would continue again, without him. The life where nothing was ever unexpected. Or inconvenient. Or unusual. The life without color, pain, or past.

He pushed firmly again at the pedal with his foot and continued riding along the road. It was not safe to spend time looking back. He thought of the rules he had broken so far: enough that if he were caught, now, he would be condemned.

First, he had left the dwelling at night. A major transgression.

Second, he had robbed the community of food: a very serious crime, even though what he had taken was leftovers, set out on the dwelling doorsteps for collection.

Third, he had stolen his father's bicycle. He had hesitated for a moment, standing beside the bikeport in the darkness, not wanting anything of his father's and uncertain, as well, whether he could comfortably ride the larger bike when he was so accustomed to his own.

But it was necessary because it had the child seat attached to the back.

And he had taken Gabriel, too.

◀ Who has Jonas taken with him?

He could feel the little head nudge his back, bouncing gently against him as he rode. Gabriel was sleeping soundly, strapped into the seat. Before he had left the dwelling, he had laid his hands firmly on Gabe's back and transmitted to him the most soothing memory he could: a slow-swinging hammock under palm trees on an island someplace, at evening, with a rhythmic sound of languid water lapping hypnotically against a beach nearby. As the memory seeped from him into the newchild, he could feel Gabe's sleep ease and deepen. There had been no stir at all when Jonas lifted him from the crib and placed him gently into the molded seat.

He knew that he had the remaining hours of night before they would be aware of his escape. So he rode hard, steadily, willing himself not to tire as the minutes and miles passed. There had been no time to receive the memories he and The Giver had counted on, of strength and courage. So he relied on what he had, and hoped it would be enough.

He circled the outlying communities, their dwellings dark. Gradually the distances between communities widened, with longer stretches of empty road. His legs ached at first; then, as time passed, they became numb.

At dawn Gabriel began to stir. They were in an isolated place; fields on either side of the road were dotted with thickets of trees here and there. He saw a stream, and made his way to it across a rutted, bumpy meadow; Gabriel, wide awake now, giggled as the bicycle jolted him up and down.

Jonas unstrapped Gabe, lifted him from the bike, and watched him investigate the grass and twigs with delight. Carefully he hid the bicycle in thick bushes.

"Morning meal, Gabe!" He unwrapped some of the food and fed them both. Then he filled the cup he had brought with water from the stream and held it for Gabriel to drink. He drank thirstily himself, and sat by the stream, watching the newchild play.

He was exhausted. He knew he must sleep, resting his own muscles and preparing himself for more hours on the bicycle. It would not be safe to travel in daylight.

They would be looking for him soon.

He found a place deeply hidden in the trees, took the newchild there, and lay down, holding Gabriel in his arms. Gabe struggled cheerfully as if it were a wrestling game, the kind they had played back in the dwelling, with tickles and laughter.

"Sorry, Gabe," Jonas told him. "I know it's morning, and I know you just woke up. But we have to sleep now."

He cuddled the small body close to him, and rubbed the little back. He murmured to Gabriel soothingly. Then he pressed his hands firmly and transmitted a memory of deep, contented exhaustion. Gabriel's head nodded, after a moment, and fell against Jonas's chest.

Together the fugitives slept through the first dangerous day.

▶ *How does Jonas get Gabriel to go back to sleep?*

The most terrifying thing was the planes. By now, days had passed; Jonas no longer knew how many. The journey had become automatic: the sleep by day, hidden in the underbrush and trees; the finding of water, the careful division of scraps of food, augmented by what he could find in the fields. And the endless, endless miles on the bicycle by night.

His leg muscles were taut now. They ached when he settled himself to sleep. But they were stronger, and he stopped now less often to rest. Sometimes he paused and lifted Gabriel down for a brief bit of exercise, running down the road or through a field together in the dark. But always, when he returned, strapped the uncomplaining toddler into the seat again, and remounted, his legs were ready.

So he had enough strength of his own, and had not needed what The Giver might have provided, had there been time.

But when the planes came, he wished that he could have received the courage.

He knew they were search planes. They flew so low that they woke him with the noise of their engines, and sometimes, looking out and up fearfully from the hiding places, he could almost see the faces of the searchers.

He knew that they could not see color, and that their flesh, as well as Gabriel's light golden curls, would be no more than smears of gray against the colorless foliage. But he remembered from his science and technology studies at school that the search planes used heat-seeking devices which could identify body warmth and would home in on two humans huddled in shrubbery.

◀ What does Jonas remember from his science and technology studies at school?

So always, when he heard the aircraft sound, he reached to Gabriel and transmitted memories of snow, keeping some for himself. Together they became cold; and when the planes were gone, they would shiver, holding each other, until sleep came again.

Sometimes, urging the memories into Gabriel, Jonas felt that they were more shallow, a little weaker than they had been. It was what he had hoped, and what he and The Giver had planned: that as he moved away from the community, he would shed the memories and leave them behind for the people. But now, when he needed them, when the planes came, he tried hard to cling to what he still had, of cold, and to use it for their survival.

Usually the aircraft came by day, when they were hiding. But he was alert at night, too, on the road, always listening intently for the sound of the engines. Even Gabriel listened, and would call out, "Plane! Plane!" sometimes before Jonas had heard the terrifying noise. When the aircraft searchers came, as they did occasionally, during the night as they rode, Jonas sped to the nearest tree or bush, dropped to the ground, and made himself and Gabriel cold. But it was sometimes a frighteningly close call.

As he pedaled through the nights, through isolated landscape now, with the communities far behind and no sign of human habitation around him or ahead, he was constantly <u>vigilant</u>, looking for the next nearest hiding place should the sound of engines come.

But the frequency of the planes diminished. They came less often, and flew, when they did come, less slowly, as if the search had become <u>haphazard</u> and no longer hopeful. Finally there was an entire day and night when they did not come at all.

▶ *What finally happens?*

words for everyday use

vig • i • lant (vi´ jə lənt) adj., alertly watchful. The <u>vigilant</u> dog barked whenever a stranger approached the house.

hap • haz • ard (hap ha´ zərd) adj., random; marked by lack of plan, order, or direction. The <u>haphazard</u> route of the bus needs to be reconfigured so that it is more efficient.

Chapter 22

NOW THE LANDSCAPE was changing. It was a subtle change, hard to identify at first. The road was narrower, and bumpy, apparently no longer tended by road crews. It was harder, suddenly, to balance on the bike, as the front wheel wobbled over stones and ruts.

One night Jonas fell, when the bike jolted to a sudden stop against a rock. He grabbed instinctively for Gabriel; and the newchild, strapped tightly in his seat, was uninjured, only frightened when the bike fell to its side. But Jonas's ankle was twisted, and his knees were scraped and raw, blood seeping through his torn trousers. Painfully he righted himself and the bike, and reassured Gabe.

Tentatively he began to ride in daylight. He had forgotten the fear of the searchers, who seemed to have diminished into the past. But now there were new fears; the unfamiliar landscape held hidden, unknown perils.

Trees became more numerous, and the forests beside the road were dark and thick with mystery. They saw streams more frequently now and stopped often to drink. Jonas carefully washed his injured knees, wincing as he rubbed at the raw flesh. The constant ache of his swollen ankle was eased when he soaked it occasionally in the cold water that rushed through roadside <u>gullies</u>.

He was newly aware that Gabriel's safety depended entirely upon his own continued strength.

They saw their first waterfall, and for the first time wildlife.

"Plane! Plane!" Gabriel called, and Jonas turned swiftly into the trees, though he had not seen planes in days, and he did not hear an aircraft engine now. When he stopped the bicycle in the shrubbery and turned to grab Gabe, he saw the small chubby arm pointing toward the sky.

---

words for everyday use   gul • ly (gə´ lē) *n.*, a trench that was originally worn in the earth by running water and through which water often runs after rains. *Every spring, melted snow and falling rain created a <u>gully</u> through the low-lying pasture.*

▶ What does Gabriel
see that he thinks is
a plane?

Terrified, he looked up, but it was not a plane at
all. Though he had never seen one before, he identified it from his fading memories, for The Giver had
given them to him often. It was a bird.

Soon there were many birds along the way, soaring
overhead, calling. They saw deer; and once, beside
the road, looking at them curious and unafraid, a
small reddish-brown creature with a thick tail, whose
name Jonas did not know. He slowed the bike and
they stared at one another until the creature turned
away and disappeared into the woods.

All of it was new to him. After a life of Sameness
and predictability, he was awed by the surprises that
lay beyond each curve of the road. He slowed the
bike again and again to look with wonder at wildflowers, to enjoy the throaty warble of a new bird
nearby, or merely to watch the way wind shifted the
leaves in the trees. During his twelve years in the
community, he had never felt such simple moments
of exquisite happiness.

▶ What didn't Jonas
experience during his
twelve years in the
community that he
does feel now?

But there were desperate fears building in him now
as well. The most relentless of his new fears was that
they would starve. Now that they had left the culti-
vated fields behind them, it was almost impossible to
find food. They finished the <u>meager</u> store of potatoes
and carrots they had saved from the last agricultural
area, and now they were always hungry.

Jonas knelt by a stream and tried without success
to catch a fish with his hands. Frustrated, he threw
rocks into the water, knowing even as he did so that
it was useless. Finally, in desperation, he fashioned a
<u>makeshift</u> net, looping the strands of Gabriel's blan-
ket around a curved stick.

After countless tries, the net yielded two flopping
silvery fish. Methodically Jonas hacked them to
pieces with a sharp rock and fed the raw shreds to
himself and to Gabriel. They ate some berries, and
tried without success to catch a bird.

**words
for
everyday
use**

mea • ger (mē´ gər) *adj.,* lacking in quality or quantity. *The evil queen gave the
young prince only meager portions of gruel
to eat.*

make • shift (māk´ shift) *adj.,* on-the-
spot; thrown-together; contrived. *Bob's
mother only had time to whip together a
makeshift costume for the party.*

At night, while Gabriel slept beside him, Jonas lay awake, tortured by hunger, and remembered his life in the community where meals were delivered to each dwelling every day.

He tried to use the flagging power of his memory to recreate meals, and managed brief, <u>tantalizing</u> fragments: banquets with huge roasted meats; birthday parties with thick-frosted cakes; and lush fruits picked and eaten, sun-warmed and dripping, from trees.

But when the memory glimpses subsided, he was left with the gnawing, painful emptiness. Jonas remembered, suddenly and grimly, the time in his childhood when he had been chastised for misusing a word. The word had been "starving." You have never been starving, he had been told. You will never be starving.

Now he was. If he had stayed in the community, he would not be. It was as simple as that. Once he had yearned for choice. Then, when he had had a choice, he had made the wrong one: the choice to leave. And now he was starving.

But if he had stayed . . .

His thoughts continued. If he had stayed, he would have starved in other ways. He would have lived a life hungry for feelings, for color, for love.

And Gabriel? For Gabriel there would have been no life at all. So there had not really been a choice.

It became a struggle to ride the bicycle as Jonas weakened from lack of food, and realized at the same time that he was encountering something he had for a long time yearned to see: hills. His sprained ankle throbbed as he forced the pedal downward in an effort that was almost beyond him.

And the weather was changing. It rained for two days. Jonas had never seen rain, though he had experienced it often in the memories. He had liked those rains, enjoyed the new feeling of it, but this was

◄ If Jonas had stayed in the community, what would he not be hungry for? What would he be hungry for?

---

words for everyday use tan • ta • liz • ing (tan´ təl ī ziŋ) *adj.*, enticing; tempting. *The <u>tantalizing</u> smell of dinner cooking made my stomach growl.*

different. He and Gabriel became cold and wet, and it was hard to get dry, even when sunshine occasionally followed.

Gabriel had not cried during the long frightening journey. Now he did. He cried because he was hungry and cold and terribly weak. Jonas cried, too, for the same reasons, and another reason as well. He wept because he was afraid now that he could not save Gabriel. He no longer cared about himself.

▶ Why does Jonas weep?

Chapter 23

JONAS FELT MORE and more certain that the destination lay ahead of him, very near now in the night that was approaching. None of his senses confirmed it. He saw nothing ahead except the endless ribbon of road unfolding in twisting narrow curves. He heard no sound ahead.

Yet he felt it: felt that Elsewhere was not far away. But he had little hope left that he would be able to reach it. His hope diminished further when the sharp, cold air began to blur and thicken with swirling white.

◀ What does Jonas feel?

Gabriel, wrapped in his inadequate blanket, was hunched, shivering, and silent in his little seat. Jonas stopped the bike wearily, lifted the child down, and realized with heartbreak how cold and weak Gabe had become.

Standing in the freezing mound that was thickening around his numb feet, Jonas opened his own tunic, held Gabriel to his bare chest, and tied the torn and dirty blanket around them both. Gabriel moved feebly against him and whimpered briefly into the silence that surrounded them.

Dimly, from a nearly forgotten perception as blurred as the substance itself, Jonas recalled what the whiteness was.

"It's called snow, Gabe," Jonas whispered. "*Snowflakes.* They fall down from the sky, and they're very beautiful."

There was no response from the child who had once been so curious and alert. Jonas looked down through the dusk at the little head against his chest. Gabriel's curly hair was matted and filthy, and there were tearstains outlined in dirt on his pale cheeks. His eyes were closed. As Jonas watched, a snowflake drifted down and was caught briefly for a moment's sparkle in the tiny fluttering eyelashes.

Wearily he remounted the bicycle. A steep hill loomed ahead. In the best of conditions, the hill would have been a difficult, demanding ride. But now the rapidly deepening snow obscured the narrow road and made the ride impossible. His front wheel moved forward imperceptibly as he pushed on the pedals with his numb, exhausted legs. But the bicycle stopped. It would not move.

He got off and let it drop sideways into the snow. For a moment he thought how easy it would be to drop beside it himself, to let himself and Gabriel slide into the softness of snow, the darkness of night, the warm comfort of sleep.

But he had come this far. He must try to go on.

The memories had fallen behind him now, escaping from his protection to return to the people of his community. Were there any left at all? Could he hold on to a last bit of warmth? Did he still have the strength to Give? Could Gabriel still Receive?

He pressed his hands into Gabriel's back and tried to remember sunshine. For a moment it seemed that nothing came to him, that his power was completely gone. Then it flickered suddenly, and he felt tiny tongues of heat begin to creep across and into his frozen feet and legs. He felt his face begin to glow and the tense, cold skin of his arms and hands relax. For a fleeting second he felt that he wanted to keep it for himself, to let himself bathe in sunlight, unburdened by anything or anyone else.

But the moment passed and was followed by an urge, a need, a passionate yearning to share the warmth with the one person left for him to love. Aching from the effort, he forced the memory of warmth into the thin, shivering body in his arms.

Gabriel stirred. For a moment they both were bathed in warmth and renewed strength as they stood hugging each other in the blinding snow.

Jonas began to walk up the hill.

The memory was agonizingly brief. He had trudged no more than a few yards through the night when it was gone and they were cold again.

But his mind was alert now. Warming himself ever so briefly had shaken away the <u>lethargy</u> and

▶ *For a moment, what does Jonas think of?*

▶ *Where have Jonas's memories gone?*

▶ *What urge does Jonas feel?*

words for everyday use   leth • ar • gy (le´ thər jē) *n.*, sluggishness; lifelessness; spiritlessness. *After a long and grueling schedule, the team showed signs of <u>lethargy</u>.*

<u>resignation</u> and restored his will to survive. He began to walk faster on feet that he could no longer feel. But the hill was treacherously steep; he was impeded by the snow and his own lack of strength. He didn't make it very far before he stumbled and fell forward.

On his knees, unable to rise, Jonas tried a second time. His consciousness grasped at a wisp of another warm memory, and tried desperately to hold it there, to enlarge it and pass it into Gabriel. His spirits and strength lifted with the momentary warmth and he stood. Again, Gabriel stirred against him as he began to climb.

But the memory faded, leaving him colder than before.

If only he had had time to receive more warmth from The Giver before he escaped! Maybe there would be more left for him now. But there was no purpose in if-onlys. His entire concentration now had to be on moving his feet, warming Gabriel and himself, and going forward.

He climbed, stopped, and warmed them both briefly again, with a tiny scrap of memory that seemed certainly to be all he had left.

The top of the hill seemed so far away, and he did not know what lay beyond. But there was nothing left to do but continue. He trudged upward.

As he approached the summit of the hill at last, something began to happen. He was not warmer, if anything, he felt more numb and more cold. He was not less exhausted; on the contrary, his steps were leaden, and he could barely move his freezing, tired legs.

But he began, suddenly, to feel happy. He began to recall happy times. He remembered his parents and his sister. He remembered his friends, Asher and Fiona. He remembered The Giver.

Memories of joy flooded through him suddenly.

---

words for everyday use

res • ig • na • tion (re zig nā´ shən) *n.,* surrender. *Though the odds were against her, Maria never showed signs of <u>resignation</u>.*

He reached the place where the hill crested and he could feel the ground under his snow-covered feet become level. It would not be uphill anymore.

"We're almost there, Gabriel," he whispered, feeling quite certain without knowing why. "I remember this place, Gabe." And it was true. But it was not a grasping of a thin and <u>burdensome</u> recollection; this was different. This was something that he could keep. It was a memory of his own.

He hugged Gabriel and rubbed him briskly, warming him, to keep him alive. The wind was bitterly cold. The snow swirled, blurring his vision. But somewhere ahead, through the blinding storm, he knew there was warmth and light.

▶ What is waiting for Jonas at the top of the hill?

Using his final strength, and a special knowledge that was deep inside him, Jonas found the sled that was waiting for them at the top of the hill. Numbly his hands fumbled for the rope.

He settled himself on the sled and hugged Gabe close. The hill was steep but the snow was powdery and soft, and he knew that this time there would be no ice, no fall, no pain. Inside his freezing body, his heart surged with hope.

They started down.

Jonas felt himself losing consciousness and with his whole being willed himself to stay upright atop the sled, clutching Gabriel, keeping him safe. The runners sliced through the snow and the wind whipped at his face as they sped in a straight line through an incision that seemed to lead to the final destination, the place that he had always felt was waiting, the Elsewhere that held their future and their past.

▶ All at once, what can Jonas see? What does he know?

He forced his eyes open as they went downward, downward, sliding, and all at once he could see lights, and he recognized them now. He knew they were shining through the windows of rooms, that they were the red, blue, and yellow lights that twin-

---

words for everyday use

bur • den • some (bər´ dən səm) adj., imposing a burden; oppressive. *The <u>burdensome</u> rules and regulations made life difficult for the boys.*

kled from trees in places where families created and kept memories, where they celebrated love.

Downward, downward, faster and faster. Suddenly he was aware with certainty and joy that below, ahead, they were waiting for him; and that they were waiting, too, for the baby. For the first time, he heard something that he knew to be music. He heard people singing.

Behind him, across vast distances of space and time, from the place he had left, he thought he heard music too. But perhaps it was only an echo.

◀ *Of what is Jonas suddenly aware?*

Respond to the Selection

What do you hope the future holds for Jonas? for Gabriel?

Investigate, Inquire, and Imagine

Recall: GATHERING FACTS

1a. How does Jonas react to seeing his father "release" the smaller twin? What does The Giver explain to Jonas about his father's actions? How does The Giver respond to Jonas's protests that his father has lied to him?

2a. At her release, what does Rosemary do herself?

3a. In Chapter 20, Jonas says to The Giver, "But don't you *want* to be with me, Giver?" How does The Giver respond?

4a. At the end of the story, when Jonas reaches the crest of the hill, what does he find? Where does it take him?

Interpret: FINDING MEANING

→ 1b. Why do you think that Nurturers are instructed to "release" the smaller of twins and babies like Gabriel who develop at a slower than average rate? Why do you think that the Ceremony of Release is kept such a mystery?

→ 2b. Why do you think she does this?

→ 3b. Who was The Giver's daughter?

→ 4b. What do you think happens when Jonas and Gabe reach the bottom of the hill? What do you think the ending of the story means?

Analyze: TAKING THINGS APART

5a. Analyze, and explain the meaning of, the following: "Of course they needed to care. It was the meaning of everything."

Synthesize: BRINGING THINGS TOGETHER

→ 5b. How are Jonas's fate and the fate of the community intertwined?

Evaluate: MAKING JUDGMENTS

6a. Do you think that Jonas was the right person to follow The Giver as Receiver of Memory? Why, or why not?

Extend: CONNECTING IDEAS

→ 6b. What type of future do you predict for the community that Jonas leaves behind? Why?

Understanding Literature

CHARACTER. A **character** is a person or animal who takes part in the action of a literary work. The main character is called the *protagonist.* A character who struggles against the main character is called an *antagonist. A one-dimensional character, flat character,* or *caricature,* is one who exhibits a single quality, or character trait. A *three-dimensional, full,* or *rounded character* is one who seems to have all the complexities of an actual human being. Who is the protagonist in *The Giver?* Is there an antagonist? If so, who is the antagonist? Which characters are three dimensional? How does *The Giver* provide a good example of the difference between one-dimensional and three-dimensional characters?

FICTION. **Fiction** is prose—*prose* is the word used to describe all writing that is not drama or poetry—writing about imagined events or characters. The primary forms of fiction are the short story, the novella, and the novel. Lois Lowry's *The Giver* is a work of fiction. Based on your reading of *The Giver,* comment on how works of fiction can teach us about real life, about our own lives.

Plot Analysis of
The Giver

The following diagram, known as a plot pyramid, illustrates the main plot of *The Giver*. For definitions and more information on the parts of plot in a literary work, see the Handbook of Literary Terms on page 200.

The parts of a plot are as follows:

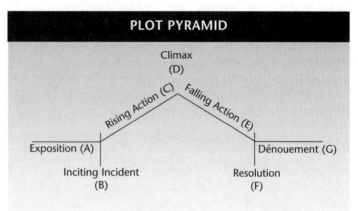

The **exposition** is the part of a plot that provides background information about the characters, setting, or conflict.

The **inciting incident** is the event that introduces the central conflict.

The **rising action**, or complication, develops the conflict to a high point of intensity.

The **climax** is the high point of interest or suspense in the story.

The **falling action** is all the events that follow the climax.

The **resolution** is the point at which the central conflict is ended, or resolved.

The **dénouement** is any material that follows the resolution and that ties up loose ends.

Exposition (A)

The Giver begins with exposition by revealing through Jonas's thoughts, the details of an event—the flying of an aircraft over the community—that took place a year before the time in which the book opens. These details provide information about Jonas and the community. Exposition continues through Chapters

1–6 as the reader is introduced to new characters and as information about life in the community is revealed.

Inciting Incident (B)

The inciting incident in this story is the selection of Jonas as Receiver of Memory. As Jonas begins his training as Receiver, his new awareness conflicts with everything he has ever known and sets him worlds apart from the people he loves. For the first time, he learns that his life—and that of everyone in the community—is not as perfect as it seems. The central conflict is Jonas's struggle to accept and understand this new awareness.

Rising Action (C)

As Jonas trains with The Giver, he gains knowledge, experience, and memory that changes forever the way he views his life and life in general. His struggle to reconcile what he learns with how he lives his life as well as his conversations with The Giver about how to change the lives of citizens of the community create the rising action of the story.

Climax (D)

The story comes to a climax when Jonas sees his father release a newchild and as Jonas and The Giver produce a plan for Jonas to escape. The climax continues when Jonas learns that Gabriel is to be released. Jonas's preparations and flight are also part of the climax of the story.

Falling Action (E)

The action of the story begins to fall as Jonas realizes that search planes have stopped looking for him.

Resolution (F)

The plot comes to a resolution as Jonas sees the red, blue, and yellow lights and experiences certainty and joy that he has reached his destination and that he and Gabriel will be welcomed.

Dénouement (G)

Jonas hears music, and for a moment, he thinks he might hear music from the place he has left . . . but perhaps it is only an echo. In this way, the story is completed, and the reader is left to interpret the ending in his or her own way.

"Secret of Life"
by Diana Der-Hovanessian

ABOUT THE RELATED READING

Diana Der-Hovanessian is a poet and translator well known for translating Armenian poetry into English. She lives and writes in Cambridge, Massachusetts.

▶ *What does the navy yard worker say about the secret of life?*

Once during the war
on a bus going to Portsmouth
a navy yard worker
told me the secret of life.

The secret of life, he said,
can never be passed down
one generation to the other.

The secret of life, he said,
is hunger. It makes an open hand.

The secret of life is money.
But only the small coins.

The secret of life, he said,
is love. You become what you lose.

The secret of life, he said,
is water. The world will end
in flood.

The secret of life, he said,
is circumstance.

If you catch the right bus
at the right time
you will sit next
to the secret teller

▶ *What will the secret teller do?*

who will whisper it
in your ear.

Critical Thinking

1. According to the navy yard worker, the secret of life cannot be passed down from one generation to the other. Why do you think he says this?
2. How does the philosophy of the navy yard worker differ from or parallel the ideas in *The Giver?*
3. Who would the secret teller be? How would this person know the secrets?

"The Past"
by Billy Collins

ABOUT THE RELATED READING

Billy Collins is the author of six books of poetry. His poems have also been included in numerous anthologies, magazines, and textbooks. Collins has received many prizes for his poetry, and in 2001, he was named poet laureate of the United States. This poem is from Collins's collection entitled *The Apple that Astonished Paris*.

There is no doubt we all had one,
waist-deep as we are in the evidence of diaries,
home movies and strange names in old address books,
not to mention Architecture and Geology,
stone clocks that measure the deeper past.

And we have anecdotes, warped beyond recognition,
and a scar on the chin from a fall,
but nothing to compare with those few vivid moments
which are vivid for no reason at all—
a face at a children's party, or just a blue truck,
moments that have no role in any story,
worthless to a biographer, but mysterious
and rivaling the colors of the present.

▶ What does the speaker compare to the act of remembering?

Remembering them is like reading a poem
that begins by carrying us, zombie-like,
down basement stairs as if to leave us in the dark
feeling the air for a light cord,

but then a little metaphor begins to grow
with such detail that it becomes a place,
a lake, for instance, cold and pine-bordered,
which we could dive into and feel nothing,
or a sunny white room where we could live
without ever having to be alive.

Critical Thinking

1. How does the speaker value anecdotes from the past?
   How do you value these? In what ways might they
   not be worthless to a writer?
2. How does metaphor grow from a memory? How do
   people create associations between memories, people, and places?
3. What is Collins's main idea about "the past"?

Newbery Acceptance Speech
by Lois Lowry

ABOUT THE RELATED READING

Lois Lowry gave this speech after winning the Newbery Medal for *The Giver* in 1994. In it, she describes how she came up with and developed some of the ideas and themes in her book.

"How do you know where to start?" a child asked me once, in a schoolroom where I'd been speaking to her class about the writing of books. I shrugged and smiled and told her that I just start wherever it feels right.

This evening it feels right to start by quoting a passage from *The Giver,* a scene set during the days in which the boy, Jonas, is beginning to look more deeply into the life that has been very superficial, beginning to see that his own past goes back further than he had ever known and has greater implications than he had ever suspected.

> Now he saw the familiar wide river beside the path differently. He saw all of the light and color and history it contained and carried in its slow-moving water; and he knew that there was an Elsewhere from which it came, and an Elsewhere to which it was going.

▶ *What is every author asked again and again?*

Every author is asked again and again the question we probably each have come to dread the most: How did you get this idea?

We give glib, quick answers because there are other hands raised, other kids in the audience waiting.

I'd like, tonight, to dispense with my usual flippancy and glibness and try to tell you the origins of this book. It is a little like Jonas looking into the river and realizing that it carries with it everything that has come from an Elsewhere. A spring, perhaps, at the beginning, bubbling up from the earth; then a trickle from a glacier; a mountain stream entering farther along; and each tributary bringing with it the collected bits and pieces from the past, from the distant, from the countless Elsewheres: all of it moving, mingled, in the current.

For me, the tributaries are memories, and I've selected only a few. I'll tell them to you chronologically. I have to go way back. I'm starting forty-six years ago.

◄ For Lowry, what are the tributaries? What is she going to tell?

In 1948 I am eleven years old. I have gone with my mother, sister, and brother to join my father, who has been in Tokyo for two years and will be there for several more.

We live there, in the center of that huge Japanese city, in a small American enclave with a very American name: Washington Heights. We live in an American-style house, with American neighbors, and our little community has its own movie theater, which shows American movies, and a small church, a tiny library, and an elementary school; and in many ways it is an odd replica of a United States village.

(In later, adult years I was to ask my mother why we had lived there instead of taking advantage of the opportunity to live within the Japanese community and to learn and experience a different way of life. But she seemed surprised by my question. She said that we lived where we did because it was comfortable. It was familiar. It was safe.)

◄ What did Lowry's mother say about why they lived in Washington Heights?

At eleven years old I am not a particularly adventurous child, nor am I a rebellious one. But I have always been curious.

I have a bicycle. Again and again—countless times—without my parents' knowledge, I ride my bicycle out the back gate of the fence that surrounds our comfortable, familiar, safe American community. I ride down a hill because I am curious, and I enter, riding down that hill, an unfamiliar, slightly uncomfortable, perhaps even unsafe—though I never feel it to be—area of Tokyo that throbs with life.

It is a district called Shibuya. It is crowded with shops and people and theaters and street vendors and the day-to-day bustle of Japanese life.

I remember, still, after all these years, the smells: fish and fertilizer and charcoal; the sounds: music and shouting and the clatter of wooden shoes and wooden sticks and wooden wheels; and the colors: I remember the babies and toddlers dressed in bright pink and orange and red, most of all; but I remember, too, the dark blue uniforms of the schoolchildren—the strangers who are my own age.

I wander through Shibuya day after day during those years when I am eleven, twelve, and thirteen. I love the feel of it, the vigor and the garish brightness and the noise: all such a contrast to my own life.

But I never talk to anyone. I am not frightened of the people, who are so different from me, but I am shy. I watch the children shouting and playing around a school, and they are children my age, and they watch me in return; but we never speak to one another.

One afternoon I am standing on a street corner when a woman near me reaches out, touches my hair, and says something. I back away, startled, because my knowledge of the language is poor and I misunderstand her words. I think she has said "kiraidesu," meaning that she dislikes me; and I am embarrassed, and confused, wondering what I have done wrong: how I have disgraced myself.

Then, after a moment, I realize my mistake. She has said, actually, "kirei-desu." She has called me pretty. And I look for her, in the crowd, at least to smile, perhaps to say thank you if I can overcome my shyness enough to speak. But she is gone. I remember this moment—this instant of communication gone awry—again and again over the years. Perhaps this is where the river starts.

In 1954 and 1955 I am a college freshman, living in a very small dormitory, actually a converted private home, with a group of perhaps fourteen other girls. We are very much alike. We wear the same sort of clothes: cashmere sweaters and plaid wool skirts, knee socks and loafers. We all smoke Marlboro cigarettes, and we knit—usually argyle socks for our boyfriends—and play bridge. Sometimes we study; and we get good grades because we are all the cream of the crop, the valedictorians and class presidents from our high schools all over the United States.

One of the girls in our dorm is not like the rest of us. She doesn't wear our uniform. She wears blue jeans instead of skirts, and she doesn't curl her hair or knit or play bridge. She doesn't date or go to fraternity parties and dances.

She's a smart girl, a good student, a pleasant enough person, but she is different, somehow alien, and that makes us uncomfortable. We react with a kind of mindless cruelty. We don't tease or torment her, but we do something worse: we ignore her. We pretend that she doesn't exist. In a small house of fourteen young women, we make one invisible.

◀ What do the girls in the dormitory do to the one who is different?

Somehow, by shutting her out, we make ourselves feel comfortable. Familiar, Safe.

I think of her now and then as the years pass. Those thoughts—fleeting, but profoundly remorseful—enter the current of the river.

In the summer of 1979, I am sent by a magazine I am working for to an island off the coast of Maine to write an article about a painter who lives there alone. I spend a good deal of time with this man, and we talk a lot about color. It is clear to me that although I am a highly visual person—a person who sees and appreciates form and composition and color—this man's capacity for seeing color goes far beyond mine.

I photograph him while I am there, and I keep a copy of his photograph for myself because there is something about his face—his eyes—which haunts me.

Later I hear that he has become blind.

◀ What happened to the painter on the island off of Maine?

I think about him—his name is Carl Nelson—from time to time. His photograph hangs over my desk. I wonder what it was like for him to lose the colors about which he was so impassioned.

I wish, in a whimsical way, that he could have somehow magically given me the capacity to see the way he did.

A little bubble begins, a little spurt, which will trickle into the river.

In 1989 I go to a small village in Germany to attend the wedding of one of my sons. In an ancient church, he marries his Margret in a ceremony conducted in a language I do not speak and cannot understand.

But one section of the service is in English. A woman stands in the balcony of that old stone church and sings the words from the Bible: Where you go, I will go. Your people will be my people.

How small the world has become, I think, looking around the church at the many people who sit there wishing happiness to my son and his new wife, wishing it in their own language as I am wishing it in mine. We are all each other's people now, I find myself thinking.

Can you feel that this memory is a stream that is now entering the river?

Another fragment. My father, nearing ninety, is in a nursing home. My brother and I have hung family pictures on the walls of his room. During a visit, he and I are talking about the people in the pictures. One is my sister, my parents' first child, who died young of cancer. My father smiles, looking at her picture. "That's your sister," he says happily. "That's Helen."

▶ What did Lowry's father forget?

Then he comments, a little puzzled, but not at all sad, "I can't remember exactly what happened to her."

We can forget pain, I thought. And it is comfortable to do so, but I also wonder briefly: is it safe to do that, to forget?

That uncertainty pours itself into the river of thought which will become the book.

1991. I am in an auditorium somewhere. I have spoken at length about my book *Number the Stars*, which has been honored with the 1990 Newbery Medal. A woman raises her hand. When the time for her question comes, she sighs very loudly, and says, "Why do we have to tell this Holocaust thing over and over? Is it really necessary?"

I answer her as well as I can, quoting, in fact, my German daughter-in-law, who has said to me, "No one knows better than we Germans that we must tell this again and again."

But I think about her question—and my answer— a great deal.

Wouldn't it, I think, playing devil's advocate to myself, make for a more comfortable world to forget the Holocaust? And I remember once again how comfortable, familiar, and safe my parents had sought to make my childhood by shielding me from Elsewhere. But I remember, too, that my response had been to open the gate again and again. My instinct had been a child's attempt to see for myself what lay beyond the wall.

The thinking becomes another tributary into the river of thought that will create *The Giver*.

Here's another memory. I am sitting in a booth with my daughter in a little Beacon Hill pub where she and I often have lunch together. The television is on in the background, behind the bar, as it always is. She and I are talking. Suddenly I gesture to her. I say, "Shhh," because I have heard a fragment of the news and I am startled, anxious, and want to hear the rest.

Someone has walked into a fast-food place with an automatic weapon and randomly killed a number of people. My daughter stops talking and waits while I listen to the rest.

Then I relax. I say to her, in a relieved voice, "It's all right. It was in Oklahoma." (Or perhaps it was Alabama. Or Indiana.)

She stares at me in amazement that I have said such a hideous thing.

◀ How did Lowry's daughter react to her comment about the incident in the fast-food restaurant?

How comfortable I made myself feel for a moment, by reducing my own realm of caring to my own familiar neighborhood. How safe I deluded myself into feeling.

I think about that, and it becomes a torrent that enters the flow of a river turbulent by now, and clogged with memories and thoughts and ideas that begin to mesh and intertwine. The river begins to seek a place to spill over.

When Jonas meets The Giver for the first time, and tries to comprehend what lies before him, he says, in confusion, "I thought there was only us. I thought there was only now."

In beginning to write *The Giver*, I created, as I always do, in every book, a world that existed only in my imagination—the world of "only us, only now." I tried to make Jonas's world seem familiar, comfortable, and safe, and I tried to seduce the reader. I seduced myself along the way. It did feel good, that

◀ What did Lowry create in beginning to write The Giver? What did she include in Jonas's world? What did she exclude?

world. I got rid of all the things I fear and dislike: all the violence, prejudice, poverty, and injustice; and I even threw in good manners as a way of life because I liked the idea of it.

One child has pointed out, in a letter, that the people in Jonas's world didn't even have to do dishes.

It was very, very tempting to leave it at that.

But I've never been a writer of fairy tales. And if I've learned anything through that river of memories, it is that we can't live in a walled world, in an "only us, only now" world, where we are all the same and feel safe. We would have to sacrifice too much. The richness of color would disappear. Feelings for other humans would no longer be necessary. Choice would be obsolete.

And besides, I had ridden my bike Elsewhere as a child, and liked it there, but had never been brave enough to tell anyone about it. So it was time.

A letter that I've kept for a very long time is from a child who has read my book *Anastasia Krupnik*. Her letter—she's a little girl named Paula from Louisville, Kentucky—says:

"I really like the book you wrote about Anastasia and her family because it made me laugh every time I read it. I especially liked when it said she didn't want to have a baby brother in the house because she had to clean up after him every time and change his diaper when her mother and father aren't home and she doesn't like to give him a bath and watch him all the time and put him to sleep every night while her mother goes to work . . ."

▶ What is the fascinating thing about the letter Lowry got from Paula?

Here's the fascinating thing: Nothing that the child describes actually happens in the book. The child—as we all do—has brought her own life to a book. She has found a place, a place in the pages of a book, that shares her own frustrations and feelings.

And the same thing is happening—as I hoped it would happen—with *The Giver*.

Those of you who hoped that I would stand here tonight and reveal the "true" ending, the "right" interpretation of the ending, will be disappointed. There isn't one. There's a right one for each of us, and it depends on our own beliefs, our own hopes.

Let me tell you a few endings which are the right endings for a few children out of the many who have written to me.

From a sixth grader: "I think that when they were traveling they were traveling in a circle. When they came to 'Elsewhere' it was their old community, but they had accepted the memories and all the feelings that go along with it."

From another: "Jonas was kind of like Jesus because he took the pain for everyone else in the community so they wouldn't have to suffer. And, at the very end of the book, when Jonas and Gabe reached the place that they knew as Elsewhere, you described Elsewhere as if it were Heaven."

And one more: "A lot of people I know would hate that ending, but not me. I loved it. Mainly because I got to make the book happy. I decided they made it. They made it to the past. I decided the past was our world, and the future was their world. It was parallel worlds."

Finally, from one seventh-grade boy: "I was really surprised that they just died at the end. That was a bummer. You could of made them stay alive, I thought."

Very few find it a bummer. Most of the young readers who have written to me have perceived the magic of the circular journey. The truth that we go out and come back, and that what we come back to is changed, and so are we. Perhaps I have been traveling in a circle, too. Things come together and become complete.

Here is what I've come back to:

The daughter who was with me and looked at me in horror the day I fell victim to thinking we were "only us, only now" (and that what happened in Oklahoma, or Alabama, or Indiana didn't matter) was the first person to read the manuscript of *The Giver.*

The college classmate who was "different" lives, last I heard, very happily in New Jersey with another woman who shares her life. I can only hope that she has forgiven those of us who were young in a more frightened and less enlightened time.

My son, and Margret, his German wife—the one who reminded me how important it is to tell our stories again and again, painful though they often are—now have a little girl who will be the receiver of all of their memories. Their daughter had crossed the Atlantic three times before she was six months old. Presumably my granddaughter will never be fearful of Elsewhere.

Carl Nelson, the man who lost colors but not the memory of them, is the face on the cover of the book. He died in 1989 but left a vibrant legacy of paintings. One hangs now in my home.

▶ Who is with Lowry as she is giving her speech?

And I am especially happy to stand here tonight on this platform with Allen Say because it truly brings my journey full circle. Allen was twelve years old when I was. He lived in Shibuya, that alien Elsewhere that I went to as a child on a bicycle. He was one of the Other, the Different, the dark-eyed children in blue school uniforms, and I was too timid then to do more than stand at the edge of their schoolyard, smile shyly, and wonder what their lives were like.

Now I can say to Allen what I wish I could have said then: Watashi-no tomodachi desu. Greetings, my friend.

I have been asked whether the Newbery Medal is, actually, an odd sort of burden in terms of the greater responsibility one feels. Whether one is paralyzed by it, fearful of being able to live up to the standards it represents.

For me the opposite has been true. I think the 1990 Newbery freed me to risk failure.

Other people took that risk with me, of course. One was my editor, Walter Lorraine, who has never to my knowledge been afraid to take a chance. Walter cares more about what a book has to say than he does about whether he can turn it into a stuffed animal or a calendar or a movie.

The Newbery Committee was gutsy, too. There would have been safer books. More comfortable books. More familiar books. They took a trip beyond the realm of sameness, with this one, and I think they should be very proud of that.

And all of you, as well. Let me say something to those of you here who do such dangerous work.

The man that I named The Giver passed along to the boy knowledge, history, memories, color, pain, laughter, love, and truth. Every time you place a book in the hands of a child, you do the same thing.

It is very risky.

But each time a child opens a book, he pushes open the gate that separates him from Elsewhere. It gives him choices. It gives him freedom.

Those are magnificent, wonderfully unsafe things.

I have been greatly honored by you now, two times. It is impossible to express my gratitude for that. Perhaps the only way, really, is to return to Boston, to my office, to my desk, and to go back to work in hopes that whatever I do next will justify the faith in me that this medal represents.

There are other rivers flowing.

Critical Thinking

1. Consider the passage that Lowry quotes from *The Giver* at the beginning of the speech. How does Lowry parallel that thought throughout her speech?
2. How might Lowry's experiences in Japan have influenced how she wrote about Jonas once he became the Receiver of Memory?
3. What do you think about the different ways in which readers interpreted the ending of *The Giver?* How did your interpretations compare or contrast with theirs?

Creative Writing Activities

Letter to The Giver

Think carefully about the ending of *The Giver.*
What do you think Jonas and Gabriel find when they
reach Elsewhere? Imagine what their lives might be
like a month or two after arriving. Write a letter from
Jonas to The Giver that tells The Giver about their
new life.

Letter from The Giver

Imagine what happens once the community finds
out that Jonas has been lost. Write a letter from The
Giver to Jonas telling him how the community
reacted to losing him and how they faced the memories that his leaving released.

Dialogue between Jonas and Gabriel

As Gabriel grows older, Jonas will probably want to
tell him about their past. Create a dialogue between
Jonas and Gabriel in which Jonas explains to Gabriel
where they came from and why they left. Imagine
the questions that Gabriel would likely ask Jonas,
and have Jonas answer those questions.

Family Dialogue

Imagine the conversation that might take place in
Jonas's family's household after his parents and Lily
find out that he has been lost. Write the dialogue for
this conversation. Include Jonas's mother, father, and
Lily in the dialogue.

Critical Writing Activities

Creating Connections

Choose one of the quotes from Echoes (pages xiv and xv) and explain how that quote relates to the ideas, messages, or themes expressed in *The Giver.*

Precision of Language

An important part of social communication in Jonas's community is called "precision of language." For example, in chapter 1, Asher is chastised for saying he was "distraught" instead of "distracted" when he stopped to see salmon killed at the hatchery. Asher, however, may very well have meant that he was distraught over what he saw. In fact, the community's rule concerning "precision of language" actually prohibited people from describing their true feelings. Skim the novel and look for additional examples of people disobeying this rule.

Many of the terms used in Jonas's community are far from precise. They are **euphemisms**—indirect words or phrases used in place of a direct statement that might be considered too harsh or offensive. Consider what the community means by terms such as "release," "Elsewhere," "feelings," and "discipline wand." What other examples of euphemism can you find in the novel?

Using your notes about euphemisms and "precision of language," write a three-paragraph essay about how the unique use of language is central to *The Giver.*

Seeing Beyond

In *The Giver,* Jonas has an ability to see beyond. His ability is to see colors. As a boy, the Giver had the ability to "hear beyond," that is, to hear music. Think about why these abilities are described as "beyond." Consider what life would be like if ordinary people were unable to see colors or hear music. Write a brief essay stating how life would be different if color and music were out of our grasp.

The End or the Beginning?

Many readers discuss the ending of *The Giver*, debating whether Jonas and Gabriel die on the hilltop, find a new community, make a circle back to their own community, or go on to something different completely. Make a chart, listing along the left edge the different possible interpretations of ending of the novel. Divide the chart in two columns, labeling one at the top "arguments for" and the other "arguments against." Fill in the chart, describing what you think makes each possible interpretation likely or unlikely. Then, pick the interpretation you believe in most strongly and write a brief essay arguing your reasons for choosing that interpretation.

Projects

Interviewing

What would it be like to live in a world free of memory, color, and emotion? Conduct brief interviews with five to ten people—classmates, friends, family, teachers—about the role that memory, color, and emotion play in their lives. You may ask questions such as the following: When do you like to recall memories? Are there memories you would like to forget? What effect does color have on your emotions? How would you feel if there were no color? Do you consider yourself an emotional person, or are you more logical? Do you think a calm life without strong emotion would be satisfying? Compile your results into a report that summarizes the basic roles that memory, color, and emotion play in people's lives. Include quotes from your interviews in your report.

Visual Representation

Form a group with two or three other classmates. For this project, you will create visual representations of Jonas and his community before he is selected Receiver-in-Training and of Jonas and Gabriel in Elsewhere. You may choose to use a large piece of paper and divide it into two spaces so that both visuals can be on the same surface. Make sure to express visually as many details of each situation as you can. For example, try to represent visually that the community lacks love, color, diversity, and pain. Try to show how Jonas changes from the first visual to the second as well. Your visual of Elsewhere will be more open to the interpretation of what you and your group members think it will be like. Once the group has agreed on how to approach the project, create! Once you've finished, present your work to your classmates.

Book Review

Write a review of *The Giver*. Your review should include a summary of the plot and the age level of the audience for which you think the book is appropriate. Comment on why you think this book is or isn't a worthwhile read. You can tailor your review to be suitable for the newspaper, radio, or TV. You may choose to present your review to your class.

Events in History

Choose an event—one from your family history or something that happened in your community, in another part of your country, or elsewhere in the world—that has had an effect on how you look at the world. Describe the event, including where and when it took place. Explain how it affected your view the world. What have you learned from this event? Were this event to be erased from your memory, what knowledge would you lose?

Glossary of Words for Everyday Use

Pronunciation Key

Vowel Sounds

a	hat	ō	go	ə	extra
ā	play	ȯ	paw, born		under
ä	star	u̇	book, put		civil
e	then	ü	blue, stew		honor
ē	me	oi	boy		bogus
i	sit	ou	wow		
ī	my	u	up		

Consonant Sounds

b	but	l	lip	t	sit
ch	watch	m	money	th	with
d	do	n	on	v	valley
f	fudge	ŋ	song, sink	w	work
g	go	p	pop	y	yell
h	hot	r	rod	z	pleasure
j	jump	s	see		
k	brick	sh	she		

ac • cel • er • a • tion (ik se lə rā´ shən) *n.*, the act or process of gaining speed.

ac • qui • si • tion (a kwə zi´ shən) *n.*, act of obtaining.

ac • quire (a kwīr´) *v.*, get as one's own; come into possession or control of.

ad • her • ence (ad hir´ ənts) *v.*, steady of faithful attachment; loyalty.

ad • min • is • tra • tive (əd mi´ nə strā tiv) *adj.*, managerial.

ad • mo • ni • tion (ad mə ni´ shən) *n.*, warning; advice.

af • fec • tion • ate (ə fek´ shə nət) *adj.*, caring, kind, warm-hearted, tender. **affectionately**, *adv.*

af • ter • thought (af´ tər thät) *n.*, idea occurring later.

am • bush (am´ bu̇sh) *n.*, surprise attack.

an • es • thet • ic (a nəs the´ tik) *adj.*, capable of producing loss of sensation with or without consciousness.

an • guish (an´ gwish) *n.*, sorrow; extreme pain, distress, or anxiety.

an • them (an´ thəm) *n.*, song of praise or gladness.

an • xious (ank´ shəs) *adj.,* worried or eager. **anxiously,** *adv.*

ap • pre • hen • sive (a pri hent´ siv) *adj.,* viewing the future with nervousness or alarm.

ap • ti • tude (ap´ tə tüd) *n.,* natural ability, talent.

as • sem • ble (ə sem´ bəl) *v.,* bring together in a particular place for a particular purpose.

as • sim • i • late (ə si´ mə lāt) *v.,* absorb into the culture of a population; take into the mind and thoroughly comprehend.

at • tri • bute (a´ trə byüt) *n.,* an inherent characteristic or quality.

be • wil • der (bi wil´ dər) *v.,* perplex or confuse.

beck • on (be´ kən) *v.,* summon or signal, typically with a wave or nod.

buoy • an • cy (bȯi´ yənt sē) *n.,* the tendency of a body to float or rise when submerged in liquid.

bur • den • some (bər´ dən səm) *adj.,* imposing a burden; oppressive.

by • pass (bī´pas) *v.,* avoid; to manage to get around.

ca • pac • i • ty (kə pa´ sə tē) *n.,* individual's mental or physical ability.

car • go (kär´ gō) *n.,* goods carried by ship, plane, or vehicle.

car • nage (kär´ nij) *n.,* flesh of slain animals or men; great and bloody slaughter (as in battle).

cha • os (kā´ äs) *n.,* a state of utter confusion.

chas • tise (chas´ tīz) *v.,* criticize severely; punish.

chor • tle (chȯr´ təl) *v.,* laugh or chuckle in satisfaction or exultation.

chute (shüt´) *n.,* a passage down which or through which things may pass or slide.

civ • il (si´ vəl) *adj.,* relating to the state or its citizens.

cli • mate (klī´ mət) n., average course or condition of the weather of a specific location.

col • lec • tive (kə lek´ tiv) *adj.,* involving all members of a group as distinct from its individuals; shared or assumed by all members of a group.

com • merce (kä´ mərs) *n.,* exchange or buying and selling of commodities on a large scale involving transportation from place to place; business.

con • ceiv • able (kən sē´ və bəl) *adj.,* imaginable; thinkable; possible. **conceivably,** *adv.*

con • firm (kən fərm´) *v.*, verify; give new assurance of the correctness or accuracy of.

con • spic • u • ous (kən spi´ kyə wəs) *adj.*, obvious to the eye or mind; striking; noticeable.

con • tort (kən tôrt´) *v.*, twist in a violent manner; twist into a strained expression.

con • vey • ance (kən vā´ ənts) *n.*, the act of transferring or delivering.

cre • scen • do (krə shen´ dō) *n.*, gradual increase; climax.

cringe (krinj´) *v.*, draw in or contract one's muscles involuntarily; shrink; flinch; wince.

deft (deft´) *adj.*, handy; dexterous; characterized by facility and skill.

de • ject • ed (di jek´ təd) *adj.*, cast down in spirits; depressed.

des • ig • nate (de´ zig nāt) *v.*, indicate and set apart for a specific purpose; denote; specify.

des • ti • na • tion (des tə nā´ shən) *n.*, place to which one is journeying.

dis • card (dis kärd´) *v.*, get rid of because of unsuitability.

dis • mount (dis maủnt´) *v.*, to come down from an elevated position (as on a horse).

dis • po • si • tion (dis pə zi´ shən) *n.*, mood or temperament one most often displays.

dis • tinc • tive (di stiŋk´ tiv) *adj.*, unusual; uncommon; remarkable.

dis • traught (di strȯt´) *adj.*, extremely troubled.

dis • tri • bu • tion (dis trə byü´ shən) *n.*, the act or process of dispensing or doling out.

drone (drōn´) *v.*, talk in a persistently dull tone.

dwell • ing (dwe´ liŋ) *n.*, a shelter (as a house) in which people live.

ec • stat • ic (ek sta´ tik) *adj.*, marked by or relating to a state of overwhelming emotion, especially rapturous delight; blissful; overjoyed; elated.

em • bed (im bed´) *v.*, make something an integral part of.

em • boss (im bäs´) *v.*, to ornament with raised work; raise in relief from a surface.

em • phat • ic (em fa´ tik) *adj.*, forceful; decisive. **emphatically,** *adv.*

em • pow • er (im pou´ ər) *v.*, give official authority or legal power to.

en • hance (in hants´) *v.,* increase or improve in value or quality.

es • ca • late (es´ kə lāt) *v.,* increase in extent, volume, number, amount, intensity, or scope.

ex • cru • ci • at • ing (ik skrü´ shē ā tiŋ) *adj.,* agonizing; causing great pain or anguish.

ex • hil • a • rat • ing (ig zi´ lə rā tiŋ) *adj.,* enlivening; refreshing; exciting; stimulating.

ex • per • tise (ek spər tēz´) *n.,* expert opinion or commentary; special skill, knowledge, or mastery.

ex • u • ber • ant (ig zü´ bə rənt) *adj.,* extreme or excessive in degree; joyously unrestrained and enthusiastic.

fal • ter (fȯl´ tər) *v.,* hesitate in purpose or action; speak brokenly or weakly; stammer.

fidg • et (fi´ jət) *v.,* move or act restlessly or nervously.

fraz • zle (fra´ zəl) *v.,* put in a state of extreme physical or nervous fatigue.

frig • id (fri´ jəd) *adj.,* intensely cold.

gen • er • a • tion (je nə rā´ shən) *n.,* average span of time between the birth of parents and that of their offspring; a group of individuals born and living during the same period of time.

ge • net • ic (jə ne´ tik) *adj.,* relating to the branch of biology that deals with the heredity and variation of organisms.

glum (gləm´) *adj.,* gloomy; dismal; sullen. **glumly,** *adv.*

grave (grāv´) *adj.,* serious; somber; grim. **gravely,** *adv.*

gul • ly (gə´ lē) *n.,* a trench that was originally worn in the earth by running water and through which water often runs after rains.

hap • haz • ard (hap ha´ zərd) *adj.,* random; marked by lack of plan, order, or direction.

hoard (hōrd´) *v.,* store up and hide away a supply for oneself.

hoot (hüt´) *v.,* shout or laugh.

horde (hōrd´) *n.,* crowd or throng; swarm.

hov • er (hə´ vər) *v.,* move to and fro near a place; to remain suspended over a place or object.

im • plor • ing (im plōr´ iŋ) *adj.,* begging; pleading.

in • ac • cu • rate (in a´ kyə rət) *adj.,* inexact; imprecise; incorrect.

in • dif • fer • ent (in di´ fərnt) *adj.,* of no importance or value one way or the other. **indifferently,** *adv.*

in • dus • try (in´ dəs trē) *n.,* systematic labor for a useful purpose or the creation of something of value; manufacturing activity as a whole.

in • tri • cate (in´ tri kət) *adj.,* having many complexly interrelating parts.

in • trigue (in trēg´) *v.,* excite interest or curiosity.

in • vig • o • rat • ing (in vi´ gə rā tiŋ) *adj.,* stimulating; energizing.

i • ron • ic (ī rän´ ik) *adj.,* meaning the opposite of what is actually said or expressed.

jaun • ty (jän´ tē) *adj.,* light-hearted; relaxed; effortless.

kin • ship (kin´ ship) *n.,* the quality or state of being related.

lei • sure (lē´ zhər) *n.,* time free from work or duties. **leisurely,** *adj.* and *adv.*

leth • ar • gy (le´ thər jē) *n.,* sluggishness; lifelessness; spiritlessness.

light • heart • ed (līt´ här təd) *adj.,* free from care, anxiety, or seriousness; cheerfully optimistic and hopeful.

lo • gis • tic (lō jis´ tik) *adj.,* relating to symbolic logic; relating to the handling of the details of an operation.

lu • mi • nous (lü´ mə nəs) *adj.,* bright; shining; radiant.

lurk (lərk´) *v.,* lie hidden.

lux • u • ry (lək´ shə rē) *n.,* indulgence in something that provides pleasure, satisfaction, or ease.

make • shift (māk´ shift) *adj.,* on-the-spot; thrown-together; contrived.

man • u • fac • ture (man yə fak´ chər) *n.,* the act or process of making products by hand or machinery.

mea • ger (mē´ gər) *adj.,* lacking in quality or quantity.

me • tic • u • lous (mə ti´ kyə ləs) *adj.,* marked by extreme or excessive care in the consideration or treatment of details. **meticulously,** *adv.*

mim • ic (mi´ mik) *v.,* ridicule by imitating.

mis • chie • vous (mis´ chə vəs) *adj.,* irresponsibly playful.

mur • ky (mər´ kē) *adj.* hazy; veiled; not distinct.

nav • i • ga • tion (na və gā´ shən) *n.,* science of getting ships, aircraft, or spacecraft from place to place. **navigational,** *adj.*

non • de • script (nän di skript´) *adj.,* lacking distinctive or interesting qualities: dull, drab.

nui • sance (nü´ sənts) *n.,* something that is annoying or unpleasant.

numb (nəm´) *adj.,* without sensation or feeling. **numbly,** *adv.*

nur • ture (nər´ chər) *v.,* educate, foster, further the development of; supply nourishment to.

ob • so • lete (äb sə lēt´) *adj.,* no longer in use or no longer useful.

ob • struc • tion (äb strək´ shən) *n.,* a condition of being clogged or blocked.

om • i • nous (ä´ mə nəs) *adj.,* threatening; menacing, boding of bad things to come.

op • ti • mis • tic (äp tə mis´ tik) *adj.,* hopeful; tending toward the habit of anticipating the best possible outcome.

out • law (out´ lä) *adj., to* make illegal; to place under ban or restriction.

pal • pa • ble (pal´ pə bəl) *adj.,* noticeable; capable of being felt.

pam • per (pam´ pər) *v.,* treat with excessive or extreme care or attention.

pa • tri • ot • ic (pā trē ä´ tik) *adj.,* inspired by love for one's country.

per • me • ate (pər´ mē āt) *v.,* diffuse through or penetrate something; to pass through the pores of; seep through; spread throughout.

per • vade (pər vād´) *v.,* to become diffused throughout every part of; permeate; saturate.

pe • ti • tion (pə ti´ shən) *v.,* to make a formal request.

pet • u • lant (pe´ chə lənt) *adj.,* rude in speech or behavior. **petulantly,** *adv.*

piece • meal (pēs´ mēl) *adj.,* done or made piece by piece or in a fragmentary way.

plea (plē´) *n.,* an earnest request or appeal.

pop • u • late (pä´ pyə lāt) *v.,* occupy, inhabit.

pre • ci • sion (pri si´ zhən) *n.,* exactness.

pro • gress (prə gres´) *v.,* develop to a higher, better, or more advanced stage; move forward.

pro • hi • bi • tion (prō ə bi´ shən) *n.,* act of forbidding the doing of something.

prom • i • nent (prä´ mə nənt) *adj.,* leading, widely and popularly known.

realm (relm´) *n.,* domain; region; arena.

re • as • sure (rē ə shúr´) *v.,* comfort; give confidence to; free from doubt.

rec • ol • lec • tion (re kə lək´ shən) *n.,* memory.

re • count (ri kount´) v., to relate in detail.

rec • re • a • tion (re krē ā´ shən) n., a means of refreshment of strength and spirit that is separate from one's work.

ref • er • ence (rə´ fə rənts) n., a mention of.

re • ha • bil • i • ta • tion (rē ə bil´ə tā´shən) n., restoration to a condition of health.

re • lin • quish (ri liŋ´ kwish) v., give up.

re • luc • tant (ri lək´ tənt) adj., feeling or showing hesitation or unwillingness. **reluctantly,** adv.

re • new • al (ri nü´ əl) n., act or process of restoring to freshness, vigor, or perfection.

req • ui • si • tion (re kwə zi´ shən) v., request or require that something be provided.

res • ig • na • tion (re zig nā´ shən) n., surrender.

ret • ro • ac • tive (re trō ak´ tiv) adj., extending in scope or effect to a prior time or to conditions that existed or originated in the past.

rhyth • mic (rith´ mik) adj., marked by or moving in pronounced rhythm.

rit • u • al (ri´ chə wəl) n., a customarily repeated act or ceremony.

sar • cas • tic (sär kas´ tik) adj., marked by bitterness and a will to verbally insult.

self- • con • scious (self kän´ shəs) adj., intensely aware of oneself as an object of the observation of others.

self-pos • sessed (self´ pə zest´) adj., composed in mind or manner; calm.

se • rene (sə rēn´) adj., calm; restful.

shud • der (shə´ dər) v., tremble convulsively; shiver.

sing • song (siŋ´ säŋ) adj., having a uniform rhythm.

sin • u • ous (sin´ yə wəs) adj., winding; marked by strong, lithe movements.

sol • emn (sä´ ləm) adj., somber; serious; thoughtful; intense.

sol • i • tude (sä´ lə tüd) n., the quality or state of being alone or remote from society.

som • ber (säm´ bər) adj., of a dismal or depressing character.

spasm (spa´ zəm) n., an involuntary and abnormal muscle contraction.

sphere (sfir´) n., globular body such as a ball.

spon • ta • ne • ous (spän tā´ nē əs) adj., proceeding from natural feeling without external constraint; arising from a momentary impulse. **spontaneously,** adv.

spouse (spous´) *n.*, married person: husband or wife.

stan • dard • ize (stan´ dər dīz) *v.*, bring into conformity or agreement with a standard.

sta • tus (sta´ təs) *n.*, the condition of a person or thing in the eyes of the law.

stead • y (ste´ dē) *v.*, to make or keep stable, firm in position, sure in movement.

steal • thy (stel´ thē) *adj.*, slow, deliberate, and secret in action or character. **stealthily**, *adv.*

steel (stēəl´) *v.*, fill with resolution or determination.

straight • for • ward (strāt fōr´ wərd) *adj.*, clear-cut, easy to understand, direct.

suc • ces • sor (sək se´ sər) *n.*, one who comes after another in office or position.

sup • ple • men • ta • ry (sə plə men´ tə rē) *adj.*, additional.

tab • u • late (ta´ byə lāt) *v.*, to count, record, or list systematically.

tan • ta • liz • ing (tan´ təl ī ziŋ) *adj.*, enticing; tempting.

tech • ni • cal (tek´ ni kəl) *adj.*, based on strict interpretation. **technically**, *adv.*

ten • ta • tive (ten´ tə tiv) *adj.*, hesitant; uncertain. **tentatively**, *adv.*

throng (thräŋ´) *n.*, crowding together of many persons.

trans • gres • sion (trans gre´ shən) *n.*, a violation of a law, command, or duty.

trans • mit (tranz mit´) *v.*, send or convey from one person or place to another; cause to pass or be conveyed through space or a medium.

tuft (təft´) *n.*, clump; cluster; a small cluster of elongated flexible outgrowths attached at the base and free at the opposite ends.

unan • i • mous (yü na´ nə məs) *adj.*, having the agreement and consent of all.

un • e • vent • ful (ən i vent´ fəl) *adj.*, marked by no noteworthy events; routine; unchanging.

un • en • dur • a • ble (ən in dyür´ ə bəl) *adj.*, unbearable; unable to be tolerated or withstood.

u • ni • son (yü´ nə sən) *n.*, at the same time, in perfect agreement so as to harmonize exactly.

un • set • tling (ən set´ liŋ) *adj.*, having the effect of upsetting or disturbing.

un • wieldy (ən wēəl´ dē) *adj.,* not easily managed, handled, or used; awkward; cumbersome.

us • age (yü´ sij) *n.,* a firmly established practice or procedure.

vague (vāg´) *adj.,* not clearly expressed, defined, grasped or understood.

ve • hi • cle (vē´ ə kəl) *n.,* a means of carrying or transporting something; a conveyance.

vi • brant (vī´ brənt) *adj.,* filled with life, vigor, or activity.

vig • i • lant (vi´ jə lənt) *adj.,* alertly watchful.

vi • tal (vi´ təl) *adj.,* necessary, essential; important.

whee • dle (hwē´ dəl) *v.,* coax, flatter.

wretch • ed (re´ chəd) *adj.,* deeply dejected or distressed in body or mind.

Handbook of Literary Terms

ANECDOTE. An **anecdote** is a usually short narrative of an interesting, amusing, or biographical incident. Although anecdotes are often the basis for short stories, an anecdote differs from a short story in that it lacks a complicated plot and relates a single episode.

CENTRAL CONFLICT. A **central conflict** is the main problem or struggle in the plot of a poem, story, or play. A conflict can be internal or external. An *internal conflict* is a struggle that takes place inside the mind of a character. An *external conflict* is a struggle that takes place between a character and an outside force such as another character, society, or nature.

CHARACTER. A **character** is a person or animal who takes part in the action of a literary work. The main character is called the *protagonist*. A character who struggles against the main character is called an *antagonist*. A *one-dimensional character, flat character,* or *caricature,* is one who exhibits a single quality, or character trait. A *three-dimensional, full,* or *rounded character* is one who seems to have all the complexities of an actual human being.

CHARACTERIZATION. **Characterization** is the act of creating or describing a character. Writers create character using three major techniques: by showing what characters say, do, or think; by showing what other characters say or think about them; and by describing what physical features, dress, and personality the characters display.

FICTION. **Fiction** is prose—*prose* is the word used to describe all writing that is not drama or poetry—writing about imagined events or characters. The primary forms of fiction are the short story, the novella, and the novel.

FORESHADOWING. **Foreshadowing** is the act of hinting at events that will happen later in a literary work.

IMAGE. An **image** is the concrete representation of an object or an experience created through the use of language. An image is also the vivid mental picture created in the reader's mind by that language. The images in a literary work are referred to, when considered altogether, as the work's *imagery*.

MOTIVATION. A **motivation** is a force that moves a character to think, feel, or behave in a certain way.

POINT OF VIEW. **Point of view** is the vantage point from which a story is told. If a story is told from the *first-person point of view*, the narrator uses the pronouns *I* and *we* and is a part of or a witness to the action. When a story is told from a *third-person point of view*, the narrator is outside the action, uses words such as *he, she, it,* and *they*; and avoids the use of *I* and *we*. In a literary work written from a *limited point of view*, everything is seen through the eyes of a single character. In a work written from an *omniscient point of view*, the narrator, or storyteller knows everything and can see into the minds of all the characters.

SCIENCE FICTION. **Science fiction** is imaginative literature based on scientific principles, discoveries, or laws. It is similar to fantasy in that it deals with imaginary worlds, but differs from fantasy in having a scientific basis. Often science fiction deals with the future, the distant past, or with worlds other than our own. Science fiction stories often take place on distant planets, in parallel universes, or in worlds beneath the ground or sea.

SYMBOL. A **symbol** is a thing that stands for, or represents, both itself and something else. Some well-known symbols are the dove to represent peace, light and dark to represent good and evil, and the season of spring to represent life or rebirth.

Acknowledgments

Harold Ober Associates. 1993 Newbery Medal Acceptance Speech by Lois Lowry. Reprinted by permission of Harold Ober Associates Incorporated. Copyright ©1994 Horn Book, Inc.

Sheep Meadow Press. "Secret of Life" by Diana Der-Hovanessian. Copyright ©1994 by Diana Der-Hovanessian from *Selected Poems of Diana Der-Hovanessian,* published by Sheep Meadow Press, Riverdale-on-Hudson, New York. Reprinted by permission of the author.

University of Arkansas Press. "The Past" by Billy Collins from *The Apple that Astonished Paris.* Copyright ©1988 by Billy Collins. Reprinted by permission of the University of Arkansas Press.